JULIE OLIVIA

IN HIS EYES

JULIE OLIVIA

Copyright © 2020 by Julie Olivia

julieoliviaauthor@gmail.com

www.julieoliviaauthor.com

All rights reserved.

No part of this book may be reproduced in any form or by any electronic or mechanical means, including information storage and retrieval systems, without written permission from the author, except for the use of brief quotations in a book review.

This is a work of fiction. Names, characters, places, and incidents either are the product of the author's imagination or are used fictitiously. Any resemblance to actual persons, living or dead, events, or locales is entirely coincidental.

Editing by C. Marie

Cover Photo from DepositPhotos

Cover Design by Julie Olivia

Dedicated to you, of course. May your sarcastic, eye-rolling, swoon-worthy words last forever. I love you.

CONTENTS

About "In His Eyes" ... ix
Playlist ... xi

1. Nia ... 1
2. Nia ... 10
3. Ian ... 15
4. Nia ... 22
5. Ian ... 27
6. Nia ... 35
7. Nia ... 46
8. Ian ... 58
9. Nia ... 63
10. Ian ... 71
11. Nia ... 80
12. Nia ... 85
13. Ian ... 94
14. Nia ... 105
15. Ian ... 123
16. Nia ... 132
17. Ian ... 143
18. Nia ... 150
19. Nia ... 156
20. Ian ... 166
21. Nia ... 172
22. Ian ... 178
23. Nia ... 187
24. Ian ... 192
25. Ian ... 196
26. Nia ... 199
27. Nia ... 204
28. Ian ... 212
29. Nia ... 220
30. Nia ... 223

31. Nia	227
32. Nia	232
33. Nia	238
34. Ian	246
35. Ian	254
36. Ian	257
37. Nia	264
38. Nia	267
39. Ian	272
40. Nia	278
Epilogue	285
Nice to See You!	287
Acknowledgments	289
About the Author	291

ABOUT "IN HIS EYES"

In His Eyes is a full-length, standalone romantic comedy! It is the second book in the *Into You* Series.

———

Unrequited crush? I've been there. Done that. Over it.

Ian Chambers is a responsible, intelligent lawyer. But I've known Ian for nine years and I can tell you that responsibility does not equal likability. Ian's also an egotistical, teasing, blue-eyed, accidentally make-you-fall-for-him kind of man. And I want nothing to do with it, thank you very much.

When he quit Treasuries Inc. eight months ago, I thought I was finally rid of him. But when I'm invited to a destination wedding as a bridesmaid and he's the best man in every sense of the word, it's not as easy to pretend he doesn't exist. And this week, he's dead-set on getting my attention just as he's tried to for almost a decade.

If he looks at me with that cocky grin and those piercing eyes one more time, I might lose control. You could say that's a good thing. But you would be wrong.

Ian Chambers can flirt with me as much as he wants, but I refuse to fall for his tricks…

Again.

PLAYLIST

"Honeybee" - Steam Powered Giraffe
"Sitting, Waiting, Wishing" - Jack Johnson
"Island in the Sun" - Weezer
"Badfish" - Sublime
"Closer to the Sun" - Slightly Stoopid
"Needing/Getting" - OK Go
"Soul to Squeeze" - Red Hot Chili Peppers
"Only In Dreams" - Weezer
"Tequila" - The Champs
"Waves" - Kopecky

1

NIA

I HAVE TWO PROBLEMS RIGHT NOW: MY CAR WILL NOT START, AND I am a bridesmaid. The two are not directly related, but at the moment, both remain in the forefront of my mind.

My ears fill with the droning sound of the car horn as I press my head against it. I'm not even looking at the ignition as I turn the key again only to be greeted by a sad engine sputtering then moaning its way into death. It doesn't help that I'm in the summer heat of the South, sweating like a prepubescent boy who just watched porn for the first time. I might even be just as anxious as one.

On the bright side, I'm fairly sure any wrinkles in my bridesmaid dress hanging in the back seat are being steamed out. At least there's that. Do I have the body to pull off the dress? Maybe. Would I normally be self-conscious about it? Not really. I'm a thirty-five-year-old woman with no more time to waste on the whole 'body image issue' thing, thank you very much—at least that's the mantra I repeat every morning in the mirror, God save my soul.

I digress. Here is the million-dollar question: Am I nervous because I want a certain someone to fantasize about me in that saucy dress?

Boy, does that deserve more of an explanation.

In less than twenty-four hours, I will lay eyes on Ian Chambers, a man I haven't seen in eight months and was relieved to be rid of once he put in his two weeks' notice earlier this year. Eight months of no snarky comments from his gorgeous mouth, no drooling over his well-fitted suits, and no constant anxiety that the one man I almost fell for will tempt me to fall again.

But, of course, he's the best man at this wedding, and I am a bridesmaid. *Lucky me.*

Sometimes I wonder if we're not being haunted by ghosts or poltergeists, but instead the spirits of those who spent their life enjoying soap operas. These particular ghosts must be working with the powers that be to engineer my worst possible reality. I'm convinced.

I crank the engine again and both my car and I make pathetic noises. I'm not sure if I'm mocking it or it's mocking me. I move my pink rabbit's foot keychain out of the way. Maybe the fur is blocking the ignition? Or maybe this is my punishment for still coveting an ancient item from the 90s, specifically one that was gifted to me by he-who-must-not-be-named.

Trust me, I *wish* I meant Voldemort.

My brother came over today so I could make him coffee one last time before I leave for the next week. Since he lives only ten minutes away, he always swings by my house in the morning to collect his to-go cup with one or two of my homemade cookies. He's normally running behind, but this morning I begged him to come early and take a look at my car. It was something along the lines of, "Please, Harry, you mechanic superstar of a man, this is a horrible start to my so-called vacation, and I might die. Help me, help me, help me!" I think using my older sister card worked as I continued to spew my pleas. That or he just felt sorry for me.

After a few seconds under the hood, Harry scratches his chin—leaving behind a five o'clock grease shadow—and concludes, "Yeah, it might be toast, Nia."

"Is that an official diagnosis?" I shoot at him from the front seat, turning the key over again while he nods solemnly as if wishing the car its best in the afterlife. "Well, great." I toss my head back. "Just great. I was supposed to be on my way to Florida thirty minutes ago."

Harry shrugs, putting his hands in his coveralls and leaning against the bare garage wall. He's a big man, blond like myself but with unruly hair that wings out from under his baseball cap, which is embroidered with the words *Smith Mechanics*. He's five years younger than me and just the right kind of chill. I've heard his mantra of *Whatever happens, happens* too many times in my life, and I'm sure he's applying that to my current situation. My opposing Type A personality refuses to see this as anything other than something I can't control. I hate things I can't control.

I step out of my car and swipe through my apps, sending a text to the bride to let her know I'm running late and may not make it to the beach at the intended time.

I get a reply immediately.

Grace: We haven't left yet if you want a ride! We're at our place. Cameron is taking his sweet time as always and the dogs need to be walked again.

I breathe a sigh of relief.

Nia: Give me thirty minutes and I'll be there.

I slam my car door and walk past Harry into the kitchen.

"Hey, can you give me a ride to Grace's house?" I ask, trying to put on my best puppy-dog eyes. "She offered to drive me down to Florida."

"Late for work. Sorry, Nia."

"You own the shop. What's the point of self-employment if you can't bend the rules?"

"Are you trying to put my business in the hole?"

I let out a sound that's a mix between a whine and a groan. Harry chuckles.

I order a rideshare service only to be told by the app that they're fifteen minutes away. *Are you kidding me?*

Harry picks up one of my homemade cookies on the counter on his stroll into the kitchen, bending down to hand a crumb to my cat, Jiggy, who gingerly sniffs it. I instinctively turn on my heel and walk back to shut the garage door while also snatching the crumb.

"She doesn't get human food."

"Spoilsport."

Exhaling and placing my phone on the counter, I take my bags and place them near the door so I won't forget. I can't think of anything else to do with my hands while I wait. I feel uncomfortable not being productive.

"I'll be back next week," I say, running my hands down my skirt to smooth it out. "Have Mom and Dad been grocery shopping yet?"

My brother takes a bite of another cookie then hops up on the counter. One snap of my fingers and he quickly hops right back down with a crumb-filled smile, instead bending to stroke Jiggy, whose actions might make you assume she's eternally attention-deprived.

"They're adults," Harry says in between bites. "Plus, they have me."

Sure. *Adults.* In their older age, my parents have fully adopted a hippie lifestyle. They've started sporting hemp clothing, growing questionably legal plants, and constantly burning candles they forget to blow out before bed. It's a blessing in disguise that my brother, at the ripe age of 30, hasn't ever moved out, though his mechanic shop in town is finally turning a profit and soon he will move out and they'll be left to their own devices. For now, though, my parents love his companionship and having their granddaughter under their roof, so it all worked out in the end. Plus, with four of their six kids spread out across the country, I'm sure they're thankful to have one only a couple thresholds away from their living room and another only ten minutes down the road.

I exhale, nod to myself, and check my bags once more.

"Hey Tasmanian devil, you're doing that thing where you act crazy again," Harry says, finishing off his cookie and slapping his hands together.

I am. I am nonstop-pacing-around-crazy-pants.

And why is that? Because of one, specific, no-good, charming lawyer.

"I'm seeing Ian," I blurt out, clearing my throat. There's a small silence before Harry laughs and I rush to the fridge, throwing my head in and inhaling the cool air. "Need more coffee? Creamer, maybe?" I pull out the carton and place it on the counter.

"You're seeing Ian?" he asks.

My brother is calm, not at all trying to avoid the subject I just broached but also not even remotely as anxious about it as I am. And why would he be? He's not the person who is constantly wishy-washy about the gorgeous lawyer.

Ian, the man who got away...sort of.

"He's the best man at the wedding," I say. "And it means nothing. Obviously."

I'm a liar. I'm such a liar. I've been dreading this week for months.

"Sure, that's why you just brought it up—because it's nothing. I bring up nothing topics all the time, like how the other day Cara learned the word 'sensual.'"

"She's five." I pause, cringing at the thought of how in the world my niece might have learned that word. "Well, if you're trying to distract me, you're doing a good job."

"Oh no, I just wanted to tell you how silly your problems seem."

"Your humor isn't hitting today," I say, narrowing my eyes.

"Yet somehow I feel like it is."

I put back the creamer I pulled from the fridge without pouring any. I turn off the coffee pot and glance at my rideshare app. *Ten minutes away.*

"Are you going to be okay?" Harry asks me. It's a good question and one I don't have an answer to. There isn't a giant cartoon piano crashing on top of me, so that's good. Could be worse.

"I'm an adult," I answer, speaking more to myself than him. I straighten my spine. "I can handle myself. Plus, I have a whole eight-hour car ride before I see him. I can build up all the comebacks I want during that time."

"I thought the proper phrase for this situation was 'kill them with kindness.'"

"I'd rather use a knife."

Harry leaves shortly after, giving me a few words of encouragement as he goes. I tell him to give my niece some love, and then I'm left with my bags, my dress, and my useless car. I check my phone again, willing it to provide an update for my ride. Nothing. Nada. I walk past my dead vehicle—not even stopping to pat it and mourn my loss—and pace my driveway, pressing a button on my keys to close the garage door behind me.

So, let me correct myself. I have three problems right now: my car is trashed, I'm attending a wedding, and my patience is wearing thin.

When my ride picks me up, I take advantage of the free time to answer emails. It's the usual suspects for a human resources manager like myself: applications for open roles, questions regarding budgetary concerns I presented, and another extended leave of absence request.

You see a lot in my field of work—horrible harassment claims, arguments regarding policies, people who can't read an email to save their life—but then there's also the good side like those who request to be more involved with volunteering or people who finish their trainings on time. I love those people, and despite the mixed bag, I absolutely love my job and my career. The people are what keep it interesting—people like Ian Chambers.

Ian was the *most* entertaining. He fell right in the middle of good and bad: kind, competent at his job, but also consistently going days without answering an email. I think he might have set up a filter to route HR emails to a junk folder, but that's just my own theory. Knowing him, he did it as a joke and then forgot about it.

Okay, calm down, Nia.

I need to stop thinking about him. I have to see him for an entire week, and I need to cherish this time alone. Find my center. My *zen*.

I make it to Cameron and Grace's house, where I find the both of them leaning against his black Jeep Wrangler, hand in hand, looking positively power-couple-like. I don't even think Cupid himself could have arranged a more compatible duo. With Grace's bright red hair and Cameron's dimpled grin, they're the epitome of sunshine, rainbows, and unicorn happiness.

The two of them met in a whirlwind office romance two years ago when Grace first started at the company. My hypocritical opinion of Grace as some office floozy didn't change until she was promoted to a management position and we worked together more closely. Seeing as I've spent years imagining what Ian looks like without his clothes on, it was slightly unfair to have judged her for seeing out her own fantasy. As it turns out, Grace is funny and motivated, and now, somehow, I'm one of her bridesmaids. Funny how life works out.

I yank my bags out of this random person's car and haphazardly try to both thank him and snatch my hanging bridesmaid dress from the back. *Come here, you slinky piece of fabric.*

"I'm sorry for being late," I say, out of breath from the humidity that makes the few feet I've walked feel like wading through an Olympic-sized swimming pool.

"Don't worry about it!" Grace says. "We're still waiting anyway."

I reach up to put my hair in a top knot, securing it in place to provide some relief against the brutal heat. Cameron loads my stuff in the back of the car, and when I reach out to help him, he waves me away with a smile.

"Thanks, Cam," I say. I look at the trunk, filled with bags, and the three of us just standing here. *One, two, three.* "Aren't we all here?" I ask. "What are we waiting for?"

In that moment, as if I just summoned a demon by saying its name three times, a jet-black Audi whips around the corner, engine revving with the sound of a smooth, well-made vehicle. This car represents confidence and class, and the man who opens the door reflects its very nature.

He's tall, towering well over six feet, and he maintains the figure of a dedicated swimmer: broad shoulders and all muscle. He wears a plain black t-shirt, and the simplicity suits him. He has pitch-black hair that's slightly curled at the ends, and I know from years of seeing this man daily that it's at the best length it can be; any longer and it just gets curlier and *bigger*. His eyebrows are thick but in a groomed kind of way, and a sliver of the left one is missing, obscured by the tiniest of scars. Apart from how he exudes the charm of a man born into wealth, his entire look still screams *bad boy from the wrong side of the tracks*.

And then I see them: his piercing, ice blue eyes, which now peek out above the sunglasses he's lowered to get a good look at me. I'm used to seeing him in glasses, but I much appreciate the change to contacts.

No. No, no, no. I cannot be admiring him already.

I officially now have four problems: my car is sitting in my driveway like a heaping pile of hot summer garbage, I have a red dress in my hand that is begging for some form of cleavage I cannot provide, my impatience has reached an all-time high, and I'm face to face with my worst enemy: Ian Chambers.

2

NIA

NINE YEARS AGO

New girl.

That's what the IT team has resorted to calling me during my first month at Treasuries Inc. The problem with a startup-style company, and with me being their first human resources employee, is that they have yet to understand my role and what will result in a lawsuit—which is exactly why, on top of hiring me, they are also recruiting for an in-house lawyer.

The owner has interviewed about a million candidates. All have been either perfect for the company culture but unqualified or, alternatively, completely qualified yet a "corporate stiff," as most of the team would put it. I've insisted on sitting in on the interviews as a second opinion, but, once again, when it's your first time with an HR professional on staff, it's hard to relinquish control and actually *listen* to HR's opinion—even if that was the point of hiring said professional in the first place.

Instead, I'm tasked with being the "face" of the organization. I greet the candidate and escort them back to the conference room reserved for the interview. I had to force my way even into this position, but at least it's a baby step toward something bigger—toward the career I enjoy.

It's almost nine o'clock and I'm minutes away from welcoming this morning's interviewee. I haven't had my coffee yet and walking is a struggle. I can see how those people in *Wall-E* ended up where they're at. I bet it was the lack of coffee beans. Even so, all of my coffee lust is halted, put in a grinder, and slow dripped down into my stomach when I see the candidate at the door.

He's well over six feet tall, gorgeous, and wearing a suit that probably cost an arm and a leg to tailor as perfectly as it has been. He looks like a model, and I wonder if maybe that's exactly what he does for a living and he just stumbled into the wrong building.

"Ian Chambers?" I ask, looking down at his resume in my hands. He turns to me and ice blue eyes stare back into mine. Paired with his black hair, he could be a human husky. *Bow wow.*

"Hello," he says, holding out his hand and flashing straight, white teeth. We shake and he gives a firm grip. I almost swoon —or maybe I actually do. All I know is I try to give him a solid handshake as well. He doesn't need to know I'm slowly melting in his presence.

"Hi, I'm Nia Smith. It's nice to meet you." Understatement. "We'll be interviewing you in the back, so you can just follow me." Once I'm turned in the opposite direction, my jaw drops discreetly into a silent "Oh my god" because, seriously, coffee couldn't have woken me up as much as this man just did.

Back to professionalism, Nia. "So, how was your drive?" I ask, turning back around to make eye contact once more. Big mistake. Those blues are like daggers into my brain.

"Good," he says. "I'm a bit far away, but thankfully I drive like I'm in the Daytona 500." He laughs. His tone is deep but still boyish and jovial, like there's some inside joke only he's in on.

"It's easy now, but just watch when school starts back in," I say conversationally. I've never been good at small talk, and when I turn to see his eyebrow lifted, I realize I am not rising to the occasion this time either.

We get to the conference room and the company owner isn't here yet. I pull out my phone and check my emails. There's a one-liner stating he'll be a bit late.

Not a problem—I'll just interview him myself! It couldn't be more perfect. This is how the company learns that HR is an important resource anyway, by us just *doing*. I belong in this conference room, and I will claim my spot here if need be.

"Looks like your interviewer is caught in a meeting, but he'll be out soon," I say, pocketing my phone into my slacks. "Make yourself comfortable. Do you need any coffee or...?"

"No thanks," he says, flashing another daring, cocky smile. Does he know he could lead the world with that smile, know armies might follow him? At least armies of women?

"Alright, perfect," I say. "Well, we can go ahead and get started if you want to take a seat over there."

I wave my hand over to show him across the table. When he passes me, his scent wafts by and its unmistakably *man*. I'm fairly sure if Brad Pitt and Ryan Reynolds were together in one room, this would be the smell in the air.

"So, tell me about yourself," I start, sitting across from him.

"Well, I'm Ian. Born and raised in Atlanta. Studied law, passed the bar, and now I'm ready for the next adventure."

"Short but sweet," I say, grinning back at him. "And what got you interested in law?"

"Once I figured out that any game worth playing can be cheated at or outsmarted, I knew law was for me."

Wait—what?

I clear my throat. "Excuse me?"

"I think any good lawyer should like to win. Isn't that point?"

I try to conceal my shock, but I still let out a mix between a scoff and a laugh. He's bold. He takes what he wants. I can't tell if the room's thermostat is high or if he's making me too hot.

"And how long did you study law?"

"Four years. Then I took two off, which I do feel I need to address. There was no bad work history or anything." For the first time, his posture slackens, he averts his eyes, and his grin gets bigger as if compensating for the awkward nature of this conversation.

It's cute. Maybe even adorable. Who is this guy?

"Personal issues," he says. "You know how life is. But, that's not common for me."

There's an awkward silence for a moment, and I'm struggling to fill it. Admittedly, that isn't my strong point. I want to ask more, but there's a line in interviewing that, if crossed, could potentially carry this conversation into illegal territory. I can't ask things like *What happened?*, *Are you okay?*, or even *Are you in a relationship?* Definitely inappropriate.

"So, do you have any pointers to give me before my interview?" he asks after a moment. I shake my head before realizing I may have been ogling him. I hope I wasn't. He leans back in his chair, slinging one arm over the rolling chair next to him, causing it to shift. He jerks his arm away and gives me a sheepish smile. How is it that I've known this man for less than ten minutes and he's already ridiculously entrancing?

"Maybe tone down the sarcasm," I say, giving a side smile and raising an eyebrow in a challenge. It comes off more seductive than I intended. *Shit.*

His eyebrows shoot up at my answer, as if surprised. He should be. I don't do this. I don't entertain taboo work relationships—especially with someone who doesn't even work here yet. He slowly nods and then his short-lived expression of surprise slowly gives way to yet another smirk.

"Noted."

Good god.

The door swings open and the man I know as Treasuries Inc.'s sole owner waltzes in with his usual swagger, the kind that can only come from someone who sports a backward baseball cap and *Pollos Hermanos* tee to work.

"Ian!" he bellows, stretching out an arm.

Ian stands and shakes his hand. "Nice to meet you, sir."

I've seen this same exchange with every candidate so far, but Ian's interaction is much more natural. His hand swings wide and shakes with a noticeably strong grip. I'm willing to bet he didn't need our warm welcome. He's provided his own.

"It was nice to meet you," I say, grasping his resume and making my way to the door.

"Hopefully I see you around," he calls to me.

I both want and very much do not need that burden in my life.

When I get back to my desk, I file his resume for record-keeping purposes. Maybe I'll look at the phone number on it? No. Unprofessional. I'll chalk up the whole experience to a one-and-done, *at least I got to see some eye candy today* type of deal.

Imagine my surprise when, that afternoon, I receive an email with specifications for an offer letter to be sent out ASAP to a Mr. Ian Chambers.

Fantastic.

3

IAN

PRESENT DAY

Do you ever wake up smiling?

That makes me sound like a weird guy, but honestly, just between us weirdos, *do you?*

When I wake up this morning, I know it will be a great day. I lie awake, staring up at my ceiling fan, and I can't help but smile. If anyone were to see me, I'm sure they would think I'm enamored with the thing. Truth is, I am enamored, but not with my fan.

Let's count the ways this week will be great. Number one, I am the best man at my pal's wedding. Number two, I get to spend an entire week at the beach, and number three, I get to spend one whole week with Nia fucking Smith.

Could life get any better?

And I don't mean that with any sarcasm intended. Nia Smith is a witty, intelligent force to be reckoned with. I have spent nine years—*nine years*—hanging out with her, playing the role of good co-worker, never making moves. I respect work-life balance enough to not cross that line; it's a recipe for disaster.

But is there room for disaster now? Not so much, friends. Well, maybe a little. I can't forget about the fact that, for some bewildering reason, Nia Smith has absolutely loathed me for the past two years.

Disaster pending, I suppose. We shall see.

My phone's ringtone goes off in my ear. I still have yet to buy a bedside table, so for years my sleeping buddy has been the buzzing phone resting on the pillow beside me. I pull it closer and look at the caller ID. It's my sister, Ramona. I answer.

"When are you getting here?" she asks before I can even voice any form of greeting.

"Well, I just woke up, so..."

"You're planning the bachelor party, right?"

"Are we going to stay on one subject?" My sister isn't one for staying on track. It's a wonder she focused long enough in school to be a psychologist of her caliber. Then again, both of us Chambers kids could be poster children for the lessening attention span in America.

"I need to know what you're doing because I'm planning the bachelorette party and there are only two strip clubs in town—not nearly enough."

"Sure." I lift my arms above my head, giving a big stretch and groaning.

"And the third bridesmaid: Nia." My heart jumps at the mention of her name. "I still haven't met her. What's she like?" Ramona pouts on the other end of the line. She likes being in the know, and missing out on meeting a bridesmaid is probably killing her.

"Didn't she go to bridal whatever stuff?" I ask.

"Grace didn't tell me she was a bridesmaid until a month ago," she says. I can practically hear the eye roll. "What was I supposed to do?"

"She's nice once you get to know her," I say with a chuckle.

"Good. So, okay, checking off the list...oh! You'll be the designated driver most of the time, right...?"

It's a silly question and she knows it; I can tell by the way the last word fades out like a sentence begging to be wiped from memory. I'll give Ramona the benefit of the doubt. It's been ten years since the car accident. We don't talk about it much in our family, but it's like a constantly healing wound. The second it's mentioned, the stitches are loosened that much more, though I, for one, do not insist on viewing it as some taboo subject. It's mostly their stitches that get tugged apart; mine are forced closed with glue.

"Drink to your heart's content," I say. "My baggage is your treasure. Is that the saying?"

"I think it's trash," she mumbles.

"Yeah, well, take advantage of my misfortune, and stop sounding uncomfortable. Of course I'm driving." I try to lighten the mood as best I can. Sheesh, if I ever want to silence family or friends, bringing up the reason I stay sober on nights out is the sure-fire way to do it.

My phone buzzes and I hold it away from my ear. *Cameron.*

"Hey, it's the groom calling," I say, thankful for the reprieve from this discussion. "I'll talk to you later."

"Do you think penis lollipops would be too much for a bachelorette party?" She gets the sentence out as one final light-hearted jab, and I switch over calls before I have to respond.

"Yell-o?" I answer, hitting the speaker button and laying the phone next to me.

"Ian, we have to leave in one hour," Cameron says. It's matter of fact, borderline demanding, and filled with exhaustion. "Can you make it on time?"

"That's a bit last minute," I joke with a grin only I can see.

Cameron pauses before letting out a heavy exhalation. I know I've pressed the wrong button. It's definitely not the morning, day, or week for this. It's his wedding week and, yes, I do mean wedding *week*. Everyone in the bridal party is receiving a complimentary one-week stay at the resort booked for their wedding, and we leave this morning.

Apparently in one hour.

"Why are you so difficult? Aren't weddings supposed to be fun?" he asks.

"Have you ever *been* to a wedding?" I chuckle.

"No," he says, slowly and skeptically.

"Exactly. Are you thinking, *Well, mine will be different*?"

"Maybe."

"Yeah, they all think that." I exhale, hopping out of bed and walking into the bathroom. "I'll see you soon."

"And what is 'soon'?"

"An hour."

I hang up and take a quick shower, throw on my Friday best, and load up my bags. With the garment bag holding my suit slung over my shoulder and the strap of my duffel over my other arm, I switch off the lights. The chandelier in my foyer takes a second to fade out like some dramatic curtain closing on the stage of my barren townhome.

I zip through the city, but even with all my special maneuvering, I'm still late when I arrive.

Damn. Cameron is gonna kill me.

I've lived here my whole life and I love the city with a burning passion, but I still have trouble anticipating Atlanta traffic. Early mornings haven't been part of my routine in months since I started working from home, living that self-employed life filled with web conferences in boxers and lots of delivered food to the house.

I anticipate Cameron's wrath when I pull in, but I don't have time to process anything he may want to say because —*holy shit is that Nia?!*

Standing on the opposite end of the driveway is the petite

woman I've been anticipating seeing for months. Being caught off guard like this, I could not be less prepared. I expected maybe some cool interaction at the resort where I pull up laughing with Cameron and Grace. *We're having a good time! See? I can be chill!*

Instead I'm running late and looking like a complete asshole, and she is absolutely stunning and out of my league.

Her white-blonde hair is a mess on the top of her head, her smooth arms still lifted up in the process of tying it. She's wearing a very conservative blue collared tank top and thigh-length Bermuda shorts that cover way too much of her beautiful, slender legs. Her knees are already pink from the sun, and her cream-colored sneakers are just one shade darker than the tint of her pure, porcelain skin.

This day could only get better if I were devouring her right here and now.

"Well isn't this a nice surprise," I say, lowering my sunglasses and raising them again. I pop my trunk and retrieve my bag to throw in the back of Cameron's Jeep, gingerly laying my suit down over it.

"Oh," is the only response I get from Nia.

"I bet if you knew I was tagging along, you would have walked to Florida," I say, giving a good-natured laugh. This only elicits a lifted eyebrow and a turn on her heel toward the rear driver's side of the car.

"Right," I say, letting out an exhalation. *I was supposed to be* cool, *damn it!*

Cameron grins back at me from the front seat. "Heyyy man," he says, dragging out the first word as if this is some really awesome coincidence that I met him here.

I nod my head. "Congratulations on marriage. Or, well, to-be marriage." I'm flustered. I just got here and I'm fucking *flustered*. I grip the car's top cage and easily swing my way in. My long legs easily scale this car's height while Nia, on the other hand, struggles to make her way in. I hold out my hand to assist, but she grips the side handle harder and pulls herself in with a determined, neutral stare. Her face is either pink from hatred of me or because she's already burning from the sun.

"Polly, you're already looking like a lobster," I say, laughing. She throws me look. It's not *exactly* a glare, but it still sends shivers down my spine. It's both terrifying and enticing all at once.

"Hopefully I'll grow claws too so I can pinch you," Nia says through pursed lips.

"So crabby," I tease.

Grace forces out a sarcastic, bored laugh while Cameron's laugh from behind the wheel is genuine. "Ha ha," Grace says. "You guys are so hilarious. What good fun." I'm willing to bet the last thing Nia is thinking is how much "fun" this week will be. I plan to prove her wrong.

"I believe this will be a week for the ages," I say with a grin. Nia's eyebrow is lifted once more, as if analyzing any hidden meaning behind my sentence. She has this eternal look to her, like she's waiting for me to present my ulterior motives out in the open—like I'm out to get her or something.

"Sure it will," she says in a flat tone.

Grace huffs and I turn to see her pointing between the two of us accusingly as she walks to the passenger side, hopping in. "Now listen to me: I don't want to deal with you two bickering the whole way down." Her finger stops in front of me. "So, control yourself, Ian."

"Me?"

"Yes, she's talking about you," Nia says, buckling her seatbelt.

"Last time I checked, you're the lobster threatening to murder me."

"If only I could be so lucky."

"No, not today," Grace says, twisting her body to look back

at us as Cameron starts the car with this big grin on his face as if he's admiring just how feisty his fiancée is. "Not this week. This is a happy time for me to marry the love of my life. I'm already irritated because we can't take our dogs, and I refuse to take in these...these additional bad vibes!"

I'm now noticing the letters on Grace's shirt peeking through her long hair: *#Bridezilla*. It looks identical to the custom shirts Ramona usually makes, and I'm willing to bet it's one of her creations. *Well, she hit the nail on the head with this one.*

I extend my hand to Nia once more to offer a truce. "I won't fight if you won't?"

She narrows her brown eyes. They're deep pools of chocolate, swirling with strings of lighter caramel. Nia is this odd mix of forced politeness fueled by a deeper, much darker personal vendetta against me. It's almost like the grudge gives her confidence.

Her posture is perfectly straight as she says, "I'll believe it when I see it."

What a woman.

4

NIA

The nine-hour drive is the opposite of what I imagined when I woke up this morning. I had intended to cruise in my own car while listening to some steamy audiobook. If I have to endure the charm of Ian all week, I could at least fantasize about some attainable muscled hunk taking me on the beach under moonlight.

Instead, I'm stuck with Ian in a tight car with a very handsy bride and groom. Every so often I look and see Ian's large hands on the center console as he leans forward to talk with Cameron. I hate that I imagine what it would be like to touch those hands, or to have them touch me in only the best of horrible ways.

Cameron keeps pulling the car over every other hour to admire various buildings. It's his architectural passion coming out, and every time it's the same deal: Grace lovingly wraps her arms around his waist as they look off in engaged bliss (sometimes I even think I see her touching just below his waistband? *Ew.*), and Ian spends his time either attempting conversation with me or staring off into the distance with his hands in his pockets, looking cool and sexy.

What a jerk.

We eventually stop off at an old roadside country store that advertises local peaches. I walk over to the covered cart, where an old woman smiles at me as if this is the most blessed day she's ever lived. Judging by the texture of her skin and her crinkled laugh lines, I'd say she's spent a lot of her life enjoying this kind of sunny weather. I smile back at her.

"Good morning," I say. Her wrinkled smile beams back. It would be a sweet moment if the chipper voice of Ian didn't come from behind me a second later and almost make me jump out of my skin.

"The weather is beautiful, eh, Polly?"

Happiness gone.

It's the same nickname he's used for years after finding out my parent's absurd naming conventions. Yes, they named their daughter Apollonia. Yes, middle school was an absolute treat. And yes, I used to sort of kind of like it when he called me that. It was like a fun little joke between us—until it wasn't.

I watch him breathe in the surrounding air, showing off his broad, muscular chest as it expands. I bet he's doing that on purpose.

"Don't call me that," I shoot back at him.

Ian is like this—pushy, cocky, always doing whatever he wants. I can't stand it. And yet...it sends some odd spark through me, like fuel to the flame I keep trying to snuff out. Let me tell you: stop, drop, and roll doesn't work. Trust me.

"Nia," he continues, grinning from ear to ear as if walking on eggshells with each syllable. "How long has it been?"

"Not long enough." Eight months and three days, actually. Not that I've been counting.

"Ouch." His hand goes to his heart in mock offense and I try to ignore the gesture as well as his defined wrists and muscled forearms. The sun has been doing him favors this summer. I shake the thought off.

Ian looks down to me—it's the only direction he can look. I am a fairly average 5' 4". He is a little more than a foot taller than me, and while that could seem like a dream for some women, I refuse to be seduced by a man based on height alone. You can shove your online dating profiles stating *I'm over 6 feet tall* someplace else.

"Well, have you missed me?" he asks with a smile. My chest constricts. It's a complicated question, but he doesn't need to know that.

I almost don't want to give him the satisfaction of a conversation, but the old lady at the register stares at me and I feel personally attacked by her judgment. She doesn't know us. She doesn't know the history.

Ian always told me he didn't date co-workers. Of course, he said that at a time when my own inhibitions were lowered, I was vulnerable, and I tried to act on my attraction to him like the silly, lonely idiot I was. I've hated myself ever since, but I've hated him even more. It's easy to dislike a man who turns you down only to find him later that evening with another, much younger co-worker—the receptionist, of all people.

I don't date co-workers, my ass.

I wanted him. It took me a bit to admit it to myself, but I did. Hell, I'd be blind to not long for him now. I had let my guard down and was strong enough to resist at the time, but seeing Ian and Saria climb into that car together? That broke me.

Years of teasing me? Just a fun game for him. It meant nothing. I meant nothing. I was the butt of his jokes, and it's hard to forgive a man who led me on for so long only to shoot me in the heart with an arrow—and not the sweet Valentine kind.

Old lady, you don't know the half of it.

But her gaze drills into me and she reminds me too much of my late grandma, who insisted on me being cordial to even the worst of enemies. So, I oblige the ghost.

"How is self-employment?" I ask.

"It's going well," Ian says, allowing my change of subject and browsing the peaches alongside me. I try my best not to let our arms cross paths, though his hand does come dangerously close. *I'm watching you, boy.* "I like being my own boss."

"You never were one for authority," I say. Understatement of the century. If I had a nickel for every time someone told Ian to do something and he came up with some snarky comment to sidestep the responsibility or just straight-up refused, I wouldn't need to work anymore. Not that I would stop working due to Ian, anyway—just on principle.

"I always respected human resources at least," Ian says. He grins down at me, and I give a sarcastic grimace in return.

"You tested the limits."

"And you let me."

His hand is on the peach right next to the one my hand is hovering over. He arches an eyebrow and takes one step closer. I narrow my eyes, daring him to try anything.

I dislike his stupid, cocky face. I dislike the way he flirts with the world as if his smile is the meaning of life. It makes me want nothing more than to prove him wrong. But, in this shack, in the heat of the summer, there is some weird greenhouse-like effect where I feel flushed, and I can't tell if it's the humidity or that silly little grin of his. There's also that annoying, ever-familiar snag in my chest at the sight and closeness of him.

The fan overhead is the only source of cool air, and it isn't doing its job nearly as well as it should. Ian is driving my blood pressure through the roof of this little fruit stand.

"Don't give yourself so much credit," I say.

We stare at each other like we're in some great war, looking across the battlefield before firing off cannons. On one side, there's me, ready to defend my land and ward off invaders with guns a-blazing. On the other side, there's Ian, a man of secret warfare with an army of spies and silver-tongued speech, drifting into opposing territory just as soft and sweet as poison.

"This is going to be a stellar trip," he declares with a grin.

He picks up the peach and takes a large bite of it. A bit of the fruit's juice slowly runs down his chin, creating a small trail through his stubble before he wipes it off. He wiggles his eyebrows as if he knows I'm watching that single droplet flow down from his lips. He drops some bills on the counter in front of the old woman and, with a wink to her—not even to me—he saunters off. Yes, he *saunters*.

I place my three peaches on the scale in front of the now chuckling woman.

"Honey, if I had a man who looked like he does..." She trails off in thought.

I slap my money on the counter. "Then you would be miserable."

5

IAN

We arrive at the resort late that afternoon. I had to expend most of my energy trying to melt Nia's ice-cold exterior. The snide comments were like a game of chess, each of us attempting to stay moves ahead of the other. I love the game. I love her sass. Even when we stopped for tacos and all of us made it through the line ordering burrito after burrito, Nia ordered a salad, probably just to spite me.

I'm more offended on behalf of the burritos.

Now listen up: I have spent weeks, months, and years pining after Nia. She was the bright, unmoving, stubborn sun that lit up my days before I left Treasuries Inc. to open my own practice. I appreciate her tenacity, but if that girl gets her mind set on something, she sticks to it, even if that dedication is focused on hating me and burritos. Those poor things.

You would think my time away from Treasuries would have eased some of the animosity between us. I was hoping maybe she would forget how much I annoyed her—in particular, those last couple years in which her hatred really turned on full blast for reasons I, quite frankly, don't understand.

We always butted heads to a degree, but we maintained a

semblance of friendship, or maybe more of an understanding. The sarcasm, the witty exchanges...it kept the days interesting and fueled some unspoken spark, but she really laid into me during those last two years. She gave me my first and second write-up when she had never given me any before. She even made me sign the updated employee handbook. She hadn't made me sign any of the updated editions since the day I started, even though I know for a fact she hounded the rest of the company to do so. In that last year, though? You bet your ass I signed each and every amendment.

But I'm done with that and ready to move on. Nia needs to know how I feel. I need to try one last time. I waited months to approach her, to have us in an environment that wasn't constrained by stupid workplace policies. I could have tried my luck during the past few months since we weren't co-workers anymore, but she would have probably been more willing to jump into the ocean and let the tide take her rather than meet me for lunch or dinner. No point in wasting my efforts then when I can put my all into it now.

I can't live life with regrets. I learned that lesson before, and I don't need to learn it again.

Buckle up, Nia Smith.

We're greeted in the resort's lobby by a very loud, earsplitting squeal followed by the *fwip-slap-fwip-slap* of sandals running toward Grace. The poor bride is almost barreled over by a bundle of curly hair. It's my sister, and she's wearing a questionably short crop top and cut-off jean shorts. Her black hair is pulled up into a haphazard ponytail and strands are sticking out every which way in what is most likely a reaction to the intense Florida humidity. Judging by the state of my own hair, I'm not surprised to see the same effect on her.

"You're getting married! You're getting married!" she yells as various vacationers turn to stare. "Girl, I am going to matron of honor this place UP!" She finally pulls out of the hug, and I notice her shirt also has vinyl lettering: *#HonorThisBitch*.

Grace and my little sister, Ramona, have been best friends from elementary school all the way through college. I've seen them through everything: the awkward teenage years and their loud sleepovers spent gossiping about boys (which they inevitably kicked me out of with a scream), Grace's rebellion stage where she came to our house to vent about her completely unreasonable parents, and Ramona's passionate love affair with her now husband Wes. That last one almost split up their friendship, but, as usual, they persevere—a joint force to be reckoned with.

"I want penis popsicles, and I will settle for no less," Grace demands with her hands on her hips.

Ramona nods in agreement, and I spot a quick glance to me with a hint of *I knew it* plastered on her massive grin. "Penis pops it is, Grace." Her arms outstretch toward me and I do the same, Frankenstein's-monster-walking my way over to her until we hug.

"Big brother," she says.

"Little sister."

She pulls back with a cordial pat and then rubs her palms together, scheming—always scheming. "Now where is that other bridesmaid?"

I glance over to see Nia already making her way to check in and completely ignoring the scene behind her. Her head tilts slightly as if she's heard her name being called, but she stays the course of waiting in line and pretending the loud girl behind her doesn't exist.

"She's hiding from you," I whisper to Ramona, throwing my thumb over my shoulder to direct her toward Nia. Ramona's face contorts into dissatisfaction, but I hold out my finger, telling her to wait a moment as I turn on my heel to walk toward Nia.

"Hey Polly, I can take your bags," I offer, extending my hand.

She finally looks over her shoulder to see both Ramona and Grace staring with their lips pursed in mock duck faces and their butts sticking out as if they were mannequins.

"I'm fun, I swear," Ramona calls over, winking. Grace is grinning back with two thumbs up. Nia's eyes widen and she suddenly looks like a child tourist seeing Mickey Mouse for the first time and realizing, *Holy shit that's an actual, real-life, giant rat*. Except Ramona is an actual, real-life, massive extrovert.

I smile. "I'll check in for you. Got your ID?"

Nia slowly lowers the strap of her bag into my hand, taking some of her tank top with it and revealing a colored bra strap. I try to hide my grin. She reaches into her crossbody purse to pull out her license, jabbing it toward me between her index and middle finger. "Lose it and you're dead."

"There's that charm." I take the ID and lug the bag's strap over my shoulder as she walks toward the two girls. Ramona squeals again and Nia is embraced before she can even protest.

"Nia, right?"

"Yes," she gets out, her face smooshed against Ramona's chest. "Hi, I'm Nia."

"I have a shirt for you!" Ramona pushes her shoulders away so she can reach into the tote slung in the crook of her arm. "It says *#BridesmaidBeast*! What do you think?"

"Cute!" Nia grins from ear to ear. I know that grin—it's her work smile. Is she *actually* happy with it, or is she being nice? I know. Because I know Nia.

"Wow, is this your natural hair color? Girl, it's gorgeous." Ramona is stroking her hands through Nia's ends.

"Never dyed it a day in my life," Nia says, and I sense a hint of pride in her voice. I would be proud too. It's gorgeous, like the hair of an angel—a hard, jawbreaker shell of an angel.

"Confident," Ramona observes, looking her up and down. "Love it."

Grace finally steps in to do formal introductions between the two. I eventually see Nia's laugh shift from uncomfortable and resistant to more genuine with every moment that passes.

"Now ladies, my sweet blonde and my firecracker red," Ramona says, throwing an arm around Nia and Grace's shoulders, "let's hit up that pool."

Wait, pool?

"Sir, are you going to move forward or what?" a voice behind me asks, and the tone knocks me out of my thoughts of Nia in a tiny pink bikini. I'm ready to turn and give this dude a piece of my mind when I'm greeted by a familiar face.

Just like Ray can fit into any girls' club, her husband Wes is a man's man. He's already pulling me in for a bear hug, and it's like a battle of arm strength as we embrace hard enough to pop the other's head off his neck.

"Truce?"

"Truce."

We let go. Wes is shorter, but what he lacks in height, he makes up for in muscle. He's like a walking brick wall, and his arms are the graffiti. When I first met him, he had a few strategically placed tattoos, but the number grew quickly and now his sleeves are fully finished pieces of art.

Cameron, appearing to be a walking coat rack with arms full of Grace's bags, walks over to join the two of us, panting as he does so. Wes is already pulling him into the test-of-strength hug ritual.

"Congratulations, buddy!" Wes says, patting his back.

"Thanks, man," Cameron says. "I'm just ready for beer. Lots of beer. And sun. Maybe volleyball?"

"Ian, you got the bachelor party down?" Wes asks, nudging my arm as I edge toward the counter.

"Have I planned the bachelor party? Get real. I'm a master

at planning bachelor parties," I say, letting out a bark of laughter. "Bars, getting arrested, strip clubs—the necessary evil—you name it, we'll do it. If I could have planned my sister's bachelorette party, I would have, but apparently that's 'not the brother's job' and would have been 'weird.'" I use air quotes as I shrug.

"You haven't planned any of it, have you?" Cameron says, shaking his head.

"Define *plan*." I grin and I pass my card along to the girl across the counter. "Ian Chambers and Nia Smith, please."

Wes sighs. "Cam, it feels like just yesterday when you mercilessly flirted with Grace at our dinner party."

"Was it that obvious?" Cameron asks with a cheeky grin.

"We all knew you were getting some that night," I say. I cringe as the concierge rolls her eyes in response and hold my hand up in apology. "Sorry."

"I like to think I was playing it cool," Cameron says mid-laugh.

"You're not even self-aware." I tsk. "Bad trait."

Cameron balks at my statement as I collect the cards and room keys, pocketing Nia's to give her later. "Who are you to talk? If I had to listen to you and Nia argue for one more minute..."

The sliding glass doors to the pool area open, and Ramona is waltzing back in, now with a giant straw sunhat and less a tote bag.

"Forgot sunscreen!" she laments, throwing her hands in the air and power walking to the elevators, arms pumping beside her.

"I'll join you," I say quickly, waving a hand back to Cameron. "Oh no, gotta go. Talk later!" I throw him a salute, having successfully avoided the conversation about Nia, and he throws me the finger.

Ramona is impatiently pressing the elevator button until

it opens, and we both climb in. I would try to make conversation with her, but my sister's tapping foot is keeping any words I could say at bay. I place my own foot on top of hers to stop it.

"Ew, gross feet," she says, lifting her leg to shoo mine away.

"Ew, gross legs."

The elevator dings and we both file out. I find my door and unlock it to drop off bags while Ramona rushes into her own room. The decor has that classic beach hotel look: cream-colored wallpaper with pastel watercolor seashells painted on them, the smell of sand and the cool tile practically seeping into my shoes, and the kitschy way every cabinet, baseboard, and chair is some creamy off-white color. In the center of the room is a seahorse bedspread on a king-sized wicker bedframe.

Yeah, very kitschy.

I unzip my luggage and pull out a pair of navy blue swim trunks. When I put them on, they're a bit shorter than they have any right to be, but with my height, it's difficult to find shorts that are long enough to hit my knee. I look down to my thigh and see my scar is showing just below the hem. I tug the shorts down a bit to try to conceal it.

No dice.

When I walk out of my room, I see Ramona's door still wide open as she audibly groans in frustration.

"Where is the *damn sunscreen*?" she wails.

"Maybe it's scared of your constant yelling," I call to her.

"Shut up, Ian!"

Ah, sisterly love.

I find Nia's room a couple doors down and unlock it to unload her luggage. When I see her wicker bedframe with the starfish sheets, I gulp. God, I'd kill to see Nia on there—splayed out, tied to the posts...

Bad thoughts, Ian.

I leave the room, adjusting my shorts at the thought, and

I'm immediately met with a face roughly running into my chest. A swirl of blonde hair greets me.

"Speak of the devil," I get out. My hard erection bumps into her hip and I try to step back quickly, but there's no way she didn't feel me. *Shit.*

"You're in my way," she says, flustered, her cheeks reddening almost instantly. *Yep. She definitely felt me. Double shit.*

"You're welcome for dropping your luggage off," I say.

She breathes in as if debating whether or not to be cordial and then responds with a very small "Thanks" that is mumbled under her breath.

Baby steps.

The door slams behind me at the same time Ramona runs out of her room with sunscreen raised in the air and yells, "Aha!"

Successes for all of the Chambers family today.

6

NIA

I'VE BEEN AROUND IAN FOR TEN HOURS AND IT STILL FEELS TOO surreal to be true.

He's gotten hotter. Is that a thing? Do men get hotter with age? Even after eight months? Maybe it's the hints of gray littered around his temples. Maybe it's his ever-growing smile —the one that gets cockier with time.

Ian is a train barreling toward me, and I'm too blinded to get off the tracks. Didn't I learn my lesson years ago? When the barriers come down, you get out of the way—you don't admire the beautiful locomotive about to slam into your face.

But he's everything I remember: witty, sarcastic, and so gorgeous I wonder if other men feel cheated in comparison.

I spend most of the late afternoon lying on the beach and soaking in the little bit of sun left in the sky. I still apply heavy sunscreen because my fair complexion is on very precarious speaking terms with the sun. I think they may have an agreement. *You come out in my territory, you get burned! Capeesh?*

While I also have Grace to accompany me in the shade, Ramona is lying starfish-style outside of the umbrella's covering. Both girls are very scantily clad in tiny bathing suits while

I, on the other hand, threw on my standard two-piece with no additional slits or cutouts. I feel almost plain in comparison, but I *dare* the sun to take a jab at me now.

"You guys are missing out," Ramona says.

"By 'missing out,' do you mean 'avoiding skin cancer'?" Grace asks, tapping around on her tablet with its pen. "Us pale girls don't stand a chance."

"No, by 'missing out,' I mean 'doing work instead of relaxing,'" Ray replies, turning over onto her stomach.

Grace and I both look down at our laps. She has her tablet and a few pieces of paper, and I'm reading a book titled *Difficult Conversations to Have with Employees*.

Whoops.

"Hey, I like my job too, but this is vacation, you guys," Ramona says. "I mean, seriously, Grace—it's your wedding. Shouldn't you be at some cabana getting fed grapes by a pool boy before you're locked in with Cam?"

"A fantasy pool boy doesn't sound too bad about now, actually," I mutter, eliciting a raised eyebrow and a slow-spreading toothy grin from Ramona.

"What was that, again?"

"Ray, I think you're projecting your fantasies onto mine," Grace interjects. "I'd prefer a coconut with a little straw in the top." She takes two fingers and mimics grasping the straw, to which Ramona laughs.

"Oh, a *little* straw? Poor Cameron."

"Ha ha," Grace says. Then she nods to me. "What about you, Nia?"

"Me?" What would be my fantasy? Some kind of sexy man with glasses, rippling abs, and a book. Yes, he would definitely be holding a book, and he would hand me a glass of ice-cold water because a girl has to be refreshed and he's a sexy, responsible man. "I don't know." I laugh. *Sexy men with water.* "Probably pineapple or something."

Grace scrunches up her nose. "Isn't that supposed to help with the taste of...you know." Her hands hover over her bikini bottoms.

Ramona laughs. "You ever tested the theory out?"

"One time I dated a guy who tried it out," I say, absentmindedly shuffling my book in my lap. "There was some bit of a difference in taste." I look up and am met with two ear-to-ear grins from both women.

"Oh really?" Grace says, scooting to the edge of her folding chair in interest with her arms cradling the tablet and papers. "You've never talked about exes before."

That's because I only have two exes. I tried online dating for a short stint, but after one particularly bad experience with a man who insisted on butt stuff after the first date, I said *no thank you* to the whole shebang. Or maybe he broke up with me? I honestly can't remember. I recall always choosing whichever restaurant *I* wanted as opposed to his preference, and I picked the movies we saw, and the positions during sex. Yeah, now that I think about it, he might have broken up with me.

I can't help the fact that I have a problem with losing control. I like knowing what I'm getting into. So sue me.

"They're in the past." I shrug. "It's not a huge deal."

"Sure, Nia," Grace says, nodding and sliding back into her chair. "Sure."

"Oh-kay, I can feel my skin melting." Ramona lifts herself off the ground and sprints out to the water, stumbling through the sand and splashing in the ocean with her hands held high.

Even from the little amount of time I've spent with Ian's sister, I can already conclude she is just as wild, open, and bold. In fact, I'm noticing a lot of similarities between the siblings—except for the one difference being that Ramona is actually really cool, and Ian is a douche.

I glance over at the guys. Ian, Cameron, and Wes are all by the beachside net punching a volleyball over to each other. I have a secret theory that they're only playing so they can flex their muscles in front of the world without judgment. It's clear all three of them hit the gym regularly, Ian especially. *Damn it.*

I admire—no, I loathe the way his shoulders connect to his upper arms and the way his forearms bulge out as he serves the ball over the net. His swim trunks sit on his hips a bit too well for my comfort, and his Adonis V dips low into his shorts, resting right below his abs that twist, turn, and ripple with every step he takes. Then I notice a scar peeking out from just under the hem of shorts. It's a couple inches long with the skin puckering in the center, but I can't get a better look before it disappears back under the fabric after he's done stretching his arms above his well-proportioned head. Do people have well-proportioned heads?

Oh shit.

Ian's very well-proportioned head turns toward me, and I bury my face back into my book, causing my sunglasses to slide down to the end of my nose. Out of the corner of my eye, I see Ian's cocky, lopsided smirk spread across his face. He caught me checking him out and, *oh god*, I can feel my face getting warm. Can I play it off as a sunburn like earlier? *Do me a favor for once, you giant, blazing star!*

I chance a look up after a couple seconds and *shit!* he's still staring back at me over his sunglasses. My heart drops into my abdomen. My exes never looked at me that way.

I return to reading the same paragraph over and over and there's no way in hell I'm actually processing the words. I can still feel his eyes drilling into me, but I refuse to acknowledge him. Then I hear a loud *thunk!* and jerk my head up to see a ball land on the sand near Ian's feet as he grips his ear. Cameron and Wes double over laughing.

Ian looks back up at me to check if I saw him get mercilessly whacked upside the head. I slowly swivel my eyes over to him with a smirk and a single thumbs-up.

You bet I saw that.

THAT NIGHT, we all decide to put on nicer clothes and meet in the hotel bar. I stall in my room, looking at myself in the mirror. I told Grace I just needed some time to check up on emails, which I did, but I'm also much too busy running my hands along my dress hem and evaluating whether I can pull off this type of cut. It's not exactly scandalous, but I figure—what the hell! I'm on vacation! I can be a bit sexy if I want to. I can be different!

It's definitely a deeper, sexier red than I would have picked out normally, and the material is thinner than my usual well-made cotton tops, but the lack of material in both the structure of the dress and the length of its skirt lends to a breezier feeling, which maybe I need.

I think about the fantasy pool boy again.

Yeah, I look like I could seduce a pool boy...or distract a man from a volleyball game.

I would kill to see that ball hit Ian's face a thousand times.

Those abs, though. That grin... He's never had much of a problem getting women, no matter how young or inappropriate the relationship is.

No, don't think about that night. You're better than that.

I hear my phone buzz on the bed and see that it's my brother, Harry.

"Are you checking in on me?" I immediately ask.

He laughs. "I have to make sure you haven't killed anyone yet."

"Now who would I kill?"

"Something something Ian something?"

"I don't need your sass. How's Jiggy?"

"Your cat is fine."

"And her food bowl is full?" There's a moment of silence, and it lasts longer than a comfortable pause. It feels weird—not at all like I'm just waiting for him to speak and confirm the cat food situation. "What?" I ask. "You're quiet. You didn't call to talk about my cat, did you?" *Oh god, is she okay?*

"Grant called." I breathe a sigh of relief but immediately tense back up.

Wait, what?

"Well there's a name I haven't heard in a few years. You're talking about Dad, right?" I say. "Surely you are."

"Unfortunately not." Harry exhales. "A mister Grant Smith, Junior."

One step forward and then three steps back to the bed where I sit on the edge, staring at the door I wish I would have walked through already.

I may have identified Ian as my worst enemy, but my eldest brother Grant might take the cake. He's the oldest out of the six of us children, and he is undoubtedly the worst. You know that one sibling who abandons the family for better things, thus breaking up the band? Yeah, he's *that* sibling.

"What does he want?" I ask. No, I think I might hiss it. Honestly, I'm too distracted to know.

"Not sure." Harry sighs. "He says he's moving back."

"Moving back?!" I yell.

Harry continues as if I didn't interrupt. "He wants to stay with Mom and Dad, and by association, me and Cara."

I stand to pace, trying to wrap my head around what I'm hearing. My brother's daughter, Cara, is a pure, wonderful child with a great heart. Taking on the role of both father and mother figures, Harry has tried to instill in her a solid work ethic and moral compass. The last thing she needs is a hotshot new uncle barging in with his arrogance and frivolity.

"He's never even met his niece," I scoff. "She's going to be freaked out by this weird man."

"Think we haven't considered that?"

"Sure, but has he said why he needs to stay?"

Harry doesn't speak for a moment, but I can hear his inaudible mumbles as he tries to find the words to say next. "I think he needs money."

"Bullshit," I snap before I can think.

Harry laughs, and I start to laugh myself. It's a ridiculous thing to imagine. Grant, a man with no money. He's *made* of money. He probably sleeps with a quilt made of hundred-dollar bills and pillows filled with quarters.

"I'll let you know when I hear more," Harry says, "but I figured you needed to know he called."

I nod before realizing he can't see me. "Right. Thanks."

"Anyway, I also stopped by and took another look at your car." He sighs. "There's nothing I can do for it. You're going to need another one."

"Not happening."

"You make enough money, more than the rest of us—apparently even Grant nowadays."

I laugh, and he can't help but let out a chuckle as well. "No, no new car, Harry."

"You're too stingy."

"No, I'm avoiding ending up like Grant. Whatever he did to screw up."

"Too soon, Nia. Too soon."

I look at my watch. I'm running much later than I should be.

"Hey, I gotta let you go. We'll talk later."

"Have fun. You need it," Harry says. "And don't kill the lawyer."

I try to respond but he hangs up too quick. *Jerk.*

I inhale and look at myself in the mirror once more.

Yes, my dress is entirely too short.

After I spend the entire elevator ride tugging down on the

garment in a struggle to get comfortable with the amount of thigh I have on display, I'm greeted by Ramona and Grace's small chorus of wolf whistles. They wear dresses similar to mine—short and fitted—but while it's clear they feel right at home in theirs, I feel like I should be having money thrown at me.

We meet up with the boys at the bar. An old couple at the opposite end, who both happen to be wearing fisherman hats and short-sleeved tropical floral button-ups, looks at our party. I'm honestly not sure if they're the same person. I wonder for a moment if maybe the old couple will take me in and we could be wonderful wallflowers together, but the fantasy is lost—*poof!*—when I stop at Ian's ice-cold eyes staring back at me.

It's hard to break away when he's giving me *that* type of look with *those* type of eyes. He's letting them wander across my stomach, legs, ankles, and back up to my chest. I feel stripped naked and suddenly very hot and uncomfortable.

"You look nice," he says.

"Thanks," I snap and cross my arms.

He laughs. "It must be exhausting hating me. Let's pretend for a second that you don't."

"I have a limited imagination," I sneer.

"Well mine is stellar."

Abort mission. Abort mission!

This isn't the first time he's told me I look nice—in fact, I wrote him up for it a couple years ago—but the way he looks at me in this moment is definitely out of the norm. I'm accustomed to goofy, pushy Ian with a boyish grin and an ultimately harmless way about him. What I'm not used to is seeing the way his eyes scour my body as if he's ready to do anything and everything to me.

But I know his games.

I bark out a laugh. "Women must eat that up."

"What?" he asks as his head shoots back up to look at my face. *Yeah, eyes up here, buddy.*

"You. This whole act." I wave my hand up and down to gesture at him. "The compliments and the staring. I thought you were just going for shock value in the office because you thought it bothered me, but god, you really *are* like this."

Ian's eyebrows shoot up and he chuckles, leaning back with his hands in his pockets like he always does when he thinks he's got the other person all figured out. It must be a lawyer thing because he also strikes the same pose when he's resolved an issue he's been working at for days. I can't count how many times I saw him pacing his office only to stop and grin to himself once he cracked something.

Yes, he's even cocky when he thinks nobody else is looking. It's infuriating.

"Well you're just pulling out all the stops tonight, aren't you, Polly?"

"I've told you not to call me that," I respond through gritted teeth.

"You're sexy when you're angry," he teases. "Keep going. Please." The tone in his voice gets deeper, as if he's daring me. I've never heard him call me sexy before. Maybe it's the dress. Maybe it's how far away from an office environment we are.

"Getting embarrassed?" he asks.

"Don't flatter yourself."

"Did you wear that dress for me?"

Maybe.

"You are so full of it."

"Well, we can discuss that—"

As I open my mouth to yell every single expletive I can think of, Ramona is already yelling, "Woah, Ian!" and Grace's arms are suddenly up in the air.

"Oh-kay!" Grace wipes her hands against each other. "I am cleansing myself of this situation."

Ian and I both jerk our heads toward her and say, "What?" simultaneously. This twin moment results in another immediate look exchanged between us—my glare and his smirk.

"I tried to warn you in the car, but I am putting my foot down now: this behavior is unacceptable and I will not have it," Grace declares. I see Ramona pucker her lips in an effort to get to the straw that's dawdling on the other side of her glass. Her expression clearly says, *This is gonna be good.*

"Get out tomorrow," Grace demands. "Leave the resort. Do not bother me or Cameron with your mess of a...whatever this is." Grace's hands are waving up and down our height, and her complexion is gradually starting to turn the same shade as her hair.

"Bad vibes," Ramona whispers. "Bad. Vibes."

"Where do you expect me to go?" Ian asks.

"I don't expect you to go anywhere, Ian. I expect *both* of you to go somewhere."

"That's the same thing," he says flatly.

"No, I mean—" Her hands curl into fists next to her head as she growls in frustration. "Both of you go somewhere *together*, and do not come back until you've worked your crap out."

My mouth gapes open. "Together? No. No, no, no. I am not spending an entire day with this guy." What would happen? We'd go sightseeing? Hit up a beach? Maybe stroll into a back alley and fight to the death? At this point, maybe.

"Only until you've worked your problems out," she amends. As if that makes it better.

"You can pick some stuff up for the bachelorette party," Ramona quickly suggests. She slurps through the straw as it hits the final remnants of drink in her glass.

Great. Perfect. I'm sure I will love going on some wild goose chase for items in stores I don't know in a town I've never been to in my life with a man I both want to ride mercilessly and also punch in the nose.

Sounds like a blast.

"And you"—Wes pokes Ian's chest—"can pick up stuff for the bachelor party you haven't planned. How perfect!" Wes flashes a cheesy smile that takes up half his face. It's endearing, but I remember that I'm mad and don't have time to let his joy rub off on me.

I dart my eyes up to Ian, who is looking down at me with one eyebrow arched in that reliably sexy way of his.

"Sounds like a plan," he says, and even though he isn't grinning like Wes, his expression still looks like he's sneaking in a bit more eagerness than I'd like.

7

NIA

EIGHT YEARS AGO

"No, Mom, we are not having tofu for Thanksgiving!"

"You ruined it."

"I offered to bring moose."

"Ew, geez, Jamie!"

"Are the potatoes ready yet?"

People all around the United States make jokes about how Thanksgiving dinners force you to spend time with your otherwise distant family. These jokes are my reality. The eclectic, the self-proclaimed political pundit, the nostalgic—every family has them, and with me being the fifth out of six children, we have just about everything.

"The potatoes will be ready when they're ready!" shouts my sister Sarah, lifting her oven mitt and shooing two of our brothers out into the living room.

"No, not on the carpet!" I yell over their continued conversation on football. "Shoes off!"

"They didn't hear you," Harry says, a black coffee already resting in the palm of his hand as his other fingers loop around the handle.

"You think?" I snap, glaring at him. He holds up his free hand in surrender while I grab the tiny vacuum off the wall.

I trudge into the living room and shove the portable vacuum against my brother Jamie's chest.

"Shoes. Off," I demand.

He's too busy showing off his new Chacos to acknowledge me. This is the same brother who denies it is winter in Georgia and says things like, "Being from Alaska, this is *real* cute." He grins and walks away with his *damn shoes still on.* I seethe the entire way back to the kitchen.

"Lighten up, Nia," Harry says, swinging his arm over my shoulder.

"I'll lighten up when I can afford to."

Thanksgiving is the only time we all get together, and as our family has grown, my parents' one-floor ranch home simply doesn't do the job anymore. So, this year, I offered to host. I just bought my first house, which has an open floor plan and is only a few miles down the road from them. It cost me a pretty penny—a pretty penny that also paid for those new carpets currently being ravaged by my brother's sandals.

"Move," demands Sarah, using her hips to nudge Harry out of the way before ripping the oven door open.

"Ouch," he says in mock offense, chuckling and cupping his coffee mug tighter while stepping out of the way. He takes a sip then sticks out his bottom lip in disappointment. "Nia, would you mind making more?"

"Sure," I say, tired of being idle anyway. I move to the opposite side of the kitchen and whip open the fridge to grab coffee grounds.

A head peeps over the top of the door, and when it closes, I see my oldest brother, Grant, examining the bag in my hand as if scanning it for anything that could be wrong. And he will find something, because he always does.

"No whole bean?" he asks.

Faster than The Flash, this one.

Grant does this thing where he places one hand in his pocket, leans in the opposite direction, and squints as if considering whether his next comment will be clever enough to say out loud and make him sound like the smartest person in the room. Everything is about image with him. He once had blond hair like the rest of us but has dyed it a deep auburn. He's not fooling anyone, though. That patchy attempt at a beard is blond through and through.

"If you're going to be picky, you don't get any," I say.

"Yes, but I'm *always* picky," he says with a grin, as if being self-aware will make his statement cute somehow.

"Wow, imagine that. Then no coffee for you, Grant."

"She put the tofu in again!" Sarah groans in front of the oven. "I'm going to kill her. This is turkey day, damn it!" And off she goes—storming past the three of us and into the living room, no doubt in search of either my mom, who will insist on tofu, or my father, who might throw out a half-assed pun like how we could *gobble* up the tofu or something.

Turkey humor. That's what I'm dealing with these days.

"What's so bad about tofu?" Grant shrugs, still eyeing the offensive ground coffee that dares to be in his presence, presumably determining if he will deign to consume it.

"It's not turkey," Harry says with a chuckle.

"If you close your eyes, it's the same thing," Grant says, running a finger through his thick locks. Our dad had a massive bald spot by the time he was thirty-six, and it's highly suspect that Grant, the spitting image of our father, namesake and all, does not have one.

"Did you get plugs?" I ask, narrowing my eyes and reaching for his hair.

Grant scoffs and takes a step back, combing through it again. "All natural, baby."

"Maybe if you close your eyes." Harry chuckles. "Are plugs the big new thing out in L.A.?"

"If you ever left this town, you would know there's so much more out there," Grant croons, his nose pointing up a bit higher than what I'm comfortable with. Last year, Grant moved himself to the opposite side of the country, where he works as a defense attorney for celebrities, goes to movie premieres, and looks at the Hollywood sign or something. Who really knows.

"You're stockpiling money, Harry. I know you are," Grant says. "Just come out to California. We'd love to have you." As if it's some exclusive club. I glance at Harry, who looks down into his coffee cup with a small smirk. True to form, he seems unfazed by our brother's comments, but I can't help being slightly offended on his behalf.

While I just bought a new house, Harry is still living with our parents and trying to get his mechanic career off the ground. He has a dream of opening his own shop, but he keeps that dream pretty close to the vest, along with the money he's saving to open it.

"Yeah, maybe, I guess," Harry says with a shrug and a lopsided smile. "But then how would I get to see Nia all the time?" he asks, throwing me a wink.

"Nia, I'm talking to you too," Grant says, leaning his weight against the fridge, knocking over a magnet and sending a picture swishing down toward the floor.

"Pick it up," I immediately demand. It wasn't supposed to come out as harsh as it did, but Grant can bend his L.A. ass over and get the damn thing.

Grant sighs as if it's such a ridiculous inconvenience to pick up something he himself knocked down, but eventually he leans over and grabs it.

"Who are these people?" he asks, examining the photo. "Wait a second, is this your *office*?" He lets out a cackle, and I roll my eyes.

"Some of us don't mind corporate life," I say, filling the carafe with water and dumping it into the maker before clicking on the power. It immediately rumbles to life.

"Did you guys make a Christmas card?" he asks, flashing it in front of me with a smug smile. I snatch it away and slide it back under the triangle magnet, straightening it in the process. The picture has the whole company gathered together in our back warehouse clutching beers, wearing tacky holiday sweaters, and grinning at the camera. I'm standing off to the side with strands of my hair poking out every which way. I had just run into frame after setting the camera on a timer. I didn't think it was possible to sense how out of shape someone is through a picture alone, but there I am.

"Yikes, that guy is tall," Grant says, pointing at the handsome dark-haired man in the back.

"That's our in-house lawyer," I say. Ian does stick out like a sore thumb, and not just because he's tall. His grin is the widest in the picture, and he's undoubtedly the most attractive. It's not that the rest of the office isn't, but let's just say he's a stallion among one-eyed sheep.

He seems ecstatic to even be there and, like myself, he's the only other person not holding a beer. I remember him toasting my water with his. It was a weird intimate moment only made more exciting by his boyish grin. I smile at the memory. In the picture, his hands are raised high in the air, exaggerating his height even more, and right in front of him, throwing a thumbs-up with an almost equally excited grin, is our new junior designer, Cameron Kaufman. He's only been working at Treasuries for a couple weeks, but Ian has taken to him really quickly.

Grant laughs. "He seems like a good time. Shouldn't corporate lawyers be stiffs? Or is that just reserved for HR?"

"And independent attorneys are better?" I deadpan.

"We get shit done. Does this lawyer guy get shit done?"

"Okay, enough questions," I say, shaking my head and going over to the cabinet to grab an additional mug for myself. I spot the handle of rum in the corner and consider spiking my drink. I even laugh to myself a little. *I'll definitely need it with a day like today.* It isn't until Grant pushes past me with an "Ooh!" and snatches it that I think, *On second thought, maybe not.*

"Hiding it from us?" he asks, unscrewing the cap and taking a large swig that's almost impressive. Though, based on how little it phases him to chug it, I sense red flags. When I glance at Harry, he seems equally concerned.

"Apparently we're having tofu!" Sarah rushes back into the kitchen with her girlfriend following behind her, arms crossed. The new girl is young, beautiful, and new to this whole Thanksgiving thing. She is clearly at a loss for where to go, and I'm willing to bet my mom has run out of small talk about tofu or *Days of Our Lives.*

"Too many cooks!" Sarah says, her eyes darting between all of us, lingering for a moment on Grant.

"We're waiting on coffee," Harry says, holding his mug in the air. I do the same. Grant shoves the handle of rum behind his back.

"Well, I was just making Thanksgiving dinner, but what do I know?" Sarah throws her arms in the air before bolting out again, going who knows where.

"She's just a bit stressed," her girlfriend says apologetically. We all nod, unable to say much else until she waltzes her way out.

"A *bit* stressed?" Grant scoffs, bringing the bottle back around to take another swig. "How long have they been dating again?"

"Who knows." I shrug. "Also, none of us are really drinking, Grant."

"Funny, I figured I was," he says, wiggling his eyebrows and throwing his head back to swallow the tipped rum. He smacks his lips and sighs. "Well, she's not just stressed because of the turkey or tofu. I also told her I'm not coming next year."

Harry and I jerk our heads to him, and Grant's eyebrows rise as if surprised the attention of the room shot to him so quickly, though I'm willing to bet that's the exact reaction he wanted.

"Why would you say that?" I ask, the question more of an accusation. Harry pats me on the shoulder and holds out his coffee mug. Even though Grant and Sarah are the real twins in the family, I've always known Harry and I have a much closer connection than the rest of the siblings. I relax my shoulders and pull the gurgling coffee pot from its holder, pouring some into his offered mug.

"Because I'm moving to Italy."

"Italy!" I bellow, and Grant instantly shushes me with his hand. "Why tell Sarah now? It's Thanksgiving, for God's sake."

"Well, it would come out eventually when I didn't stroll in next year with a turkey in hand."

"You didn't even do that this year!"

"See? Expectations are already lowered."

"I like that you were just going to just wait until the 'Whoops, where's the turkey?' moment." Harry chuckles.

"You're ruining Sarah's Thanksgiving!" I hiss, darting my eyes to the living room, where she's sitting on the couch with her arms crossed.

"She took it well enough." Grant shrugs.

"Why are you moving?"

"Work, opportunity, adventure." He shrugs yet again. "Does it matter?"

To Grant, probably not. Nothing ever matters when it comes to our family. When he went off to college at an Ivy League school up north, he promised to call us daily. After the first month, the calls went from daily to weekly, eventually fading to never. When he received a scholarship to study abroad, we said, "Bon voyage!" with our various instant messaging apps open for communication. In six months' time, we received not one message, and when he moved across the country saying he would simply text us, we didn't believe him anymore. We were right.

"Whatever. You can do whatever you like," I huff. "You're an adult."

"Ever the pragmatist," Grant says, lifting the handle to his lips once more.

"Stop it," I say, snatching it from him and shoving it back in the cabinet with a *bang!* He reaches in to grab a mug and fills it with coffee from the pot.

"Oh, are you going to join the commoners with our ground coffee?" I say, flattening my palm against my chest. He grimaces at me, but it only lasts a second before Sarah is blasting through the kitchen again, opening the oven, groaning, and then leaving with only the remnants of her irritation remaining. The no-name girlfriend walks in for a moment, sees us, peeps out some noise that's a mix between "Oops" and a whine, then exits.

"Seriously, what is her name?" Grant whispers.

"I think it's Sara," Harry says with a straight face.

"Get real," I laugh. "Sarah and Sara?"

"Maybe if you lose your biological twin, you have to date another," Harry says, lifting an eyebrow at Grant, barely making it through the sentence before breaking out in a smile.

"See? I'm so replaceable," Grant says. "Anyway"—he turns his body toward me—"when are *you* going to bring someone to Thanksgiving?"

This is why everyone hates the holidays.

"Why me?" I shoot back. "Why not ask Harry when he'll get a girlfriend?"

"Leave me out of this," Harry says.

"We're talking about you, baby sister," Grant insists. I rest my weight on my hip, assuming a *Watch what you say* stance because if I know anything about my brother, it's that his filter is nonexistent. "You must have someone you can bring. You're pretty now."

There we go.

Harry lets out a low whistle.

"*Now?*" I ask. "What do you mean *now?*"

"Come on, you can't have your controlling personality without it being paired with looks," Grant says, drinking his coffee nonchalantly as if he didn't just call me out.

"I have more than that going for me," I say through an exhaled breath. "And most other women do too."

"Nia is studying for her HR certification, actually," Harry jumps in, throwing an arm around my shoulder again.

"That's good!" Grant says, but it still feels patronizing. Last time I checked we were having Thanksgiving in my new house *paid for by me*, not that it matters to Mr. Italy-bound.

"Yeah, so I don't really have time for dating right now," I say, not hiding my hint of a sneer.

Grant smiles, and I'm not even sure he's picking up on how condescending it looks.

"Everyone has time for dating," bellows a deep voice. Our middle brother, Lawrence, comes in with his football jersey draped over his muscled shoulders, rifling through the cabinets.

"What are you looking for?" I ask.

"Snack," he grunts.

"We're about to eat!" I say, slapping his hand off the cabinet door, hoping to close it before another brother of mine steals my rum.

Lawrence shakes his wrist in mock pain. "Not according to Sarah," he says, nodding his head over to the living room where Sarah's head is in her hands. Other Sara strokes her back.

"Fruit of my loins!" Our dad comes around the corner, the thick sleeves of his cross-stitched sweater rolled up to his elbows and his hands raised in the air like a messiah ready to liberate his people.

"Gross," Lawrence mumbles, scrunching his nose.

"Your mother wants to order pizza instead," Dad says.

"She what?!" I throw out my hands. "No, I am not going to spend my first time as holiday host playing the role of a glorified pizza-ordering operator!"

"You won't," Dad says innocently, tossing his thumb over his shoulder. "The place down the road will."

"Why pizza?" I groan. "It's Thanksgiving. What about home-cooked food?"

"You're starting to sound like Sarah," Harry mumbles over his coffee, and I shoot him a glare.

"Which one?" This from Grant.

Harry moves his mug over his mouth to hide his laugh.

"Because..." My dad shuffles in, his hands still raised as if continuing to declare his presence. He pulls the oven door open and looks back to us. "The tofu looks gross and your saintly mother insists on pizza."

"Father Grant," Lawrence says, slinging his arm over our dad's shoulders. "Please tell me we can have pineapples on this pizza."

"That's where we draw the line," he replies, taking Lawrence's face into his hands and tilting it down to kiss his forehead. "Nia, dear, will you call it in?"

I moan. "Sure." One by one, the boys shuffle out into the living room, Grant taking another mug full of coffee, leaving only me and Harry.

"Just think," Harry says, "it could be worse. Dad was just waiting for someone to call out Grant's name so he could pretend he's confused." Harry's eyes grow wide and he looks from side to side, pointing at his own chest, mimicking our father.

"Very true. He thinks that's absolutely hilarious."

"Hey, Nia?" he asks.

"Yeah?"

"You really should get back out there."

"I'm studying—"

"I know," he says. "After your test, I mean."

It's been a while—one year, really—since my last ex and I parted ways, and he was quite a doozy. Note to self: tattooed men are beautiful, but they're more trouble than they're worth. Well, at least that man was. No offense, beautiful, nice tattooed men of the world.

In any case, I spend too much time at work to focus on dating. The only eligible bachelor near me nowadays is that designer Gary who just sits in his corner desk eating junk food. Oh, and Ian Chambers.

Damn. Ian Chambers. He makes me want to punch a wall, and I don't even think I'm a particularly angry person. He's like Grant: egotistical, sarcastic, and thinks he's much too clever for his own good.

"I'm not really into dating right now," I say, pulling open a drawer that already contains a disproportionate amount of takeout menus considering the short time I've lived in this house.

"Just a thought," Harry says.

"I'll put myself out there, but only if you do the same. Or, even better, look into that lot nearby." I rise up on my toes, poking at his chest. "I think you could get it for a steal right now. Your own shop? Finally?"

I want my brother to find a place for his dream mechanic shop much more than I desire a man in my life.

"Well, that's the plan," he says. "You get your certification in

HR, gain all the employment knowledge in the process, and then I can just use you as a consultant for my business."

"Was that the plan all along?"

"Of course." He winks.

I smile and pick my phone up from the counter, tracing my finger across the menu for the number.

"Happy Thanksgiving," Harry says, lifting his coffee cup to me. I roll my eyes and dial the local pizza place. He laughs. "Remember: tofu, not pineapple."

8

IAN

PRESENT DAY

It's been nine years since I met Nia Smith. Nine years of admiring from afar, keeping my distance because, as the in-house lawyer, I knew better than to pursue her. Nine years, and I'm finally not working for Treasuries Inc.

I go down to the lobby, taking in deep breaths, and step out to see Nia already waiting for me.

"Ready for a day of fun?" I ask.

"No funny business," she says sharply. "We buy what we need, and we come back."

"Nooo." I exaggerate the word. "The entire point is for us to get along. Did you not hear the bride?"

She walks off, not acknowledging me. I'll admit, I feel bad. I don't mean to make her uncomfortable. I didn't even think my comment was all that offensive.

I follow her, pulling out my phone to preemptively request a ride.

"Do you know where you're going?" I ask. She shakes her head with pursed lips. "I saw some local place with a giant shark statue out front. Could be cool."

"Whatever you want to do."

The sentence makes my heart jump, but I keep myself composed for the time being, though it's hard with her skirt flowing behind her. The wind is doing me favors because I see a slight peek of her black thong when the thin material pushes against her backside. *Thank you, Florida breeze.*

The rideshare service arrives and takes us down the street. Nia looks out the window the entire time. I can't help but chuckle at her determination to have a horrible time.

The shark statue outside the souvenir shop is much bigger than I anticipated. I ask that she take my picture with it then stick my arm in the statue's mouth and cringe, pretending the shark is biting me.

"Is that your new dating profile pic?" she asks, handing me my phone back.

"Nah, I don't do dating apps," I say. "Do you want a picture too? Maybe spruce up your profile?" I ask, hoping she says something to contradict the idea that she's active with other men.

"I'm not on the apps anymore," she says. *Score.*

"Why not?" I ask, trying to stay nonchalant. I see a small smile tug at the edge of her mouth, and my heart leaps. "Do you have a dirty little secret?"

Her smirk instantly disappears. "Let's just say I'm a bit tired of stupid men."

"Good thing I'm smart."

I wink and she pushes past me into the shop.

We browse through, and while I'm having no luck with my bachelor party shopping, Nia is zooming through Ramona's list, picking up items whose relevance to a bachelorette outing I can't even imagine. We walk down another aisle where she picks up a wiggling hula girl and places it in her basket.

"What the hell does Ray have planned?" I ask.

"I honestly don't want to know," Nia says, exhaling.

I smile, looking at the rest of the aisle. There are bobblehead dogs in floral button-ups, a variety of seashells, and at the end, displayed across the entire wall, samples of airbrushed designs.

"We *have* to get one of these," I say, walking up to the counter and flipping through the binder with sleeves of design pictures: stick figures in bikinis, stylized animals of every variety, surfboards, skateboards, boogie boards—you name it, they have your board of choice.

"That's silly," Nia says. "Those shirts are a total waste of money. You wear them during the trip then they never see the light of day again."

"Yes, but did you even go to Florida if you didn't get a tacky airbrushed shirt?" I say with a grin. She seems less than amused.

"I'm not wasting cash on that."

"Oh well, I guess I'll just buy yours then." I shrug, flipping through the book again.

The man at the counter approaches, splaying out both hands. "Whatcha lookin' for?" he asks, his accent thick and gritty.

"We'll have the two girls in a bikini," I say. "One with a yellow top and the other in pink. Short black hair on one, long blonde on the other. What size do you wear, Nia? Small?" I turn to look at her, scanning up and down. Her arms are crossed with one leg stuck out and the weight in her hips fully distributed to the other side. Yet, with all of that, she actually has a hint of a smile on her face.

"You're putting yourself in a bikini?" she asks, raising an eyebrow.

"Only fair since you're in one," I respond, raising mine in response.

She waits a moment then exhales. "I wear a small."

My chest rises at the satisfaction. I crave more of that—the participation, the secret enjoyment tugging at her lips.

"You heard the lady." I slam my hand down on the counter then point my other index finger at her and squint. "You're having fun, Nia."

"I am not," she insists, turning on her heel to walk back down the aisle. With every swing of her hips, I'm convinced each movement contains a little less contempt for me. And, maybe I'm dreaming, but is she showing off her backside on purpose?

Twenty minutes later we receive our shirts and they are everything I had hoped for. Our names are scrawled across the top in gaudy airbrushed cursive—hot pink and ready to take on the day. I tug off my shirt in the store, making Nia's face flush a deep crimson. I relish it before pulling on the new shirt.

"Aren't you going to wear yours?" I ask, holding her tee out. I can tell she's considering it, but all I get is her snatching the shirt and knotting it around her crossbody purse securely.

"In your dreams," she says.

"Suit yourself."

I throw my old shirt over my shoulder and continue walking through aisles with her. She somehow hasn't found all the stuff on her list, and I'm wondering what we could possibly be missing. Once we're stopped, having walked across the entire store at least three times—and these souvenir stores are far from small—I peek over her shoulder and scan the piece of paper. A slow smirk spreads across my face when I read the rest.

*Penis popsicles, tiny silicone dildos, streamers with dicks...*the list goes on for a while.

She moves her shoulder to shrug me off, and I flash her a grin that she does not return.

"That's some risqué stuff you're avoiding," I say.

"I'll buy it another time," she says, shaking her head and pocketing the list. "Let's head out."

"But we're still pseudo-fighting, and what the bride says goes, so what better time than now to finish up that list?" She narrows her eyes at me. "There's only one place to get all of that."

"I am *not* going to a sex shop with you, if that's what you're implying," she says.

"But look, I'm already searching." My hands deftly swipe across my screen as I browse the area looking for any store with a title containing *dirty*, *secret*, *hideaway*, or any combination of the three. And, much to my satisfaction, there is a shop within walking distance.

"A quarter of a mile away. Our lucky day," I say, turning my phone to show her.

Her nose scrunches up.

I can't tell where her mind is, but I try my luck. "Think of it this way: if you get all your shopping done for Ray, you don't have to hang out with me tomorrow."

She looks away from me, eyeing some random spot on the wall, no doubt considering the pros and cons of this situation before meeting my gaze once more and muttering, "Fine, but we get what we need then we leave."

9

NIA

I have never been to a sex shop, head shop, or adult store. This week was not the time I expected to change that, but here I stand, facing a storefront conspicuously placed at the end of a run-down, grungy shopping center. The sign above the front doors looks weather-worn, paint peeling off every edge. Its faded hot pink logo and the black—now almost gray—halo circling the first letter gives it the feel of a joy once hoped for but now long forgotten, probably just like my image of this wedding party vacation.

"Are you ready to go inside?" Ian asks. His eyebrows bounce up and down.

"Not really," I say. He gives me a slight nudge to my upper arm with his elbow, and it seems my life is an odd tragedy where I'm doomed to always shudder under Ian's casual touch while also being angry that it happened to begin with.

"We'll get deep in there," he says, and I groan. I try to pass it off as annoyed, but I think my ovaries just collapsed. I overcome my apprehension of being alone in this shop in favor of walking away from him so he can't see me blush.

I open the heavily tinted door and find that the inside is

much the same as the outside. The carpet (*Who the heck would put carpet in here?*) is matted down from years of use, the walls look like the inside of an old convenience store with slots running along them to hang hooks for merchandise, and the lights seem much too bright for an atmosphere where I would rather be shopping with a baseball cap and a hood over my head, maybe even sunglasses.

Then I notice the items for sale. There are two walls of DVDs that easily rival the stock of a closed video rental store. *God, I hope these can't be rented out...* They have movie titles ranging from silly puns to...well, lots of *questionable* sex poses.

"At least they don't beat around the bush," Ian says.

Hardy har har, Ian.

One wall displays an array of rubber circle things and vibrators. There are different speeds, colors, and sizes. There's even a mold of the penis of some famous porn star I've never heard of. My eyes drift over to the section with a purple painted wall, and I'm overwhelmed by handcuffs, leather suits, and whips. I feel my face grow hot and am suddenly very unsure if I can follow through with this.

"So, what's on your list?" Ian asks, making me jump a little. He grins at my skittishness, and I throw him a glare in return before pulling the piece of paper out of my pocket once more. I feel like I'm in some alternate universe. *One time there was a shop with Ian Chambers and cock rings...* It's like the start of a bad joke, or a fantasy.

I hold the list out to him and look both ways before stepping forward as if trying to cross the street without getting hit by a car—or getting pelted in the face by a floppy dildo.

"Don't be shy," Ian says. "Just think: if you see someone you know, you get the satisfaction of seeing they're just as dirty as you."

I flush once more. At this rate, I'm bound to look like I did receive a horrific sunburn.

"This is way beyond my comfort zone," I admit in a whisper, but he smiles, walking backward with his hands in his pockets. I would rather he stay close to the walls, but of course he walks through the center of the store where everyone and their poor, nasty grandmother can see him.

"Don't leave me!" I hiss louder, instantly covering my mouth with my hand when Ian holds a finger to his lips. I power walk to him using a mix of running and ever-careful tiptoeing.

He scans the DVDs a bit before pulling one down from the wall.

"*Backdoor Babes*?"

I choke and start coughing, and Ian lightly slaps me on the back. I look around and see nobody notices a thing. They're all too wrapped up in their own purchases. There's a man with long hair wearing a bandana, an old woman with a cane and her wild, gray hair tied into a bun poking through magazines, and then another couple like Ian and me, perusing condoms in the corner.

A couple like Ian and me. I shove the thought from my mind. We are not a couple, this is uncomfortable, and, damn it, I just want to go back to my hotel room and curl into a ball in the shower.

"Put it back," I whisper, grabbing the DVD from him and shoving it back onto the shelf. I take a deep breath and stalk over to another aisle, desperately looking for bachelorette party items in the hopes we can leave as soon as possible.

I find the section nestled in the back corner of the store, filled with more niche items than even Ramona probably could have dreamed of. I start to blindly grab things, hoping for the best. She'll be happy with whatever I bring, I'm sure of it, and she's definitely paying me back for every bit of it, or at least splitting the cost.

The faint scent of woodsy cologne wafts around me and Ian

reappears, rummaging through a box of tiny rubber penis erasers. "Do you want pink or blue?" he asks.

"Blue," I say, mostly because I really need him to stop talking this instant. We're drawing attention to ourselves. I swear that old woman keeps flashing us a grin.

Ian hands me a blue eraser and narrows his eyes then looks away with a nod as if deciding on something.

"What?" I ask.

He shakes his head. "Nothing. Just not surprising you like blue balls."

I scoff, "What is that supposed to mean?"

"I don't know. Makes sense. You seem like a tease." He shrugs, starting to walk away. "Like you enjoy the control of it all."

Why I oughta...

I choke out a laugh. "I absolutely do not."

"Come on, Nia. Knowing you have that kind of power over a man? Imagining he's sitting in front of you, so turned on and just begging you for release?"

My temperature rises and my heart thumps louder in my chest. I'm hoping my face doesn't give me away, but once I feel the heat creep up my neck and into my cheeks, I know it's beyond obvious. This afternoon is too much.

"What am I supposed to say to that?"

"That it's true," he says, "because I know it is."

"You don't know me," I insist, following him down the aisle with my hands full of an assortment of trinkets.

"Weirdly enough, I think I do," he responds. It's that same confidence that both turns me on and also makes me want to punch him in the face about ninety-nine percent of the time. "I've worked with you for almost a decade," he says. "Did you know that? You're Apollonia Smith. Organized, controlling, Type A, secretive. When are you going to open up to me? In another decade?"

"I don't owe you anything," I say, trying to keep my voice down. I almost feel bad.

No, he totally deserves the cold shoulder.

"You don't, but I'm probably the longest sort-of friend you've had, aren't I?"

I stand there, pulling every relationship from the back of my mind and trying to recall the last time I contacted that person. My best friend from high school is in South Africa, I think. She might be doing some mission trip, but I honestly don't know. My roommate from college? I think she's married now. Might have kids.

In reality, my closest friend outside of family is Grace, and though we get lunch together during the week, my social life outside of work has become pretty barren.

"I'm close with my brother," I say, cringing the instant it leaves my mouth. How pathetic.

"That doesn't count." He laughs. "I've known you the longest and you know it."

"But are we *really* friends, Ian?" I ask, lifting an eyebrow. I'm asking the question almost to myself as well. We were something like friends before. He hung out in my office more than anyone else, and I looked forward to it.

I looked forward to it. Christ.

"I would hope so after all this time," he says. "So, tell me something I don't know—a secret."

"I don't have secrets," I say.

Lie.

"Tell me a dirty secret, Nia." I hold back a laugh, causing him to smile...his genuine, warm smile. "Come on, we're in the perfect place for it."

"I don't know," I say, walking between aisles as he follows behind. Why do I kind of *want* to tell him something dirty? It's taboo, and he's a hot guy desperate to hear these things. When was the last time that happened? My stomach churns.

I absentmindedly pick up items from the shelves then put them back, just needing something for my hands to do while we talk. This isn't a conversation I imagined having with Ian, and now that it's happening, I'm trying to do anything I can to distract myself from it.

He's confident. *Sexy*.

I hate it.

"I'll tell you one of mine," he says, straightening his posture. My breathing increases and I try to hide it by consciously holding my breath and letting it out in increments to mask the steady acceleration of my heart rate. I've never realized how much work it takes to pretend to breathe normally.

"Fine, go for it," I say.

"I had sex in the law library," he says.

"Of course you did."

Did he press her against the shelves? Were books falling with each hit? Did he cover her mouth so the librarian wouldn't hear her moan?

Fuck—*was* it the librarian?

He grins and a small smile spreads across my mouth. I push it down, lowering my head and continuing to walk on.

"Your turn," he says.

"I didn't agree to that," I say, turning to him and crossing my arms, holding the items I've collected in both hands.

"Don't ruin this," he says, taking everything from my grasp to hold them instead, relieving me of the burden. "I shared, so now you share."

I smirk and start walking again. It's odd, this feeling of entertainment and semi-enjoyment around Ian. It's been too long since I've let my guard down around him. I almost miss it. "When I was in middle school, I found my mom's romance novels."

Ian laughs. "And, let me guess—you returned them?"

"No," I shoot back. "I...well, I'll have you know I was obsessed with them."

"Go on," he says, looking around as if ensuring this is a private conversation. It's almost a gentlemanly gesture, trying to conceal my secrets while holding my contraband.

"I learned what an orgasm was," I say, feeling goose bumps run down my arms. "But, obviously, my expectations for sex were a bit high after that." *Wow, I just said that.*

"I'm sure they were," he responds, inhaling sharply. "And has someone lived up to that expectation?"

I turn to face him, his body much closer now than it was just a minute ago. I can feel the warmth radiating off him. The low hum of his voice is sending shivers down my spine. I wonder what other words can come out of that mouth with that same tone.

"Yes," I lie, and whether he believes me or not, I don't care. Those scenes in romance novels are just fantasy. What guy actually demands sex on the beach? What guy realistically makes you climax with just oral? Happy endings are just for those who are in their twenties hoping for their Prince Charming. Prince Charmings do not exist, but hunky men in romance novels do.

And, unfortunately for me, so does Ian.

He looks me up and down as he has been want to do lately then smirks. He passes me, saying nothing, and heads to the DVD wall again. I walk faster, attempting to keep up with his long legs. When I catch up, he's already pulled a movie down with his free hand.

"I dare you to buy this," he says, shoving it toward me. Oh goodie for me, it's *Backdoor Babes* again.

"This isn't truth or dare, Ian," I say, shoving it back to him.

He shakes his head in protest. "It could be. Have a good sex life. Indulge."

"I have a good sex life," I insist.

Lies! Why are you such a silly liar, Nia Smith? What sex life? I haven't had sex or any form of intimate contact since…hell, God knows when.

"Sure you do," he says, nodding in clear disbelief. "But buy the movie."

"But I have a good sex life," I repeat.

"Saying it again won't make it true."

"Buying the movie won't prove a thing."

"What do you have to prove if your sex life is so good anyway? I think this will prove you're confident enough in your level of enjoyment of romance novels that buying some simple, dirty movie is just an afterthought."

I narrow my eyes and snatch the movie from his hand, turning it over to read the description. Surprisingly, *Backdoor Babes* is not exclusively about butt stuff but instead about construction workers. Who would have thought?

"Will it make you leave me alone?" I ask, peering up at him.

"No, but you're too prideful to not buy it now."

"I hate you."

"I know."

10

IAN

When we return to the resort, I'm carrying both a small black bag containing only a couple gag gifts for Cameron's bachelor party and my internal satisfaction that a tiny pornographic DVD is somewhere in Nia's goodie bag as well.

We drop the items off at our respective rooms and head down to the beach where the rest of the group are packing up. Grace's hair whips in the beachside wind as she stomps toward us.

"Please tell me the fighting is over," she groans, tote bag slung over her shoulder. "You're best friends now, right?" The sand engulfs the heels of her sandals with every step, and poor Cameron is catching the brunt of the backsplash. He holds up his hands to protect his eyes.

"We're friendly, at least," Nia responds. I look for a smile, but she grants me nothing. Then I see something—a little hint in her eyes that tells a different story. It's a slight glimmer, but not in her usual I-hate-you-please-leave-me-alone kind of way. It's as if we share some secret that nobody else can know, not that I would be the man to tell everyone else she has porn anyway. That's a fun fact I'm keeping for myself.

"How was it today?" Ramona asks from behind me. I take her folding chair from her and tuck it under my arm. I wait until Cameron, Grace, and Nia are out of earshot before responding.

"She's not at my throat anymore," I mumble, giving a nod to Wes once he appears on the other side of Ramona, taking the remainder of the items she's holding. We look like glorified bellhops.

"I like her," Ramona says with a grin much too similar to my own. We both have that happy-go-lucky look about us as if things could always be worse. She looks to Wes, who exhales. "Wes? Thoughts?"

"Well, I just haven't gotten enough time with her," he says. "I'm sure she's great, but she does seem like she has it out for you, man."

"I'll admit, I've given her bad impressions over the years," I say.

"No kidding," he responds with a sharp laugh. I chuckle with him, letting my own self-inflicted misfortune wash over me.

"She's definitely a bit more closed off," Ramona says as I push the glass door open with my feet. I hold it while Wes squeaks both himself and the oversized flamingo float across the threshold. "But she doesn't put up with any of your shit, which I totally dig."

"Well, I *totally dig* that too," I agree with a mock surfer accent, letting the door swing shut behind me. "It's like she's got some separate, confidential life itinerary that she won't let anyone see."

Ramona taps the elevator button. "You know, you don't need to understand everyone, Ian. People are complicated."

"I don't want to understand her," I say.

Wes's eyes widen with realization. "That's why you like her

—because she's a well-kept secret nobody can crack, and neither can you."

"No," Ramona corrects with a smile and an index finger raised in a knowing gesture. "It's because he can't control her."

"You guys are doing that thing." I point accusingly between them, but this doesn't hinder their stares. "That psychologist thing." Even though they're both therapists, they keep this fact wrapped up pretty tightly. Overall, the two of them are very chill, down-to-earth people, but occasionally they work off the clock, and I hate it every time.

"That's it!" she says with a grin, that same Chambers family grin I'm sure Nia wants to slap off my face at all times. I see why. "It's thrilling to not worry about something, isn't it?"

"Stop," I warn.

"You like the idea of an autonomous, strong partner. It would be nice to have someone in your life not bending to your will like every other woman fawning over the big, tall lawyer man, wouldn't it?"

"Stop psychoanalyzing me," I grumble, loading into the elevator the second the doors open and placing my palm over the opening to allow Wes in.

"Why is being in control so important for you?" Wes asks, glancing to Ramona as if she might have the answer—which, regrettably, she does.

"He's needed to be in control of everything since...well, you know." Her voice drifts off as she looks up to me.

I can already feel myself seething. "I don't want to talk about that," I say, shifting uncomfortably.

"It was a pretty big thing," Ramona says, putting her hand on my shoulder. I shove it off.

"You were fifteen," I say, "You didn't even know what was going on past boys and your best friend Grace."

"But I saw the aftermath."

Wes's eyes absentmindedly shift down to the edge of my

shorts, resting inches above my knee. The cinched skin on my thigh is just barely visible, the edge of the scar from the crash peeking out slightly from under the bottom.

"You two are nosy Nancys," I say, walking out of the elevator once it comes to a stop.

"Who's nosy?" asks a matter-of-fact voice from behind me. It's Nia with her leg stuck out, weight rested on one hip, and her arms crossed—the classic *I look annoyed even though I'm just existing* stance. Even her blonde hair is secured into a tight bun. Then I notice the deep blue dress with thin straps resting delicately on her collarbones, just the smallest sliver of a lacy white bra peeking out from underneath. She looks pure, almost like an angel dropped from above to explore the dirty underbelly of Earth. I want to be her tour guide.

Damn it, I'm too flustered by the conversation and the way she looks to come up with anything clever. It's like my brain just turned off and I'm left looking like an idiot in front of this goddess in front of me.

"Now where are you going, hot stuff?" Ramona asks, checking out Nia's dress. Wes squeezes out of the elevator with the float and pats me on the back.

"I was coming to get you," she says. "Apparently, clubbing is on the schedule tonight."

Wes doesn't even let Nia finish explaining before he's punching the air in victory, shoving the float into my chest, and running off to his room, yelling out whoops of joy.

"You've never been to a club, have you?" I joke. She's either standing with her arms crossed because she's uncomfortable, or because she's simply being Nia.

She smirks. "No, but I do as the bride says, remember?"

"Well, you look nice," I say, and her smile immediately falters. Without a word, she turns on her heel to walk back to her room, letting the door swing shut behind her.

Baby steps.

I HAVE a theory that clubs might be some of the happiest places on Earth. Think about it: What is happening at nightclubs? Your friends are dancing, inhibitions are lowered with fruity, semi-fantastic drinks, and someone is flirting with another person just looking for a tumble in the sheets. What isn't there to love about it?

Nightclubs are places to let loose, be your best self, but most of all—and most interesting to me—it's a perfect place to people watch. I love imagining strangers' lives, their interests, and ultimately their problems. As a lawyer, I always wonder what I'll be hit with next, and there's nothing like people watching to help predict upcoming trends.

I see Grace and Cameron dancing in the crowd, smashed between others. Ramona and Wes make out in the corner on a couch like they're a new romance just beginning to take flight. It's sweet, and yet the last thing I want to see is my sister getting her face sucked.

I look around for our other party member, but she is nowhere to be found. She hasn't even danced yet. I'm only hoping there isn't another man attempting to hit on her. I'm not even sure how I would act. The thought itself makes my blood boil. I try to turn my attention elsewhere.

Yes, people watching is definitely preferable.

"Can I buy you a drink?"

I'm snapped out of my thoughts—having focused too long on a middle-aged couple grinding on the dance floor with their parent bods shamelessly on display—and am greeted by a black-haired beauty attempting to talk over the loud, thumping music. She's stunning in three-inch heels and a dress fitting every hourglass curve of her body.

"You could, but I'd have to buy you one first," I say.

"Gentleman and a devil," she says with a wink. Then, out of

the corner of my eye, I finally spot the blonde wearing deep blue at the other end of the bar, and it's obvious the bombshell in front of me is wasting her time.

"Actually..." I sigh, feigning disappointment, my brain completely on board with this plan while another part of my body is fighting every urge to leave. Thankfully, my heart is thumping louder than the blood quickly flowing down south. "See that girl at the end of the bar? My friend is having a rough time."

"Oh," she says, not hiding her obvious disappointment. She even sticks out her bottom lip and, god, if I wasn't mentally taken, I would cave. Alas, my cheesy, mushy soul is too enraptured by the ball-busting woman who hates me right now. Rookie mistake in love. "Maybe next time. Are you from around here?"

I chuckle. "Maybe next time." She nods and accepts the rude rejection like a champ. *Yep, definitely deserves better than me.*

I get up and make my way over to where Nia is sitting by herself, her finger pushing the small umbrella of her drink around the edge of the glass. It doesn't even look like she's had one sip.

"I was always told not to play with my food. Does that also apply to drinks?" I say over the music, sitting on the stool next to her.

She notices me, revealing no expression aside from an exasperated, heart-crushing sigh. Even though I can't hear it over the deafening hum of the crowd, I can see the dread coming from her open mouth.

"Wow, I could have sworn we formed some connection today," I say, drawing my lips up in a lopsided smile, almost mocking her disappointment with my presence.

She shakes her head. "You aren't *that* bad."

"I'll take that as a compliment. So, why are you moping at a club?" I ask.

She straightens her back and, yes, there's that defiance I'm so accustomed to. "I'm not moping. I'm thinking."

"Always thinking, even at a place of enjoyment."

"I enjoy thinking," she says, smiling. "Ever considered that?"

"What are you thinking about?" I ask, tilting my head to the side. She slides her drink to me in response, and I slide it back reflexively.

"Are you not drinking?" she asks, clearly avoiding my previous question. Her eyes drift behind me and then back to me.

"Driving," I say, turning to look behind me, spotting the black-haired, gorgeous succubus sipping a drink through her straw, chest stuck out.

"You have an admirer," Nia says with a smile.

"I'm focused on someone else," I say, causing her smile to grow wider and her face to flush, all the while still rolling her eyes in contempt as she picks up her glass. She's finally letting down her guard, and I could soak her in all night long.

"I want no part of whatever game you're playing, Ian," she says, placing her drink down with a hard drop as if to prove a point.

I laugh. "What game?"

"Your whole thing," she shouts as the music pumps louder, matching the tempo in my chest. "Your cocky, 'I'm the best' thing. You get off on being liked, on having women fawn over you."

Even after all this time, she doesn't really know me.

"Get to know me," I say, leaning in closer to her. She doesn't move, but she does throw an excellent smirk at me.

"You're a man with an agenda."

"Wrong."

"A lawyer who likes winning."

"Well, who doesn't?"

"Finding out how far you can push limits and what you can get away with."

"Okay, maybe a bit," I say, tilting my hand side to side.

"A man who gets off on shocking others."

"Do you want to find out?" I shoot her a grin, but she shakes her head, scoffing. "Come on, let's pretend we're getting to know each other. Twenty questions."

"Ah, but I already know you," she says.

"Tell me one fact about myself," I test. She might know some things, but it's only the tip of the iceberg.

"You're an alcoholic."

I feel my face fall, but I immediately compensate with a smile. "Easy assumption, but wrong."

It's hard not to let the feeling take over, but I promised myself long ago that I would disregard doubt. I'm better than that. I've learned my lesson. She doesn't need to know the real truth—that I'm not an alcoholic, just irresponsible.

"Incorrect?" she says, her eyebrows raised in surprise. "But you never drink."

"Personal choice. Who's to say I don't love being DD?"

"Nobody enjoys being designated driver."

"I might."

She pauses. "So, no alcoholism?"

"Sorry, Polly," I say with a shrug.

Her hand goes to her chin and she narrows her eyes. "Okay, fact attempt number two."

"I love that you're calling it an attempt now."

"You come from a wealthy family," she says, ignoring my comment.

I grin. "Got me there. And, let me guess, you do not." I think I'm being clever with the response. *Because opposites attract* is what I would follow up with, but she doesn't give me the chance.

"What makes you say that?" she says, taken aback.

Because opposites attract. BECAUSE OPPOSITES ATTRACT.

"I...I don't know," I stumble. *Why won't the words come out?*

Her eyes widen and all pretense of potential familiarity and budding enjoyment of my company fades. *Wrong thing to say, Ian. Wrong. Thing.* "That's unfair."

"What's unfair?" I ask. *Shit shit shit.* I'm digging my hole deeper. I've got a problem with not keeping my damn mouth shut.

"Do you always speak before you think?" she sneers.

"No." *Yep.*

"Okay, let's pretend I didn't mention that," I continue, waving it off, but she's already twisting on her bar stool to face the dance floor. I don't want this. Why couldn't I keep my fucking mouth shut? "I genuinely want to get to know you."

"And I genuinely think I know you well enough," she snaps.

"I'll tell you why I don't drink," I say. At this point, I'm desperate.

"I don't care." She gets up and walks onto the dance floor. Grace notices her entrance and immediately grabs her hand, tugging her into their dance party. Nia adapts as well as she can, still visibly irritated, but her hips start to move to the music, and I shift uncomfortably in my chair. I've never seen— nor would I have expected to see—her roll her body in those type of movements. Her dress pulls at each curve and her sharp bun starts to unravel just a little bit, letting wisps of blonde hair frame her face.

She shoots a look at me and, for just a second, I wonder if she's tempting me on purpose.

11

NIA

Seven years ago

It just wouldn't be a proper employee termination if we weren't slapped with a lawsuit a couple weeks later.

I'm in my office, court order in hand, sifting through older emails and trying to pick through documentation when my door is kicked open by Ian. In one arm, he balances two coffees, and in the other he holds a box, lid open and revealing donuts.

Today he's wearing a suit, which normally dictates the worst days. It means he's going to court later. The only plus side to this is that I am graced by his presence in a tailored suit. It's like sex just wandered into the room. With donuts.

Be still my heart.

"Morning, Nia," he says, gearing his leg up to knock the door shut again. He places the items on my desk, on top of papers that definitely did not need donut glaze on them. I dig them out from underneath the sticky box and put them aside. "Whoops," he says with a shrug.

"Thanks for that." I take a strawberry-coated donut from out of the box and then look around for somewhere to put it.

Finding nothing convenient, I place the glazed treat on a blank piece of paper next to me. "Did you forget plates?"

"Can't have it all," Ian says with a chuckle before settling himself down on the chair across from me.

"And you didn't bring your laptop?" I ask. I shouldn't be shocked he comes unprepared, as this is not a new thing. At least he brought breakfast.

"Nah," he says before poking his index finger to his temple. "It's all in here."

"Every single law?" I deadpan. He smirks, slightly lifting the corner of his mouth. It creates a small crease beside his lip.

"Try me."

I roll my eyes and print out a few emails I've saved, walking him through the evidence I've accrued for the case so far and communicating potential risks and items of concern. His head is angled at the wall beside him as he nods slowly, soaking all the information in. I can see the wheels turning in his head. I can also see that his hair is perfectly curled at the ends with a hint of styling gel still in it. He's started trimming it shorter on the sides. And did he shave today too?

"So, what are we concerned about?" he asks after a moment of silence.

I exhale. If only he could pay attention. "Were you even listening?"

"I heard every word, but my question is, what is the concern? He has no case."

"He was terminated with a disability," I say, repeating myself with irritation. "We have paperwork from his physician a week before he was terminated. We also have performance reviews stating he's been underperforming and unreliable, but they're outdated."

"But he wasn't fired *for* the disability," he corrects. "And that's the case his lawyers are presenting."

He's smart, and it's so darn attractive that I might curl into a ball and die.

Ian's eyes shift to the wall behind me, and after a moment, he leans forward. "Is that your name?" he asks, pointing. I turn around to see that he's looking at my college diploma. I framed my Bachelor of Arts in Sociology, as well as my Master of Science in Human Resource Management. On both of them is my full name: Apollonia Smith.

"Yes," I say, turning back to look at him.

"That's Greek," he says. I nod. "But you're not Greek." I nod again. "Doesn't that name mean 'destroyer'?"

"Okay, why are you analyzing my name?" I ask.

He shrugs and sticks out his bottom lip. "No reason. Just seems weird you'd have a Greek first name. Although—" he laughs, "the meaning is accurate."

While my parents may have pegged my future controlling personality with absolute accuracy, I'm pretty sure my very non-Greek mother simply lost a bet to my also incredibly non-Greek father when it came to naming their bouncing baby girl. By the time you're birthing your fifth kid, I guess you run out of ideas and disregard compassion for your child's elementary school well-being, but hey, I'm not bitter or anything.

"Thanks?" I say. "My dad is a history teacher. He thought it was a good, strong name for a woman."

"I like strong women," Ian says, picking out a donut for himself and taking an arrogant bite out of it. How can a man take an arrogant bite, you ask? Just trust me. He does.

"That's inappropriate," I say, reaching to take the printed emails back from him.

"How so?" He cocks his head to the side in innocence and tightens his grip on the papers, causing me to jerk it out of his hand.

"We're co-workers," I say.

"I wasn't talking about you, though," he responds. "Plus, I

have a girlfriend, so that automatically negates any additional connotation."

I feel sorry for the sad girl who's stuck with Ian and his personality, but my stomach also shifts a little. Maybe it's because I notice that, yes, he did shave. I want to run my hand over his jawline…

"Who's the lucky lady?" I ask.

"Well, now, *that's* inappropriate," he says with a smile.

"You're the worst."

"I'm kidding, I'm kidding." He laughs. "Lighten up, Apollo."

"Never call me that again."

"I'll try something different next time."

I think he throws me a wink, but honestly, I'm unsure. I clear my throat and stack the papers, setting them to the side.

He picks up his coffee to sip it and hisses as it hits his lips. "Too hot."

This elicits a small smile from me—completely involuntary—and I pick my own coffee up, cradling it in my hands and lightly blowing on the lid's opening.

"Are you dating anyone?" he asks over the top of his cup. I can see the edge of his smile peeking out, and I want to change the subject. In fact, I know I should. Talking about dating situations is a big no-no. Additionally, talking about dating situations with a good-looking, confident man like Ian is completely off limits. Well, maybe my HR training didn't exactly specify that, but I'm drawing my own line in the sand.

"Let's get back to the issue at hand, shall we?" I say, narrowing my eyes, but he leans forward, and I can tell he has a different idea in mind.

"You aren't, are you?"

"I am not talking about my dating life"—*or lack thereof*—"with you."

"What happened, Apollo? Who hurt you?"

"This isn't appropriate."

"Apparently nothing is."

"Nothing with you." The statement slips out before I can stop it, which catches me off guard. But, true to form, Ian doesn't seem fazed in the slightest.

"Not the first time I've heard that," he says.

"Can we please focus on this case? I'm busy today and can't deal with you this early on a Monday."

He chuckles. "Sure thing, Apollo."

"What did I say about calling me that?"

"Right. Sorry, Polly."

12

NIA

Present day

Ramona insists we all go to a bridesmaid brunch the next morning, and I am more than happy to leave the hotel and go to a place that is any distance away from Ian.

To say last night was a disaster would be an understatement. And to think—I was actually sort of getting used to his presence again. But, in true Ian form, he opened his mouth and said something ridiculous and inconsiderate. Sometimes good looks simply can't save a person.

The bell above the door dings when we walk into the breakfast eatery. It resembles just about every other restaurant in the local area: lots of seashells, wicker chairs, and a general musk of seaweed and coconuts—though that might be artificial. Are there even coconuts here? Do they put it in the vents and just let it waft around the seaside?

I fully expected Ramona to greet us with shirts saying *#BridesmaidBrunch*, but I was happily surprised to find her with only the black bag of stuff I dropped by her room yesterday. I made sure to take the dirty movie out and slip that under my pillow. Though now that I think about it, I wonder if housekeeping will find it. I exhale.

Grace settles in her seat with her eyebrows drawn in. "You okay, Nia?" she asks.

"Yeah, perfect." I breathe out with a forced smile. The corner of her mouth tugs into a half-hearted attempt at returning the gesture, but her concern is apparent. I don't even know how I feel. Upset? Angry? Flustered? *Well, I have a porno in my bedroom that I bought due to pressure from a handsome man who makes me want to stab my eyes out.* Well, maybe not my eyes since he's pretty easy on them, but *ugh*, my emotions are too much for me right now. I'm a walking Cathy cartoon.

"How did yesterday go?" Grace asks.

"Ooh, yes!" Ramona says, pulling her own chair up to the sticky table, which I'm already consciously making an effort to not allow my elbows to rest on. This place oozes syrup from every crevice—the walls, the chairs, the tabletop. Even after the hostess wipes it down with a rag, the remnants of the syrupy meal prior to ours is glued to the table, and no amount of scrubbing with an equally sticky, damp, mop-water rag is going to rid us of its almighty reign.

I place a napkin in my lap. "Fine."

"If you don't tell me you're the best of friends, I want nothing to do with either of you," Grace says with a joking smile.

"It's impossible to be best friends with Ian," I say, glancing over to Ramona in hopes that she isn't offended, but she's already nodding her head solemnly in agreement.

"It is known," she says, patting my knee with her eyes still closed, as if in prayer.

"I mean, don't get me wrong," I start, trying to defend him. I'm not sure why—he doesn't deserve my defense after last night. But, admittedly, okay, sure, I had a teensy bit of fun with him prior to his asshole behavior. "He's okay, but he's still infuriating."

"I'll take that rather than you guys' constant hate-fest," Grace says.

"I'm sorry," I respond. "He opens his mouth and I just—*rrg!*" I shake my fist in anger, and Ramona busts out laughing.

"Welcome to my life," she says, wrapping her hair up in a haphazard fluffy bun.

"I'm sure being greeted by him after your car broke down wasn't the best," Grace says. I forget how absolutely wonderful she can be behind that fiery exterior.

I wave my hand. "No, don't even apologize. I should be thanking you for the trip."

"Damn right," Grace says with a laugh, scooting the new water toward her and ordering us a round of mimosas, specifically making a point to order a fourth.

"Who is joining us?" I ask, looking toward the door.

"Oh, my cousin Corinne. She's the third bridesmaid," Grace says. "I didn't want a lot of bridesmaids, but I would feel weird if she wasn't here."

"Oh, you'll love her, Nia," Ramona says. "She's really interesting. Blonde like you. Very, very Khaleesi."

"How can someone be 'very Khaleesi'?" I'm suddenly aware that my *Game of Thrones* knowledge is lacking, and I can't help but feel judged by Ramona's gawking stare.

"Shame, shame, shame!"

"Okay, enough with the references," Grace says, batting down Ramona's hand, which looks as if it's ringing a large bell at my forehead. "Oh, there she is!" Grace says, getting out of her chair and rushing toward the woman walking into the restaurant.

She looks strikingly similar to me with light blonde hair tied back in a ponytail, a braid trailing up the side. Her eyes, unlike mine, are remarkably blue. They're not reminiscent of

Ian's ice blue, but they're vibrant and captivating. She wears a long, flowing skirt and a tan crop top with a purple bralette peeking through. She immediately embraces Grace.

"Corinne!" Ramona screams.

Before I know it, they're hugging, I'm being hugged, and it's just one giant squealing hug-fest.

"It's so great to meet you!" she says. "Not at all Greek like I thought you'd be!"

"It's the name," I say.

"*Love* the name," she responds, swatting her hand at me as she sits.

Of course she's the sweetest person alive.

"Do you go by Polly?" she asks. Memories of Ian from last night begin drifting back. I have to exhale to push my angry thoughts to the dark corners of my brain.

"Nia, actually," I correct with a fake smile. *She does not deserve your anger, you jerk. Tone it down.*

"Oh, sorry!" She grins sweetly. "I'm sure you get that mistake all the time."

Ramona lets out a sharp laugh. "Ian's the culprit for that."

"Ian!" Corinne practically squeals, clapping her hands together. "Is he coming?" My heart rate increases at her obvious joy that he is present, but *why?* I am much too old to be playing comparison games with another woman. My feminist bones are mad at myself for even flirting with the idea.

"He's at the beach with the guys," Ramona says. "He'll be so excited to see you again!"

"Oh, how long has it been?" Corinne says wistfully, her eyes glancing toward the ceiling. "Three years? Four?"

What does that mean? How do they know each other? Do they have a history? What does she know that I don't? Admittedly, probably a lot. I only know him as co-worker, lawyer man Ian. She probably knows him on a much deeper level, a more personal one. I gulp to keep my stupid irritation at this cute girl from invading my mind.

"It's definitely been a while," Grace agrees. I'm about to ask how Corinne and Ian know each other, but Grace is already taking the newly arrived mimosas and lifting hers. "Thanks for coming, you guys. I know Cameron and I are a lot of responsibility sometimes. We're a mess and a half, but it means a lot that you're on this journey with us."

"Ew, gross," Ramona says. "*Journey.*" She scrunches her nose and gulps down half of her flute before we can even toast. Grace clinks her glass against Ramona's with probably a bit more force than is necessary.

"Your love is beautiful," Corinne says. "We're happy to be a part of it and to be cringing at your cheesiness together."

"Hear, hear!" Ramona says, clinking her half-full glass with the rest of our untouched ones.

They spend the rest of the morning downing bottomless mimosas, which I'm fairly sure get less and less champagne as time goes on, but I'm continuing to drink my water. Grace seems to be on the same page as me, nursing water the entire morning as well. I've never been one for heavy drinking, and I'm sure even two small mimosas would have me knocked out by the end of the afternoon.

Corinne and Ramona have settled into a giggle frenzy by the time we're heading back to the hotel. I escort the women up the elevator because they all insist on changing and going to the beach. When we walk down the hall, I hear a closing door and see Ian wiggling the handle of his room to ensure that it's locked behind him. He's much too handsome in his simple gray tee and striped beach shorts. Slightly below the hemline is the puckered edge of his scar, and even higher up is the section of the bathing suit that is leaving absolutely nothing to the imagination. It almost angers me to realize I'm staring at his crotch. Why did my stupid eyes immediately drift there?

I look up and see the corner of his mouth quirked up in a smoldering smile, and I relive every word he said last night.

Asshole. Remember he's an asshole.

"You okay, Polly?" he asks, his eyebrows joining in the center. I must have been glaring.

"I don't think she prefers that name," Corinne says from behind me with a giggle.

Ian's eyes dart away from mine and his face immediately brightens. His eyebrows shoot up and a grin spreads across his whole mouth.

"Corinne!" he yells, rushing over to her and wrapping her in a large bear hug. She's just tall enough to look picturesque beside him. Yes, just two models waiting to pose naked on a beach. I feel sick at the thought. "Wow, it's been...what? Three or four years?"

Why is everyone so hung up on the number of years they've been apart?

"Still a knockout," he says, and my stomach drops.

"You're exactly the same," she says, and I feel like such a third wheel and the most naïve woman in the world. I'm falling into the same trap as I did years ago. He was flirting with me and then found another younger woman.

What's new?

"I should go," I say, pointing my thumb to the door. At this, Ian's expression goes from absolute joy back to concern. "I'll meet you guys downstairs after I change."

Corinne's arms are still wrapped around Ian's neck as I wave my goodbye. I unlock my door and close it behind me, glancing one more time at Ian's mockingly ice-cold blues before letting it shut and eliminating my perfect view of his stare.

I exhale the moment I enter my room, resting my back against the door and closing my eyes. What am I thinking? What are these stupid thoughts ripping through my brain? Am

I jealous? There's no way I can be jealous. It's just Ian. He's the classic image of a tall, dark, and handsome man, but he's also annoying, judgmental, and a complete, absolute tease.

And yet... *how do he and Corinne know each other?*

I hear my phone buzz in my purse, and I pull it out. *Harry.*

"Hi," I say, relieved to have the distraction.

"Heh-lo," he answers, a slight singsong tone to his voice. "How's vacation?" he asks. I can hear clinking on the other line. He must be in his workshop.

"Just came back from brunch."

He gasps. "Dare I ask if there were mimosas? Drinking during the day?" He tsks. "Who even are you?"

"I'm on vacation," I say, bouncing down on the bed. "And I only had half a mimosa, so no worries, I'm still a prude."

"A delightful prude, though."

I think back to the sex shop with Ian...a prude who likes control...

"Why did you call?" I ask, clearing my throat.

"Well, I'm about to ruin that post-brunch high of yours," he says. I hear a rolling sound and imagine him scooting out from under a car. "Guess who is staying on the couch as we speak?"

"It's not my sweet niece, is it?"

"Guess again."

"I'd rather not."

"It's Grant."

My breath catches. "He's home?"

"Yeah, and he looks like a mess," Harry says.

"How bad?"

"Well..." He exhales for a moment, and I'm a second away from insisting he continue when he finally answers me. "From what he's told me, his wife left him."

"He still has a wife? Bless that woman."

"Well, not anymore."

"Why?"

"Why do any wives leave their husbands?"

"Please don't tell me he cheated." I know it's true the second the words leave my mouth.

"Okay, then I won't." But there it is. My mouth opens and closes, trying to find words, but I can't. There we go. I guess my oldest brother really was—well, *is* a prick.

Grant has always been a ladies' man. He's provoked girls with sentiments that remind me of Ian's constant barrage of compliments, so why am I surprised? I remember being in elementary school and him half babysitting me at the park while handing a mixtape to some swooning senior clutching her heart over his sensitive "I'll Be Yours Forever" persona.

"Oh, and not to make it worse," Harry says, "but I'm pretty sure he's coming down from some high."

My chest drops and my head swims. Drugs have never been much of an issue in our family unless you count Mom and Dad's recent foray into "medicinal" solutions with plants. Sometimes I look at their lone plant in the refurbished garbage can with a heat lamp overtop and think, *Maybe it's just parsley.*

Maybe Grant just likes parsley.

"What? High? Since when?" I ask.

"I don't know," he says. "He said something about it last night but then he fell asleep. Eyes red, kind of out of it... I don't know."

I run my hand through my hair and shake it out. The buzz of a text breaks the silence, but neither of us can seem to find the words.

I haven't spoken to my older brother in years. I couldn't even tell you what he looks like now. Probably streaks of gray and some aging, but mostly a mystery.

"You're really letting him stay with you?" I ask with a tone of reverence I'm unwilling to hide.

"He has nowhere else to go. Cara just started school, so

she's gone most of the day anyway. Plus, Mom and Dad don't know about...the things."

"That's what we're calling the problems of our mess of a brother? 'The Things'?"

"It's probably best to keep it a secret from them," Harry says. "They're just happy he's home. Mom is even agreeing to relinquish the remote."

"At least there's that," I groan, and Harry chuckles.

"Listen, I was just filling you in, but don't worry about us," he says. "He'll definitely be here when you get back, so you can give him a stern talking-to then."

"I'd rather punch him in the face."

"Nia..." he warns.

"Fine." I exhale. "I'll talk to you later. Let me know if you guys need anything." I feel another vibration of a text against my ear.

I look down at my phone as it returns to my home screen after the call ends. Texts come barreling through from Grace, and I'm unsurprised by the words.

Grace: KARAROKE!

Maybe karaoke will be a good distraction. I'm still trying to process whatever I just heard. It's hard to not feel some sort of disdain for Grant. He's always gotten everything he wants—every woman, every job, and every bit of success he can reach for. The rest of us Smiths are just as motivated, but it's like he's been blessed with something more, like he made some deal with the devil.

Tonight, I think I need to indulge in my own sins. I need a drink.

13

IAN

Corinne suggested we all go to a karaoke bar tonight and, while I had planned for karaoke to be at the rehearsal dinner outing, I will never protest performing karaoke two nights in one week.

Grace's cousin knows my drinking habits—or lack thereof—and she's considerate enough to suggest activities even the sober people can enjoy. Plus, Corinne is a great karaoke partner, and it's been much too long.

So far tonight, I've been on and off the stage three times, sometimes with the addition of someone for a duet and sometimes just rocking out on my own. All the same, I still have the wedding party to cheer me on from the bar. Cam and Grace are chatting; Nia and Corinne hang out beside them, sipping their mixed drinks together; and Ramona and Wes order new drinks, joining the conversation as well.

I let my gaze settle on the two blondes in the middle. It's hard to ignore the similarities between Nia and Corinne. They're both beautiful, yet they're each confident in their own way. There's Corinne with her jubilant smile, bouncing on the bar stool enthusiastically, with every single man—maybe even the married men—looking her way. She's youthful with long, model-length legs that have this sheen about them, and she seems happy.

Then there's Nia, small and petite with her body leaned against the bar and chest stuck out in a no-nonsense pose. She's all attitude, and I eat that shit up. Men look at her, but she's definitely getting fewer glances than Corinne. When she's standing with such an off-putting demeanor next to the girl in her twenties who is excited to be here, complete with bouncing tits, I can't help but understand why she's subsequently getting less attention.

But that's just my kind of woman.

Ramona was right: I can't pin Nia's personality down, but that's the last thing I would want to do. I like how much she challenges me. She's intelligent. Sexy.

Corinne is just another sister to me at this point. My little sister's best friend's cousin. Yeah, basically just another sister. We can sing karaoke together or joke about tits on other women, but Nia is the mystery, the fire I would beg to burn me inside and out.

When I walk up to the group at the bar—the bride and groom excluded given that they're now in a competition to see who can eat whose face harder—Corinne is distributing bright, lime-tinted shots from a tray. Ramona, Wes, and Corinne clink their glasses together, nudging Nia to insert hers into the toasting circle. After doing so, three of them slam their drinks on the counter and slosh them back with gusto. They're drinking pros. Nia, on the other hand, is still attempting to gulp hers down with one hand pinching her nose and the other clenched around the glass in a vicelike grip as the contents slowly drain out. Once she finishes, they pat her on the back, and Ramona twists her finger in a circular motion to order another round.

Nia coughs, waving her hand in front of her face and

shaking her head side to side.

"Not much of a drinker?" I ask, tilting my head, and she rolls her eyes in response. "Come on, back to square one? I said I was sorry."

"Actually, you didn't," she says.

"I'm sorry," I amend.

She takes the drink Ramona gingerly slides to her around my back since I've nestled in between the two of them.

"You should have apologized sooner," Ramona mumbles out of the side of her mouth.

Nia says nothing, but she does smirk. Even in the dim glow from the string lights roped around the exposed beams in the bar, I can see the glimmer of her captivating brown eyes. The color is rich, like a pure cocoa treat from the chocolatiers in those tourist trap fudge shops I have yet to hit up and let rob me blind.

"Ramona can vouch for me, right, Ray?" I say, lifting my arm to wrap my sister in a side hug. Her arms wrap tightly around me in return, and she flashes a grin at Nia.

"He's an ass," Ramona mumbles through a puckered mouth as our cheeks smush together.

The glass, now filled with misty pink liquid, touches Nia's plump lips. I'd kill to be that fucking glass. In a few determined gulps, it's empty, and she's already turning to order another.

"Going a bit fast, huh?" I observe, releasing my grip on Ramona, who splays her hand across my cheek to push me away from her. I'm too entranced by Nia's new habit to notice.

"It's been a weird day," Nia responds, tapping her finger on the counter as I slowly nod in response.

"Want to talk about it?" I ask.

"Poor people problems," she replies. "You wouldn't understand."

"I deserve that," I say, and she nods in agreement, her small smile lifting her cheeks. I'm fine with the blunt trauma of her insults if it grants me a smile. Probably not healthy, but I never claimed to be a well-adjusted man.

She snatches her next drink off the counter once it arrives, black napkin stuck to the bottom and all. It's down in one go, and I'm noticing she's getting bolder with each drink.

"So, is everything okay?" I ask, trying to get the conversation rolling again. She looks up at me, and I can see the gears turning in her mind, the flutter of her lashes. I wonder if I'm close to having her open up to me…but then the moment is broken by a shove into Nia's shoulder.

A man pushes past her shoulder with gnarled, leathery hands coated in a layer of thin white hair and a face that is the human equivalent of a mountain goat, hair on his chinny chin chin and all.

"Excuse me," he grunts with zero actual regard as to whether Nia has budged at all.

"Rude," Ramona mutters from the other side of me, leaning her head back to catch a glimpse at this hobbit-sized man and placing a hand on her hip.

"What was that?" the man snaps, his jowls jiggling under his sloped chin.

"She said you're being rude," Nia says, straightening her back. "Why don't you just let us order your drink for you? That would be the most productive option considering we're women and this is a bar."

The goat man narrows his eyes at her, and honestly, I'm impressed she's still as loquacious as she is given what drink number she is on. But, I'm also clenching my fists, readying my reflexes to reach for Nia should I need to steal her away from the irrational drunk goat man.

Maybe he bleats when he's angry.

Okay, now I kind of want to find out...

"Fine. Let me get a drink," he grumbles. The old man gestures to the bar, sweeping his arm across the exposed wood where Nia was leaning just a second ago. "Are you finished, *ma'am*?" he asks, his unwavering sarcasm echoing through the insincere nicety.

"No," she replies, knocking her hip against his to move him out of the way so she can hop on the bar stool his stance was blocking, diplomacy gone. I can't help but let out a laugh.

"Charming," he sneers. The goat man is looking between the two women, then to me and Wes, who hold our hands in the air, ready to let them handle the situation on their own.

Finally, a grin cracks the goat man's stubbled face, showing dirty teeth, as well as his lack thereof and the dregs of God knows what remaining in the gaps. "Girly, I could drink you under the table." He chuckles, rapping his knuckles on the bar and whistling to get the full attention of the bartender at the opposite end.

"That's a weird challenge to make," I say.

"I'm a weird man," he grumbles toward me.

Nia's hand suddenly slaps the counter beside her, making all of us jump.

"Listen here, *sir*." Her faux pleasantries are just as convincing as his, though she has a wild grin on her face. "We're trying to enjoy karaoke. Now are you going to sing or what?"

"Sing?"

"Sing, *sir*," she repeats.

Yeah, she's definitely drunk.

———

An hour later, we're all singing, even Nia, whose voice is quite possibly the worst I've heard all night. She's like an angel with a broken harp and missing sheet music, but she's putting her all into every belted note and each Celine Dion impersonation. She butchers it like any good karaoke performer. I'd almost be disappointed if she didn't.

Her high bun has slowly deflated into a mid-to-low tangled mess of hair somehow still secured in the hairband. Her makeup is bleeding a bit to reveal the light spattering of freckles on the bridge of her nose granted to her from her short stint in the sun yesterday. It's adorable.

"You want that broad," a voice says beside me through a wheezed laugh. I turn and there he is, the goat himself, with his crooked smile and equally crooked teeth.

"You're terrifying," I say.

"I get that a lot." He nods solemnly as if mourning his own appearance then nudges my arm with his scrawny elbow. "So, when are you bagging that?" He tips his drink toward the stage, where Nia is now bending in half trying to belt out the lyrics to "I Will Always Love You." It's both horrific and fantastic.

I smile. "'Bagging' simplifies it a bit too much."

"You're a good-lookin' fella, though." He squints, making me bark out a laugh.

"She has higher standards than me. Much higher standards."

"Let me tell you a story," he starts, swaying closer to me, lifting his drink into the air again and breathing straight vodka into my face. "I was a gross younger man."

"Infinitely difficult to imagine," I mumble, tipping my glass of water to my lips.

"Thank you. But I dated this woman named…god, what was her name…my first wife…"

"Jesus." I sigh, and he lifts his hand to hush me.

"Stella!" he says, his eyes bulging in realization. "I loved that woman. I loved her so much. She wanted nothing to do with me. Gorgeous woman. Tall, lean, gorgeous."

"You've said that."

"Gorgeous."

"Uh huh, and?"

"Wanted nothing to do with me, but I just...let go, you know?"

"No."

"I told her everything about me. I let her *in*," he says, emphasizing the last word, and to be honest, I'm actually not sure if that's a double entendre or not, but half of what he's saying isn't making sense anyway. I doubt he's lucid enough to complicate his speech any more than he already is.

"How'd that work out for you?" I ask.

"We married," he says, slowly moving his head up and down. "Best years of my life. Then she left me."

"I'm sorry, man."

"My fault. We all have our vices," he says, exhaling, and I feel like I see him sober up in the split second it takes for him to admit that.

"We all have things to atone for," I agree, patting him on the back. He knocks me in the shoulders in return. His eyes glaze over, hat twisted so I think the back is now the front—although it's hard to tell with these fishing hats—and his hand is shaking to the point where his drink is spilling a bit.

We do all have things to atone for, and I'll be trying to pay mine forward for the rest of my life.

"Let me give you a ride," I say, more of a demand than an offer.

"Nah, I've got my keys," he says with a wink.

"Oh, is that a bottle opener keychain?" I gasp, holding my hand out. "Let me take a look."

"Sure thing." He drops the keys into my palm, and I close my grip around them, shoving them in my shorts pocket.

"You're coming with us, dude."

"Should have seen that coming."

"Probably."

We stay out much later than probably any of us intended to. We're even present for when they turn the lights back on for last call. It's blinding after the hours of misty darkness. I successfully corral Corinne, Ramona, and Wes to the bar where Nia and the goat man are talking with each other—or more like slurring things *at* each other.

"I see absurd tourists and damn wedding parties all the time out here," the man murmurs. "You, missy, ain't half bad though."

"Let's not try to make her your fourth wife, pal," I say, tapping the bar and waving my credit card. "I'll pick up whatever they haven't paid for."

Nia lifts her drink glass, rolling her fingers over the side and stroking the lip of it with the pad of her thumb. "You're buying drinks for me now, Ian?"

I exhale the energy that was welling inside me from watching the small beads of condensation run down the edge of the tumbler.

"I'd buy drinks for you all night if you'd let me," I say.

"He wants you," the goat man grumps, and I point my finger at him in warning.

"Inappropes," Ramona says, leaning against Wes, who is barely standing himself. Thankfully, he's built like a paper weight, so as long as he isn't trying to go anywhere, I think they're both stable.

"You know what? I don't want you with us anymore." Nia declares it as if her word is law, narrowing her eyes and pushing the goat man's drink away from him in a childlike manner.

"Nia, he can't drive," I say. Even with the amount of drinks she has in her, she's still maintaining impeccable posture, looking like she owns this bar, and hell, she probably could. "And I have his keys."

"He can call a ride," she says, crossing her arms in defiance.

"Do I look like I own a phone?" he says, and well, no, I guess if I had to pick any one person as someone who wouldn't own a modern-day invention, it would be this guy with his beige, tattered boating hat and roughed-up Hawaiian shirt. Even his shorts, with their plethora of compartments meant for holding items, seem to be lacking any at all.

"We're taking him home," I insist. Even if he's the biggest asshole in the world, ready to slug the next person who walks past us with his tiny, dwarven hands, I'm still going to load him in the back of Cameron's Jeep. No person will drive drunk if I'm here to offer an alternative. No person needs to put themselves in that situation. Not again.

The goat man gets up to go the restroom, and Nia nudges me slightly. "We're actually taking him?"

"Yes, Polly, we're actually taking him."

"Why?" she whines.

"Because he needs a ride," I say with a shrug. "And that's what I do."

"Designated driver," she says softly, almost to herself. "Better hero than Batman."

"I try to be," I say, smiling. I can't even help it; she's feeding me compliments, and I'm eating them up like kibble. "Now let's find the bride and groom and get out of here."

Ten minutes later, it's like herding cats into the Jeep. Wes and Cameron are in the back with Ramona and Grace in their laps and Corinne shoved between them. Nia sits in the passenger seat next to me and leans her head back against the headrest.

I plopped the goat man in the back, his knobby knees shoved to his chest and his hat clutched in his hand, revealing wisps of white hair on his mostly bald head coated in liver spots. I somehow got his address from him before he passed out. It's unsurprising he lives so close to the bar, and the drive is barely a few miles down the road.

I'm focusing as best I can with the commotion of drunken laughter, but out of the corner of my eye, I see Nia's phone light up and buzz in her lap. I take a quick glance and see the name *Harry* pop up. I nudge her and she takes in a sharp breath of air. I must have woken her up.

"I think your brother is calling," I yell over the wind rushing past our ears. She nods slowly and picks it up to answer.

"Hey, wonderful," she slurs. I love seeing this side of Nia, the unguarded and loving Nia who isn't bound by work policies and rules. The thought of her answering one of my phone calls and nicknaming me *Wonderful* tugs at my brain.

"Not drinking. Drunk—past tense," she says with a giggle. "You're what?"

I bet it's hard to hear with this wind. I try to listen in more, but in the rearview mirror I see the goat man trying to stand, so I snap my fingers, yell "HEY!", and demand he sit the fuck down. For an arrogant old guy, he complies surprisingly quickly.

"I can't hear right now," Nia says. "We'll talk tomorrow. Bye-bye." She hangs up her phone and exhales, leaning her head back against the headrest and rolling it toward me. "I think I underestimated you."

"Most people do." I grin.

"You're good-looking, you know that?" she says through a slur.

"Weirdly enough, yes," I say, lifting an eyebrow at her as she scoffs in response. My heart pounds in my chest. I just thank God she's drunk enough to think that joke was funny.

When we arrive at the old man's house, I try to load him out of the car and unlock his front door. He's mumbling things to me I can't understand and I'm just nodding and saying, "Uh huh," to make him feel heard. Then right before I leave, having placed his keys in the entryway bowl, he whispers from the couch, "Just be open with her. Be honest."

Godspeed, weird goat man.

14

NIA

Houses, houses, houses, hotel. Houses, houses, shopping mall.

I believe the world is gradually becoming clearer as we make our way back to our resort, but once I stand to exit the vehicle, I know I am sadly mistaken. The world is far from clear, and my body is not in a state to be walking.

Ian runs around the car and tries to hold out his hand to assist me. I accept the gesture. God, he's warm, and his hands are big. What do they say about big hands, again?

With Ian? Bigger ego.

When we're inside, Corinne throws her long arm around me and kisses the side of my face. "Your singing was beautiful tonight," she compliments. I lean my head against her arm, as she is much too tall for me to rest my head on her actual shoulder. I want to dislike her, but she's just so darn sweet.

We all ride the elevator up and a couple people are groaning, though it's hard to determine who. Once we're on our floor, Ramona and Wes immediately disappear into their room and Cam tries to lead himself and Grace off, but she's too busy clinging to me and Corinne in some form of a group hug.

"You guys are the best bridesmaids," she says.

"We're okay, I guess," I slur. "I would say we're probably run-of-the-mill bridesmaids." Honestly, I might lean a bit more toward best bridesmaid for me because, last time I checked, I went to a sex shop and none of the rest of them did, but I can't really put myself on a pedestal like that. Ramona seems like the best maid of honor, and damn if Corinne isn't the kindest soul I've ever met. She sang multiple songs with me tonight and we rocked the heck out of them. She will definitely be my future partner in all Styx covers moving forward. *Domo arigato, Mr. Roboto.*

I roll my lips together and try to keep my thoughts inside. I'm having trouble with that tonight. My mouth feels like it's necessary to blurt out every idea my mind has. Maybe, if I try hard enough, I can put just enough pressure to have my mouth stay shut.

We all nod against each other and Grace finally follows Cam into their room. I hear faint giggles before the door closes.

"You're swaying," Ian points out, watching me move back and forth, which I just realized I'm doing. "You know you're not on a boat, right?" he asks, lifting an eyebrow and grinning. His smile is gorgeous. He has those teeth, you know? The kind that obviously reflects years of orthodontia. They're all uniform too, like they've been shaved down to the exact same length with the exception of maybe the canines. Is it genetics? I think Ramona has perfect teeth too, but I haven't really been paying attention to her as much as I have to Ian. That's because his looks make him practically a god among men. *Shit, I did not just think that.*

"She's had one too many," Corinne stumbles, patting me on the back. "You have keys?" Her tone is almost motherly. I rifle through my purse pocket, pull out the keycard, scan it because I'm a total expert at this—*no help needed, thank you very much*—and finally enter.

"Thanks, Corinne. Bye, Ian."

I turn around before the door shuts and see Ian's bright blue eyes staring right back at me.

Goodbye, beautiful.

I stand in the foyer of my room. Yes, Ian was correct. I am definitely swaying. The bed is up then down then…shaking? I don't know what to do now. Lying down feels like a waste of time, but I'm too drunk to do anything else. Maybe I'll answer emails, do some work. No, that's a liability waiting to happen…

A solution is provided for me when my phone vibrates in my purse. I pull it out and see that it's my parents. What the heck are they doing up this late? It has to be two o'clock. Maybe three? I've lost track of time. Maybe they're indulging in their newfound "plant hobby." The thought gives me pause, but I answer anyway. Bunch of old kooks.

"Hi," I say.

"Nia." The voice on the other end speaks, and it's not my mom's cheery voice or the goofy tone my dad uses when he starts a phone conversation as if it's the beginning of a stand-up bit. The voice isn't even comforting like Harry's or higher pitched like Cara's. It's gruff and raspy with an edge to it.

"Who is this?" I ask.

The person clears his throat. "Grant. It's Grant."

My stomach sinks, and even though I want to sit, my knees are locked, and I'm cemented to my place in the foyer.

Grant is using their phone. My brother. This stranger I used to know.

"Why are you calling me?" It's all I can get out.

"Thought I'd say hey to my little sister. Long time, no talk."

"And what is there to say?"

"Tell me about your life," he says, exasperated. "Work, your cat, who cares. Whatever."

"You called me at three in the morning to talk about Jiggy?"

"You named him Jiggy?" He laughs.

"Her," I correct.

"Well, either way, no. We can talk about your job instead. Or your shitty car. Who cares."

I feel like I'm at a bus stop carrying on a conversation with the chatty person in the corner of the depot revving up for any social interaction. Unfortunately, not only am I barely capable of having a decent discussion at the moment, Grant is the last person I want to talk to.

"Fine, I heard you cheated," I say. "And that you're on drugs."

There's a pause followed by Grant's punching laugh.

"Where did you hear that? Harry?"

"Is he not a reputable source?"

"I've fucked up, but so have all of you. Last time I checked Harry has a child with a runaway baby mama. Didn't see that coming."

"Shut up," I snap. "She didn't run away. She's busy and professional...but that's beside the point!" I grumble. "I don't have time for this right now." It's the only excuse I can come up with, and it's a flimsy one at that. *I may be drunk, but I am in control of this situation.*

"It's three in the morning," he drawls. "Of course you have time."

"No, I don't," I insist, shaking my finger in the air. "I'm hanging out with people. I'm still young, you know. I have a life."

Okay, control is slipping. Bring it back in, Nia.

"I just wanted to talk."

"We'll talk when I get back. How's that?" The last thing I want to do is speak with him, but if he's living with Harry and my niece, it's unavoidable.

"You sound like you're talking to a child."

"Maybe I am."

Then, *boom!* Silence. Deafening silence. Is that even possible? Do those words go together? I don't know, but I want the silence, which is now quickly veering into awkward territory, to end—and fast. "You've been a child forever," I say in an effort to achieve that. The words leave my mouth before I can stop them, as if the alcohol is pushing them from the depths of my subconscious.

Shit.

"You want to run that by me again?" His tone is sharp and demanding, offended. I really, *really* don't have the mental capacity to handle this right now.

"I can't do this tonight."

"No, we're going to talk, Nia."

"Talk to Harry."

Before either of us can saying anything else, the background tone dies, and I see he's hung up.

I mull in the foyer for a minute or two—heck, maybe even thirty minutes, I really don't know—before standing in my room no longer seems good enough. The night is still young and damn it, I really want to go on a walk. I need the beach to help me wind down and sober up, and reevaluate my life choices.

I involuntarily nod as if I'm agreeing with my wildly irresponsible decision, stop to pocket my key, and then waltz back out into the hall where Ian is inserting his keycard into his own door. He pauses when he sees me.

"And where do you think you're going?" he asks with a black eyebrow lifted.

"I could ask the same," I blurt out, looking both ways down the hall.

"Bed," he replies slowly, moving back from his door and putting the keycard in his pocket. What? Does he think we're going to be talking here forever?

"But where were you?" I insist.

"I went on a walk," he says, squinting at me in suspicion. "Where are you going? And why so late at night?"

"A walk as well, *sir*," I quickly announce, ignoring his second question. How dare he question my motives. This is none of his business.

Ian exhales with a smile. "Well I guess I'm joining you."

"Excuse you?" I ask, my head jerking back. "I am an independent woman, and if I want to go on a walk alone, I will do just that."

"Well that's fine and all, but it's dark."

"I'm not afraid of the dark," I scoff.

"Okay," he says, "but what about the washed-up trash you can't see on the shore? The animals with stingers?"

"I'm a human. They are fish. They don't even have thumbs. I think I can handle myself." I walk to the railing and, out of the corner of my eye, see him take a step forward with one hand out, as if ready to catch me.

Psht, I'm not going to fall.

"What are you doing?" he asks, laughing.

"Checking out the ocean," I say, looking out at the dark beneath me. I don't exactly hear waves, but it's hard to see much at night anyway.

"That's the parking lot." *Right.*

"Fine," I say, twisting to see him. How irritating and wonderful all at once. Shorts, well-fitting shirt...his normal look. And, yes, those are some big arms that could potentially protect me should I encounter a shark on land. Doesn't punching a shark in the nose protect you? Does that still work outside of water?

"A guide would be alright, I suppose," I declare, my head raised.

"Then let's go," he says. His hand goes to the small of my back, and even though I'm compelled to clock him in the face just like I would do to a shark if one were to come at me right now, I let the gesture go.

It has been much too long since I've had the feel of a man's hand on me. I like it. His is large, warm, and like a small blanket draping over my lower back. I wish it would rest just a little lower. I wonder if it would if I asked him to. Thankfully, my mouth doesn't blurt this thought out.

We ride down the elevator and I'm stroking the side rails, noticing the smudges against the bronze. Too many fingerprints. *Gross.* I jerk my hand back in disgust, and he laughs. I find him staring at me, leaning against the railing on the opposite side of the elevator.

"You're a funny drunk," he says.

"I'm glad you find me amusing."

"I do." A single eyebrow rises once again, this time the one with the scar across it.

"You can raise both eyebrows independently," I observe out loud. "I can only do one. That's talent."

"Is it?" He gives me a sideways grin. It's got that underlying sense of mischief, like some wood nymph. *Why am I thinking of wood nymphs?*

"I play flute, you know," I say. *Just like a wood nymph.*

"Is that so?" He chuckles quietly. He's flirting with those stupid arms and that stupid eyebrow with the stupid scar he probably got from being an asshole and getting punched in the face.

"I was in band all throughout high school," I continue. *Stop talking about stupid band stuff, Nia.* "I was first chair flute." *Stop bragging about an achievement from almost two decades ago.*

"That's cute," he says. My knees buckle a bit, but I hold the rail.

"I'm actually delightfully average."

He stares at me for a moment then deepens his half-smile. "I don't think so."

I turn my head away from him as my face flushes, and then I realize I'm touching the railing once more, smearing more fingerprints onto it. *Ew.*

The walk to the shore is a struggle. Ian has to escort me down the stairs with his cell phone flashlight leading the way. We both take off our sandals once we reach the deep sand, and I finally get the common sense to whip out my own phone as well. By then, we're already strolling on the beach, shining our lights on the walkway of sand in front of us with our shoes in the opposite hand and saying nothing.

"How long are you going to walk with me?" I ask, breaking the silence.

"Until you don't want me to anymore," he answers.

"That's really nice," I comment. "Like, really nice. You're a lot nicer than you seem."

"I like to think I'm a fairly nice person." He laughs. "You've just made up your stubborn mind to dislike like me over the years."

"Because you're annoying," I groan exasperatedly. This only makes him laugh again. I look down and see a washed-up, curled piece of plastic. "Ew, what's that?" I ask, shooting my finger out to point at it.

He grips my wrist to pull me away before I can touch it. When I lean closer, I see that what I thought was a sheen from the plastic appears to be something entirely different.

"That's a condom, Polly," he says.

"Gross!" I yell, and he shushes me while snickering.

"Not a fan of beach sex?" he asks.

It's a good thing it's dark and he can't see my expression because I feel my entire face grow hot again while my mouth stretches into a grimace. If only he knew the fantasies I've been having. I let out an awkward burst of laughter, unable to contain the unrest bubbling within me.

"Oh, so you are?" he says with surprise, his phone light

lifting from the ground to point at me. I swat it back down before it can reach my reddened face.

"I've never tried it," I mumble, "but I've read about it."

"In those romance novels?"

"Shush." As the tide rushes in, the water wets the sand beneath our feet, causing our toes to create deeper footprints. If we were having sex right here, I wonder if our asses would leave prints on the sand. I wonder if my toes would curl and gather sand around me and if Ian's hands would make indentions on either side of my hips. No, these are inappropriate thoughts to be having about stupid Ian Chambers...but it's hard not to notice how, with every step, his thigh muscles tighten and release. I bet they have a lot of power in them.

With each additional step, his shorts skim his toned thighs, and then I see it again: the cinched scar peeking out beneath the hem. His skin waves inward like the edge of a crumpled piece of paper, leaving a sort of shallow dent the farther up it goes.

I flash my light to it. "You've never told me about that," I say.

He hesitates before saying, "You've never asked."

"Well, what happened?"

I hear a faint gulp from him as if he's contemplating whether or not to answer, and I wonder if I've crossed some sort of line. He finally breaks the silence with a short, two-word response. "Car crash," he croaks out, followed by a small chuckle as if he's in disbelief he said anything at all.

"Was it your fault?" I ask. He's silent again, and I get a small tinge of anxiety in the pit of my stomach. I'm starting to remember that this is why I never drink. "Oh god, I'm sorry." I burrow my face in my hands. "I'm so rude. This is so rude. What am I even asking?"

I hear a *thunk* and see my phone dropped into the sand. Ian quickly snatches it up before the tide comes in to claim it as its own. I see the hint of a smile when the light from his phone passes across his face. Okay, he's smiling, so maybe I'm not crossing *too* many lines, more like lightly placing my big toe on one side.

"You're too drunk for your own good," he says. "And I fully intend to take advantage of this."

HUH?

"What?!" I bellow.

"No! Not like that, Polly," he says, dragging out the words with a small chuckle. "Geez, you're so testy."

"I don't want to be…be…" I struggle to find words and let out a groan. "I can't talk."

"That's because you're drunk."

"Well, I hate being drunk!" I yell. He quickly places a hand over my mouth and shushes me, laughing.

For whatever reason, I stick out my tongue and lick his palm, hoping it will cause him to move it away from my lips. To my surprise, he keeps his hand there, instead turning on the spot to face me. I bump into his chest and the smell of his cologne wafts over me. Sandalwood…bonfire…*man.*

"You've got to stop yelling." He laughs, finally releasing my mouth.

I grumble nonsense words in response.

"What was that again?" he asks, bending a little to reach my level. My eyes must have adjusted to the moonlight because I can make out his features just slightly: the sharpness of his jaw, the manly stubble that's formed over the past day or so, and the flop of his curls, no doubt fatigued by the humidity. He's breathtaking in every way a man should be.

"You're close," I whisper.

"Does this bother you?" he asks. His voice is low, causing me to squeeze my legs together as nerves flitter down between my thighs.

"It bothers me that you're good-looking," I blurt out.

"That might be the nicest thing you've ever said to me," he

whispers. "Can I tell you a secret?" The gruffness of his voice seeps into my chest. I gulp.

"What?" I say.

"I like you, Nia."

My arms cross, but my hands are getting clammy and I'm curling my toes in the sand, barely able to contain the rush of attraction flowing through my veins. I've almost forgotten how it feels to be wanted, especially by a man of Ian's caliber.

"You're playing with me," is all I can get out, and judging by his sly grin, he knows I'm borderline speechless.

"I wish I were," he growls. It's animalistic. I need him to make the noise again.

Wait—no, I don't. Remember Ian? Ian, the man who turned you down? The man who ogles every woman? You don't want that Ian. That Ian does not actually like you, at least not in that way.

But he's licking his lips, and I'm biting mine because I'm trying anything to stop this building tension.

"You look like you want to kiss me," I comment before I can even stop myself. My whole body gets giddy at the thought, but I swallow it down. "I mean—*I* don't, just stating the obvious." *There we go. Good cover.*

He grins. "Lucky you, I don't kiss drunk women. Not my style."

Of course he doesn't, because he's too perfect for that, isn't he? I respect him for it, but admittedly, I'm also a small bit disappointed.

"Good," I say defiantly, causing him to let out a laugh.

He's a very intelligent man. I know this, and I'm wondering if he can see through my drunk, uncaring, nonchalant façade. I wonder if he's feeding off it.

"But if you want to flirt with a woman, go somewhere else," I say, barely getting the words out through my tipsy stupor. "Go flirt with Corinne or something."

"Corinne isn't exactly into me," he says with a small eye roll, as if I'm the idiot who should have known that.

"Don't treat me like I'm stupid," I snap, and he laughs again. "Ha ha," I mockingly reply. "I'm glad my...my drunken state is funny to you."

"Maybe, but last time I checked, I've been looking at you, not Corinne, or that girl at the bar."

I'm exhausted. He likes me, he doesn't...do I even care?

"How do you know Corinne?"

"Old friend."

"Old friend you used to date?"

"Yes and no. I liked her once. But now she's like a sister to me. That's in the past. What did I just say? I'm looking at you."

"Why are you doing this?" I ask, exhaling.

"You know why," he says. "You're smart, Nia. Take a guess."

The words are coming out so easily for him, and I don't understand how, but I know it's all a ruse, just a game from a man who plays them knowing he can win. He's just a man seeing how far he can take a woman before she caves. I've seen this with my older brother Grant and all the girls who swooned over him, all the girls who got their heart broken—including his poor, nameless wife.

I refuse to end up the same way.

"Can I tell you another secret?" he continues.

I don't want him to. I want to push him away from me and go back to the hotel. How far did we walk, though? Am I stranded? I wonder if I should start walking back on my own. He can endure the land sharks by himself. Maybe if I walk fast enough, I can outrun them, but I also can't stop imagining Ian's touch, and that is the real terrifying scenario.

"Sure, tell me a secret," I say, clearing my throat and lifting my chin in the air. This means nothing. This means *nothing*.

Curiosity killed the cat.

"I liked going to the sex shop with you," he says. The words run through my body like venom. He's the snake biting me, and I'm succumbing to the pain.

"Why?" I ask.

"Because I can imagine things."

The words stab into me, fill my head with no-good thoughts, making my stomach drop. It's a wonder I'm still standing. His lips look so soft as they hover near me, his curls so willing to have hands running through them.

I take a step back and feel the water run over my feet. The sand depresses under the weight and my heels dip lower. Next thing I know, I'm losing my balance, toppling over, and my arms are helicoptering in the air as I try to right myself. Ian grabs my arm just in time, wrapping his other hand in my shirt to hold me in place.

I hear my phone plop onto the damp sand for the second time tonight. Unfortunately, it is not as lucky this time as it was the first. Though not taken by the ocean, it is still soaking wet by the time I haphazardly shuffle to get it.

"No," I moan before letting out a louder cry of, "What the HELL!"

Ian is grabbing his stomach in laughter, bending over and trying to contain himself.

I can't believe two seconds ago I was actually considering kissing him, wondering what it would be like to be with him. I'm such a sucker. I'm actually happy he's being such a jerk again. It's reminding me why I've avoided him for six years. Seven? Eight? Ugh, I don't know how many! *Too* many, that's how many.

He sees my irritation and tries his best to stop laughing as he says, "It's fine. Just put it in rice."

"Oh, sure, I'll totally find freaking rice at three o'clock in the morning," I sneer. I'm just about done with him. I don't want to hear any more of his misleading comments, and now I have a stupid, wet phone thanks to him. How am I possibly supposed to get back home? I want to leave. I want to get out of here. Stupid wedding, stupid week, stupid Ian.

"Well, it's four o'clock now," he corrects. *Smartass.* "But I actually *do* have rice."

"Stop lying," I snap, making my way through the sand, moving away from him. Just another joke, and it's not even funny.

"I'm not. I always bring a bag of rice to the beach," he says. "It's saved me too many times."

"That's stupid."

"You won't think that in a few minutes."

I stomp the rest of the way back, clutching my phone in a near death grip. Ian is a few steps behind me, pointing his phone in front of him to guide my way. Even though it prevents me from tripping up the wooden stairs, I refuse to be thankful for it.

We get back up to the rooms, exchanging no words in the elevator, and he tells me to wait, placing a hand on my arm as if to gently coerce me into being patient while he retrieves his imaginary rice. The gesture works, and that pisses me off even more.

Lo and behold, he returns two seconds later with a freaking bag of freaking rice. Is this guy even real?

"What the heck?"

"Told you." He holds out his hand, palm up, and I reluctantly place the phone into it. When I do, my fingertips graze his skin. I can feel the ruggedness of it. His hand is so giant in comparison to my petite, slender fingers. I jerk my hand back, causing him to flash a smirk at me. The man can totally read my mind.

The phone is dropped in the bag of rice, zipped shut, and shaken up.

"This will soak up the moisture." He hands the bag back to me. "Leave it in there overnight."

"Neat trick," I mumble, shuffling the rice around. Admittedly, it *is* a neat trick and a very good precaution to take. I appreciate responsible men, and he probably just saved my lifeline to home. Though, after my conversation with Grant, maybe I should let the thing die.

"You're welcome," he says, putting his hands in his pockets and leaning back in triumph. What does he want, some type of reward? It's not like I owe him anything. The edge of his lip is curled into a cocky smile. While he is making me exceptionally angry, my body is also betraying me by having my nipples harden and press against my bra. They're suddenly so sensitive. I wish our hands would graze again.

It's silent between us with only the sound of rice bunching together in my hand as I absentmindedly squeeze and release the bag.

"What was it about the sex shop that you liked?" I suddenly ask.

It's been a weird night, and for some reason I feel like I need to hear this. I haven't received this type of raw attention in so long, and my body is having a hard time resisting.

He inhales sharply, shoving his hands deeper in his pockets.

"I don't know," he says, giving a small chuckle after. Is he as nervous as I am right now?

I feel like I'm in college again, in the beginning of a relationship, that magical time where you're just getting to know one another. There are butterflies zooming through my chest, just waiting for the next comment that will drive my mind insane.

"No, really. What?" I say, voice nearly a whisper. I'm scared someone will overhear us. The last thing I need is Grace or his sister coming out of her room.

"You looking at DVDs," he says. "Picking up penis erasers." He laughs.

My mouth twitches into a smile. I roll my lips in to push it away. I both desire and resent this conversation. I need to get out of here.

But why? He's no longer my co-worker. He's just Ian. But, that's it exactly—he's Ian Chambers: a liar, a man who, despite saying he doesn't date co-workers, I have seen do the opposite. I remember that night years ago. He didn't see me standing there when he broke that sacred rule, the one he promised me he never broke.

And I'm not gullible. I can't be.

"Have you ever thought about...us?" he asks.

That comment is exactly what I need to prompt me to shake my head, step back, and make my exit.

"Get over yourself," I scoff.

"Wait, hang on—"

"I'm not here to be just another girl you've duped into thinking they're special."

"I'm not teasing you, Nia."

He says my name, not some stupid nickname like Polly or Apollo, just Nia. It has a different meaning to it. It's intimate coming from his mouth, but this will not break me.

"I'm no different," I say.

"Yes, you are."

"I'm going to bed." I exhale, nodding in a matter-of-fact manner and rummaging through my pocket to retrieve my keycard. His hand reaches out to grab my elbow and I turn on my heel to look at him. "What?" I snap, irritated. What else does he need? What other stupid, fun game can he play with me?

"Do you still have that movie?" he asks. My heart sinks.

The movie from the sex shop. I haven't touched it since we got it. It's still under my pillow, like a secret tooth ready to be stolen by the tooth fairy.

"No, I threw it away," I lie. He smirks. He knows I'm not telling the truth.

"You should watch it," he says. His voice is both a plea and a request. My knees shake and I realize I want him to plead with me more.

"I don't have it," I repeat, tugging my arm away and inserting my card. I twist the handle and walk in, but before I shut it, I turn back around, and there he is. He's looking at me, piercing me through deep into my core, and I can't help but take in a deep, shaky breath.

I imagine it all: his naked body, his strong arms, his sloping Adonis V, the gift waiting at the end of it.

He winks, and it's a *knowing* wink. So, with that, I slam the door in his dumb, smirking face.

I trudge into my room, pacing and throwing my keycard and bag of phone rice onto the table, running my hand through my hair while I kick off my sandals in disgust. They're covered in sand and beach water and stupid memories of tonight.

I almost let my guard down. I hate that I was almost just *that* weak enough. I hate his rough hand on my arm. I hate his gorgeous stubble. I hate his muscular body with its toned thighs. I hate how feverish my own body is, reeling with my blood pumping deeper down, desperate for release. All due to Ian Chambers.

My eyes jerk over to the pillow and my heart races faster.

No. I will not do it. Porn is disgusting.

I storm over to the pillow and toss it to the side, revealing the movie with its cover depicting actors in compromising positions, body parts intertwined like two octopuses trying to wrestle one another.

What a sorry way to spend time. How sad to feel like you need to watch random people get it on just to get your kicks.

I press the movie into the DVD player's opening and mash the button on the TV to turn it on.

It's ridiculous that people stoop to this level of entertainment.

I see a woman with her arms pressed against the chest of a bulky man. His muscles ripple even through his tight-fitting white shirt. He's wearing a utility belt and a hard hat. She's wearing a thin tank top with no bra underneath. His hand goes to her nipple, rolling it in his fingers. I mirror the same movement on myself, lifting my shirt over my head.

This is such a silly movie. Look at him, saying corny words and pushing her onto the workbench. Do your job, carpenter! You're fixing her house!

I lean back on the bed, sliding my hand under my panties and closing my eyes. Carpenters leave my mind instantly.

I imagine the beach at night and the glow of a flashlight. There's a tall, muscled, shirtless man hovering over me. His hands are placed on either side of me, centering himself just below my hips. He's kissing my neck, nibbling my earlobes, and running his hand to my center as his fingers gently slip inside me.

I can imagine so clearly how he exhales over me, as if unable to contain how much I turn him on. He tells me to open my eyes so he can see me when I release. I oblige.

And I picture ice blue eyes staring right back at me.

15

IAN

Six years ago

"I'm tired," Cameron says. "Please let me go home."

My long arm blocks the aisle leading away from Cameron's desk. A couple months ago, he negotiated with the former desk occupant to get the coveted corner area. Although he says it helps him focus more, it's also working against him in this moment as I passively block his route out. Unless he barrels through me—which he could—then he's staying right where he is.

"I'll buy you dinner," I say, hoping this will convince him because he's a damn cheapskate, but he only shakes his head in response.

"No," he says. "I'm already working late, and Abby is pissed she has to take Buddy on a walk as it is."

"Come on," I plead. "A steak." I'm shuffling side to side as he tries to move past me, blocking every attempt he makes to slip by. "I'll buy you a steak at that fancy-pants place. You know the one."

"No."

"Please."

Cam stops trying to dodge me, adjusts the strap of his work bag over his arm, and then smirks. "Promise steak."

"I promise."

"Fine, just let me call Abby first," he says, pointing at me and using his shoulder to push past as I pump my fist in the air in victory.

I'm not exactly holding Cam hostage from his girlfriend and puppy, but I selfishly kind of am. I just don't feel like going to my house yet. While Cam rents a place with his small family, I decided to be a big boy with my big boy lawyer money and purchase a fancy new townhome...and now I'm just a poor lawyer with his entire savings shot to shit. Because of this, I have an undressed mattress plopped in the center of my living room and a mounted TV over the fireplace. Not exactly the most exciting place to call home.

Mostly I'm tired of going back to the same oversized townhome only to lie on the bare mattress and stare at the vaulted ceilings and *think*.

I hate just thinking. It leads to places I'd rather not go. You would imagine that, after a few years, certain memories would no longer haunt me. You would be wrong.

I'll splurge for a steak if it will keep my mind off of a swerving car and the bright lights of a hospital room, blurred from tears.

Cam and I pull up to the restaurant and he whistles low. I realize this place never lost its luster. It's not exactly a large building, and it's a bit secluded from the restaurants surrounding it. It's not much to look at from the street, but once you get closer, the ornate decorations on the outside and large wooden double doors—which must be a couple inches thick—show the quality of the square footage over quantity.

My parents used to take my sister and me to this steak restaurant when we were younger. We really had no idea we were eating such luxury food until we were old enough to try to go on our own with our silly college jobs. Yes, a forty-dollar steak will humble you real quick.

The valet takes the car from us while Cam runs his hand through his hair, slicking it back and almost stumbling over the curb once the car drives away.

"You've got to call me 'Daddy' while we're here if I pay for your meal," I joke with a grin.

"Sure, Daddy," he deadpans.

We walk in and easily get a table because who else is at this place on a Tuesday night? While we're being escorted back, I see a shock of white-blonde hair appear out of the corner of my eye. Two white-blondes, actually. One of them is a bulky woman with shorter hair and the figure of an Olympic athlete, and across from her is undeniably our HR manager, Nia Smith, sitting with an elegant smile across her face. The heels of her palms meet at her chin as her fingers splay across her cheeks. Her hair is twisted into a bun, and she wears a modest, flowing short-sleeved top.

Wow, she's stunning.

"Nia!" I yell over to her. The sound of my voice causes her eyes to widen and her back to arch like a cat. I walk to her table, abandoning Cam and the hostess in favor of getting closer to Nia and her blonde friend.

"Oh, Ian." She still seems to be in some shell-shocked state. "Hi."

"What brings you and your friend here tonight?" I ask, turning to direct my smile at the woman across from her. I realize my mistake immediately.

As it turns out, the bulky girl across from her is actually a dude with incredibly good hair that hits just below his ears. However, despite his naturally luscious locks that could rival Fabio's, he also wears an ill-fitting turquoise polo that has small smears of...*what is that? Grease? Dirt?*

I tense. Is Nia on a date? With *this* guy?

"I'm at dinner, Ian," Nia says, her voice stilted and terse. "What are *you* doing here?" I'm still looking at her date, who has a good-natured smile on his face with kind eyes that already seem to be laughing before his body can catch up.

"I'm Harry," he says, standing and leaning over the table with his hand extended.

"Ian," I respond. His eyes widen as if my name means something to him. He even passes a glance over to Nia, whose mouth is in a permanent straight line. Jealousy zaps through my muscles as I shake his hand.

"Nia, what a surprise!" Cam calls from behind me, jogging up to greet the table.

Nia's face drops more. "Crazy," she says with zero enthusiasm. Maybe this was a much more intimate dinner that we interrupted. Third date, maybe? My chest feels like it's curling in on itself, and I do the only thing I can think to do.

"Two chairs over here!" I yell out.

"Oh, no, we were just..." Nia starts, but the muscled surfer-looking dude across from her waves his hand in protest.

"Sure!" he bellows, picking up his glass of wine from the table and raising it toward us. "The more, the merrier! We're celebrating anyway, aren't we?"

Nia buries her face in her hands, and in thirty seconds, two new chairs are added to this already crowded round table, much to the chagrin of an uncomfortable server who can tell this will never work with plates. I nestle in between Nia and Harry with Cameron situated across from me, immediately engrossed in the menu.

"What's the occasion?" I ask. Engagement? A baby? Maybe he just lost his court case and this is their last meal before he's locked in jail for a few years? One can hope.

"She just passed her certification exam," Harry says, reaching across the table and slapping Nia's wrist to coax her out from behind her hands. She peeks through her fingers and I see a slight smile forming on her face.

"That's great!" I say, grinning from ear to ear. "What's it for?"

"Human Resources Senior Certification," she mumbles through her hands, as if trying to hide from the embarrassment.

"It's a big deal," Harry says out of the corner of his mouth, the back of his hand slanted against his lips as if sharing a secret even though he is not speaking quietly at all. The small smile tugs at the corners of her mouth again.

How does he keep making her smile? What type of unseen power is that? It irks me even more that he knows her well enough to take her out to a celebratory dinner. New boyfriends don't do that.

"That's awesome!" I toss my hands in the air in a touchdown-style pose. "Congratulations!"

"Thanks," she grumbles with an awkward laugh, sipping at her glass of wine and looking around the restaurant, almost as if to assure herself nobody is watching this charade.

"So how do you all know each other?" Harry says, pointing between the three of us.

"Work," I respond. "Yeah, Polly and I have been working together...how many years again?"

Harry spits against his glass, sputtering red wine against the other side. I get a small ounce of joy at how silly this makes him appear. He wipes his chin with a nearby napkin. "Apparently long enough for you to call her by a nickname." He looks at her. "You *hate* nicknames."

What nicknames has he tried to call her? Baby? Dearest? And what does she call him? *Big daddy?*

I shudder.

"I *don't* like it," Nia insists, leaning forward to hiss the words at the table as if daring anyone else to use that nickname. Or maybe she's avoiding the potential for a precedence to be set with this guy. Good; I like being the only one to call her Polly.

The server lifts the wine bottle from the middle of the table and displays it to me, but I shake my head and point to another choice on the menu.

"Oh, no, you shouldn't," Nia protests once her eyes spot the name. Sure, it is a bit more expensive, but who needs furniture for a townhome when you can treat a woman to some damn good wine? It's not like I'm trying to one-up her date, but fuck it, maybe I am.

"My treat," I insist, gesturing for the apprehensive server to continue getting the bottle, much to Nia's dismay. "It's a celebration!"

She leans back in her chair with her arms crossed. "Why are you two here?" she snaps, making Harry's eyebrows rise.

"That's rude, Nia. He just bought us wine," he says. *If only he knew.*

I respond with a wave of my hand. "I've gotten used to Nia being irritated by me."

"I thought you liked work," Harry says with a smirk. A pink tint crawls up Nia's neck and cheeks. *So, she* does *like us.*

"We test her limits, I think," I say, tossing her a wink. Her face progresses to a deeper pink, stark against her ivory skin. "In truth, I just had a long day. Needed some relaxation." I shrug, throwing my arms up and behind my head to lean back in my chair in some relaxed pigeon pose or whatever. (I've only done yoga twice. I don't really know what it's called.)

Nia's mouth gapes open for a second until she regains the composure to close it again. Harry's eyebrows are raised almost to his white-blond hairline, but he still wears a lopsided smile, as if amused by my answer.

"Wait, so you're saying you just come here on a whim?" he asks. "*This* place?"

"Yeah," I say. "Why not?"

I look between the two and it dawns on me that this was the incorrect answer if there ever was one. His ratty shirt, her hair in an uncharacteristically elegant top knot, the wine bottle that is definitely one of the less expensive selections on the menu... I'm suddenly embarrassed.

"Are you guys getting steaks too?" Cameron asks, laying his menu down on the table with a toothy grin.

Damn it, man. Read the room.

"Uh..." Harry says, peering down at the menu again.

"Haven't decided, huh?" I jump in with a quick laugh, trying to cover my ass as best I can, but I've already made my obvious privilege apparent, and I'm cringing internally. He laughs back, clearing his throat and tossing a glance over at Nia, who is now shooting daggers in my direction.

I feel absolutely horrible. This schlub just wanted to take a beautiful woman out to dinner for a huge accomplishment, and I'm the entitled asshole who ruined that. Hell, I wish I had thought to take her out to dinner first, although that would have required me even knowing she was studying for some big-shot test.

"They have good sandwiches," he says offhandedly, perusing the menu and clearing his throat again. "Isn't tofu your favorite?" He flattens his menu to the table as she narrows her eyes at him.

"Hush, you," she shoots back.

"Tofu?" I ask, shaking my head. "I didn't know you like tofu."

"I don't," she says, lifting her menu again. I hate feeling out of the loop, but it's clear they've got their own language going on. My hair stands on end and chills run down my spine in irritation.

"How long have you guys known each other?" Cameron asks before I get the chance. Probably for the best. I've been dominating this conversation and I know it, but I'm desperate to know the answer as well. I can't tell if I'll hate him more or less if I find out they're in a long-term relationship.

I shouldn't be the jealous one here. He should be shaking in his work boots. Aren't I the man who visits her office first thing in the morning five days a week? Aren't I the man she kicks out thirty minutes later? He should be so lucky to be the guy she loves to hate.

"You could say we've known each other a while." Harry laughs, staring me right in the face.

My blood boils. He's just so damn *chill* about this whole thing. Is that what the kids say now? Chill? Maybe not, but how does someone have that much *chill*?

"Great," I say, drawing the word out. "And by 'a while'... would you say that's like...five years? Ten?"

"How long, Nia?" he asks, as if consulting her on their intimate history. She starts to smile back at him, and I just imagine they're loving this game. They won't tell me. Why won't they tell me? What is it about their relationship that makes them seem like they can't tell one simple date in time in which they met? Was it in college? Was it last year? Did I know her first? And why does that seem like an important detail?

"Weird how time flies by, right?" she says, a smile tugging at her full lips again. They're sharing some secret. They're looking at each other in that way, the way that implies they're lost in each other—or teasing me.

"Weird how?" I ask. Am I out of breath? Is my heart pounding? *Just fucking tell me how you guys met.* Why is this a secret? I don't understand these cute glances at each other. Is it really that special? "Did you meet at a bar? A club? Website?"

Across the table, Cameron is lifting an eyebrow at me. I can practically see the thoughts of *Dude, what the hell* written on his face. I might be sweating.

"He's my brother," Nia groans loudly, leaning her head back

in frustration. "He's my brother, Ian. Geez, stop with the inquisition."

"Oh."

Right. The identical white-blond hair. The inside jokes. The celebration dinner.

"Pleasure to meet you, Nia's brother," Cameron says with an exhalation, shaking hands with Harry over the menu. He shoots a wide-eyed look at me as if the entire interaction exhausted him beyond belief. Harry takes the hand then chuckles, also tossing me a look.

He's laughing at me. I have clearly been very jealous of this innocent dinner with his sister, and everyone at this table can glean that. I look like a fucking idiot.

His sister.

Jealous.

The pure rage I just felt at Harry, such a relaxed, down-to-earth guy with his long hair and easygoing demeanor...it was uncalled for. I've never had that type of reaction. Is it because she's out of my league? Because she so clearly is. She's interesting, and I'm just a lawyer. She's still getting certifications while I just passed the bar and called it a career.

No, it's the look she gives me—the one she's shooting in my direction right now—that sets my soul alight. My reckless behavior doesn't make her swoon like it might other women. Instead, she builds walls between us—not just walls, but houses, buildings, neighborhoods, cities constructed through sarcasm and contempt.

I didn't realize until this moment just how bad I want to see through the stucco.

16

NIA

PRESENT DAY

I'm hot.

Really hot.

Seriously—why is it so hot?

I'm in hell. It's happened. I *masturbated* to Ian Chambers. This is a very real thing.

Beads of sweat run over my head, chest, and stomach, and not in an attractive way. I open my eyes and immediately shut them when I'm greeted by the glare of the sun trying to blind me. *Ow.*

The bed and I are like ants under a magnifying glass in the window-filtered sunlight. Rolling my body over to the other side of the bed, I feel the coolness of the now shaded sheets, smooth against my shirtless chest. *Much better.* I flop onto my back and stare up at the ceiling.

So, am I really in my bed? Well, of course I'm not in my true bed, the one with numerous pillows and a fluffy cat, but am I still in a hotel bed under my name, one that's...*not Ian's bed*?

It's surreal that I am actually concerned this may be an issue.

I slowly sit up on my elbows, cringing at the effort of it all while trying to ignore my nauseating headache, and look around. All the blankets are bunched near my feet with only the fitted sheet clinging on for dear life; my shirt is tossed a few inches away from me, also crumpled into a mess; and a DVD case is teetering on the edge of the TV stand with very naked people on very full display.

Oh.

I lower myself back down—making sure to keep one eye on the DVD just in case because I'm fairly sure it's taunting me now—and rest my hands on my stomach as I try to parse through the events of last night.

"I'm no different."

"Yes, you are."

It would have been all too easy for me to waltz back into Ian's hotel room last night. Just one hand placed on the correct spot on my lower back or only a few more sweet, well-placed words, and I might have been a goner.

Oh god, I was a mess.

I throw my hand over my face and groan. I don't know the last time I was that drunk. In college, I was never much of a drinker or a partier. I wanted to study, save money, and make sure those red pens scribbled shiny As on all my essays. Did it sometimes stop me from having a healthy, normal-twenty-something social life? I like to think instead I just experienced an alternative route to my thirties that involved fewer hangovers and more worry-free visits to the gynecologist, but this life also prevented me from building up my alcohol tolerance and learning how to deal with confident, sexy men like Ian Chambers, and I'm feeling the brunt of both now.

Congratulations, Ian Chambers. You won. And what do I get now? A hangover and a full day of guilt.

Thanks a lot.

As much as I would love to sit here and wallow in self-pity, complaining about how I gave in to some wild, gorgeous man's wishes, there's no point in doing so. The best thing to do now is to move forward with my head held high and to see that the naughty DVD is thrown out. I swear the actors on the case throw me a wink like, *We know what you did, you naughty bitch.*

Okay, first things first: work emails.

I pat the space next to me, hoping to feel the comfort of a glass screen. Instead, there's just blank space. I twist my head to look and—yep, no phone.

I sit up again, a little less graceful this time, and clutch my head. Pain radiates from my shut eyes outward to my temples, resting there like a carpenter bee drilling into the side of my head. I creep my eyes open once more and spot a bag of rice tossed on the desk in the corner.

Right. I almost forgot I used Ian's "phone in rice" trick. This better work or he's going to get a tongue-lashing from yours truly. Heck, maybe I'll do it anyway just to prove a point. My muscles tense. Maybe it's best not to think of Ian and "tongue-lashing" in the same sentence right now...

I slip off the bed and pad over to the table, stripping open the plastic bag to dig out my phone.

Dry as a bone. *Well, would you look at that.*

I turn it over in my palm and press my finger down on the side button to turn on the power. Just as the screen lights up, I hear a knock at my door.

I jerk my head toward it and my ears ring. I didn't think I was on edge before now, but the sound of the knock indicates one of five possible wedding party guests who could be at my door—unless I'm lucky and it's just hotel staff. The possibility that one of those visitors could be Ian is unsettling, and I am less than prepared to be dealing with him this early in the morning. Wait—is it early? I pull my wrist up to see the time.

"A little after one o'clock?!" I shout in disbelief, and from the other side of the door, I hear a small shot of laughter followed by a raspy feminine voice.

"So, you are alive!" Grace calls. I run my fingers through my hair, trying to finger-comb any craziness out before rushing to the door and whipping it open. I blink several times to adjust to the outside light. *Yes, this is what hell feels like.*

Grace stands there in a semi-sheer black t-shirt dress, hands on her hips, hair knotted in a low-hanging ponytail, and mouth scrunched to the side as if she's caught me doing something I'm not supposed to.

"Shirt," she says.

"What?"

"Shirt."

It takes me a second to feel the cool coastal breeze glide over my chest and realize that *god no!* I left my shirt off. I slap my hands to my boobs and hold them like some makeshift human bra while I turn around and steal the closest t-shirt lying on the desk nearest the door.

After I put it on, Grace busts out into laughter and points at it. "What in the world is that?"

I look down at my chest and recognize the airbrushed stick figure versions of both myself and Ian. The text reads *Big Beach Bash 2019* with my full name written in looping cursive along the top. The I is dotted with a heart.

I exhale and nod. "Ian and me in bikinis." As if this is an everyday occurrence.

After a beat and a few blinks to process both the shirt and the words coming out of my mouth, she simply responds with, "Sure, okay." I'm waiting on her to say more, but she takes a couple more moments of admiring the design with a smirk before continuing. "So, how are you feeling?" she asks.

"I'm feeling like I need an aspirin," I groan.

"Good, then I have a surprise for you." She holds out her

hand and gestures for me to do the same. I extend it with my palm open, and tablets drop into it from her fist.

"Thanks," I say with a sigh, popping the pills into the back of my throat and dry-swallowing them as she sidesteps me into the room, shutting the door behind her.

"I figured you probably packed your own pills," she says, "but oh well."

My mind is always so clouded with work, deadlines, and emails, it's easy to forget how seamlessly Grace and I have formed this friendship over the past few years—and how well she knows me.

Our relationship is best described as "work friends," but with the amount of time we both dedicate to our jobs, she might as well be a roommate. After one too many run-ins in the breakroom following normal working hours, we eventually started meeting in the more spacious boardrooms with comfy couches and projection screens so as to take advantage of each other's company. She would work on her projects and I would clickity-clack emails and run payroll, occasionally giving her my candid uncreative thoughts on the designs she was producing. She's never taken my suggestions. Let's just say I'm more suited for HR.

"I haven't seen much of you around," Grace says, aimlessly walking through the room then stopping at the DVD case. She holds it up to me. "Oh, but now I see why." She raises and lowers her eyebrows with a sly, Grinch-like smile.

I cringe and make a low noise resembling that of a bruised whale, or maybe even a deflating balloon.

"Ian." I exhale before throwing my hands in the air in a *What the hell else is there to say?* gesture.

Grace gingerly places the movie back down like it's some precious commodity. "Don't worry, I won't hurt your prized possession."

I'm sure my embarrassment is a real treat.

"Sorry I made you guys hang out," she says, though her apology is punctuated by a couple ill-suppressed hearty laughs. "But, good lord, that *fighting*!" Now she's the one throwing her hands in the air in a similar *What do I even do?* motion. That seems to be a common gesture when referring to anything regarding Ian Chambers.

"No, I'm the one who should be apologizing." I sit down on the bed and lie back. She mirrors the motion and turns her head to me so we're lying side by side. "It's your wedding week and I'm over here not letting old habits die. I'm just so used to constantly fighting with him that I don't think I know anything else."

As soon as the words leave my mouth, I realize how true they are. I never stop fighting with Ian, and even if we're not outwardly arguing, I'm internally carrying on this itch of a grudge. It's insatiable. Maybe I just have an obsession with hating him.

"He can be crazy, but he's really one of the nicest people I know," she says.

I want to tell her I know that. I want to say how we almost but not really kissed last night, how he wouldn't because I was too drunk, but that would open a can of worms type conversation that would easily squirm out of control through my fingers.

"We both know he likes to get under your skin. The problem is that you let him." She pokes my face, and the tip of her finger sinks into my cheek as I smile.

"Let's stop talking about Ian, please," I say. "What have I missed with you?"

She grows silent, lolling her head side to side and exhaling.

"What?" I ask.

"I want to tell you something, but you can't tell anyone." She twists the fabric of her dress near her stomach, and instantly my sensors go off. "Seriously. Not a soul." Her belly shows zero signs of bloating or life of any kind, but her mannerisms all point to the possibility. "I'm pregnant," she says, her eyebrows scrunching toward the center. "But, don't tell anyone!" Her hand lands on my wrist, which is attached to the hand now covering my mouth. She looks panicked, and I wonder if this is the first time she's admitted it out loud.

"When did you find out?" I ask.

"Yesterday. I wanted to tell you. I wish I hadn't sent you away…"

I laugh. "You didn't send me away. Sure, I was with Satan himself, but it's not like you banished me." This makes her laugh, and before I know it, she's rolling on the bed. Whether it's a mix of admiring any actual humor I may have, or if she's just letting out her nerves, I don't know. I let her have her moment.

"Who all knows?" I ask, knocking her out of her giggle fit and causing her to wipe her eyes with a smile.

"Just you," she says.

"Why me?" I ask, lifting an eyebrow as she lies on her back and gives me a simple shrug.

"You're the most rational person I know," she says. "I needed to tell someone, and I figured you would be the only one to not freak out or start planning baby showers."

"Then you've made a wise decision." I smile. "Does this mean I'm the godmother? Finders keepers on information?"

"Ha!" Grace barks out a laugh and then widens her eyes as if coming to a realization. "Yeah, actually you probably are the most responsible of the bunch. Maybe Corinne is too, but she's young. I mean, we're like sort of the same age," Grace continues, still in thought, "but she's six months younger or something. I'm not sure."

I zone out, eyes wide, staring at the ceiling and thinking of Corinne.

She is young, young enough to entice older men like Ian.

What is their age difference? Ten years, possibly? I want to feel something akin to hate or anger, but it's difficult to muster up any true disdain for her when she was such a genuine friend last night. Still, I see the way she and Ian look at each other, like old friends with history, and history commonly repeats itself.

The thought of Ian with another woman after I pictured him with me so vividly last night almost feels like infidelity, but I have no claim over him, and I don't even want one. *So why am I overthinking this?*

"Something wrong?" Grace asks, squinting her eyes.

No, Grace, I definitely wasn't brooding at the thought of tall, handsome Ian skipping hand in hand down the beach with model Corinne.

I shake my head with a smile. "No, not at all! I'm just happy to be your baby's secret godmother."

"Tentatively," she corrects. "I'll tell Cameron tomorrow. He's got the bachelor party tonight and he doesn't need any more stress."

I almost forgot the bachelor party was tonight. Then it hits me that there will most likely be strippers. I feel sick.

"Seriously, what's wrong with you?" Grace asks, scrunching up her nose.

I let out a nervous laugh. "Nothing!" I protest, batting at her. "I'm just wondering how much trouble those boys are going to get in."

She narrows her eyes at me, a small smirk tugging at her lips. "You're worried about Ian."

"No, I'm not," I lie, but I am a terrible liar. I can hover around the truth for days, avoid questions and give diplomatic answers, but straight-out lying? My cat could probably pick up on that.

Grace gasps loudly, sitting up from the bed with a jerk and rearing back to punch my arm.

"Ouch!" I yell, trying to be calm, but *damn!* That girl doesn't know how much strength she has!

"You like him," she says, a grin spreading across her face. She looks giddy, as if I've just presented her with a new puppy, or hell, as if *I* was the one who just told her I'm pregnant. "You have a thing for Ian."

"No, I don't," I say with a nervous laugh, which I did not expect to come from my mouth. *What the hell was that?*

"You're a crappy liar," she accuses, and I give her a smug half-smile.

"I don't have any feelings for Ian."

"He's loved you for years," she says breathlessly. "This would be fantastic. You should totally go for it."

I stop. The world stops. Bees stop buzzing. Flowers wilt. Is the apocalypse here?

Wait, he's *loved* me?

This man doesn't love me. He doesn't even know me. No, Ian messes around with other women—not me. Not Nia Smith. But then why the hell did that sentence come out of her mouth...?

"He doesn't love me," I insist. "You're getting too excited about something that is not—will never happen."

She leans her weight to the side and rests her palm on the bed. Her head rolls against her shoulder as she examines me. "What's holding you back?"

"Do I need an excuse to not want to date someone?"

Admittedly, I have a few. Ian is cocky and proud. Plus, I can never tell when he's making fun of me, which may or may not stem from my lingering awkward middle schooler complex, but I'm no psychologist.

And, what about the future? What happens with men like Ian? They end up like my brother Grant: lying on his parents' couch, most likely going through a divorce because he neglected to be faithful to his wife and couldn't be rational about his vices.

At my silence, Grace slowly nods. "Fine, I'll leave it alone," she says, hopping off the bed and waltzing toward the door. There's no tone of offense to it, so I'm comfortable flashing her an innocent smile as she turns to face me again. "You up for the beach today?" she asks. "I think Ramona is wanting to hash out some last-minute bachelorette party details."

"Well I did buy your coveted penis lollipops," I say, pointing to the black bag resting on the desk next to the TV. The dirty DVD's presence still mocks me.

She follows my gaze over to it then peers out of the corner of her eye with a knowing smile.

I exhale. "Not my idea, I swear."

She holds up her hands in surrender. "Hey, what you do in your free time is none of my business, Miss Smith."

I stand up, grab the movie off of the table, and immediately toss it in the garbage with as much disdain as I can muster. "See?" I say, gesturing to the newly trashed DVD. "No emotional attachment." *Only the emotional scars from the knowledge of having watched it.*

"Hang on, wait a sec," Grace says, tiptoeing toward the trash can and picking it out. "Bachelor party present." She winks, waving it toward me.

"I'm sure Cam will love that," I say, but she continues waving it at me with insistence. "What?"

"*You*—you should give it to Ian." Grace grins, waving it faster until it looks like a small blur in the air.

"Absolutely not." I balk, trying to appear nonchalant about it, but my heart starts pounding. How am I supposed to hand this stupid movie over to Ian after I told him I disposed of it? And what could I possibly say to make it not weird? *Enjoy the bachelor party with this fun movie*? *I hope you and the strippers can watch it together*? The thought makes me shudder.

"Well if you don't gift it to him, I will, and I'll say it's from you with *love*." She holds the DVD close to her chest. The facial expressions of the actors on the back cover make me uncomfortable; they look much too happy being in such close proximity to Grace's boobs. No person should be hugging that movie.

"Give me that," I say, snatching it from her in both a sense of responsibility to protect this pure, younger woman and also because I wouldn't put it past her to actually gift it to Ian with my name attached. "I'll do it. Whatever."

"Future baby is rooting for you," she says, cupping her stomach. Her hand resting there suddenly makes it feel so real.

"You'll be a good mother," I say, giving her a lopsided smile.

"And you would be good for Ian."

The sentiment is cute, but I'm not buying it.

17
IAN

CAMERON IS PACING THE LENGTH OF AN EMPTY CONFERENCE ROOM we found in a corner of the resort, mumbling to both himself and maybe us. I honestly can't tell. This room is the only place we could find to talk bachelor party specifics that also accommodated his anxiety.

Wes's sandaled feet are propped up on the long boardroom table as he leans back on two legs of a flimsy wooden chair. I notice the twisted edges getting strained. It's clear that even though this resort has invested money in a lot of the amenities, the secret boardroom was apparently not on their list of priorities.

"That's gonna break," I comment, glancing down at the legs then back up to him.

Wes shrugs nonchalantly followed by a small, "Nah."

"It's just nice to know Grace and I will have each other's backs," says Cam. "Just in case things get crazy." He's only talking to himself at this point; I'm not even sure he cares whether we're paying attention or not.

With the bachelor party being tonight, Grace and Cam planned to have the bachelorette party the following night, the day before the rehearsal dinner. It's back-to-back celebrations of some sort until the wedding day, and I commend him on at least attempting to be responsible about the schedule.

And, if I'm being honest with myself, I like that I can be available should something happen to Nia at the bachelorette party. She may not be my wife or fiancée like Ramona and Grace are to Wes and Cam, but there's some weird sense of responsibility I feel like I have with her.

I can't tell if that thought sounds obsessive or caring.

"Not that I don't support this—because I do—but what crazy thing could possibly happen with strippers?" Wes asks, lifting an eyebrow.

"Well, I'll be sober," I offer, "so at least I can drive. That will tone down the potential for crazy."

"Yes, but you're a wild card," Cam throws back at me pointedly. "You pick up strays."

"Hey, I resent that. I try to keep things fairly reasonable, and that goat man from the other night was nice enough," I say.

"He was on drugs." Wes laughs.

"Actually," I correct with my index finger pointing in the air, "he was just super drunk."

"The point is," Cam says, exhaling heavily, "I would like backup just in case, and the girls have agreed to be available."

"I guess it's probably for the best," Wes says, leaning farther back with his hands behind his head. The chair creaks. "The other Chambers kid is a wild card too."

"You people and not trusting the Chambers family." I shake my head as if in disbelief. "I am, quite frankly, appalled."

"Do you remember that time Ramona just disappeared? We all walked up and down the interstate looking for her."

"Sure," I muse, "but she made it home just fine."

"She hitchhiked, Ian, and somehow had a stuffed bear when we found her?"

"The origin of that bear is still a mystery."

"Still not as bad as you," Cam says. "Didn't you streak in a park?"

I bark out a laugh. "Hey, I made sure nobody was there, but yeah. That was a good time, thanks very much."

"Necessary precautions, my friend," Wes says, slapping my back.

"Okay," I say, "so it looks like the night's events are as follows." I look down at my phone, where I've been attempting to take notes. "Strip club, bar, bar, pier?"

"What is this, Duck, Duck, Goose?" Wes laughs. "And why is the strip club first?"

"To get it out of the way," I say with a raised eyebrow.

"Good call," he replies, a bit too quickly.

"Agreed," Cam interjects. I can see the relief in both his and Wes's eyes, and I wonder why the heck we're even choosing to go if none of us want to.

"I mean, we can skip it—" I start before immediately being interrupted by the others.

"It wouldn't be a bachelor party without it."

"Absolutely not."

"Have to."

"Okay," I say slowly, looking between them then back down at my phone again. "So, strip club, bar, then pier?"

"Did you take out a bar?"

"Why is the pier last and not a bar?"

SNAP!

I look over and down goes Wes, butt flat on the floor with the chair splayed under him in various chunks and splinters, a full-on gregarious laugh erupting from his throat.

"This is…going…to be…a shit show, isn't it?" he asks between laughs, and both Cam and I look at each other with a smirk.

Absolutely.

I SPEND most of the late morning and early afternoon trying to relax by the pool with my most recent read, but it's hard to concentrate when I keep wondering what time Nia will arrive. It's almost three o'clock before she wanders out of the resort's sliding glass doors and, good lord, she's as gorgeous as ever. No other woman can pull off a conservative bikini like this woman, and I never really thought I'd say that. It's probably those long legs still on display. Even at her shorter height, she's seventy percent legs. Couldn't hide those even if she tried.

I pop out of my pool chair with my book placed under my arm once she passes, following right behind her as her blue skirt billows next to me.

"Afternoon, Polly," I say, sidestepping the fabric. "How are you feeling?"

"Not dead. At least there's that." Her tone lacks the familiar underlying bite of irritation that I'm used to. Dare I say it has a slight sweetness to it? I can get behind this change.

We walk down the stairs that lead to the beach. She removes her sandals to pocket them in her tote bag. She eyes me for a bit then slightly opens the bag as if to invite my own sandals in as well. It's weird how such a simple gesture can cause my heart to swell three times as big.

"Wow." I slip my sandals off. "I like this new politeness. What's gotten into you?"

"I'm trying this new thing where I try not to completely hate you," she says, a sly smile tugging at the corner of her lips. *Is she flirting with me?*

I use my hand to widen the bag's opening and drop the sandals inside. Just as they plop in, I catch a glimpse of a DVD. *The* DVD. My jaw drops.

"So, you *do* still have it," I say, and her head jerks toward me, face flushing red.

Her eyebrows rise above her dark sunglasses. "I take it back," she says, her mouth twitching into a constrained half-smile. "I still hate you."

"Tell me why you have it," I prod, a grin spreading across my face.

This woman is effectively carrying pornography just a foot or two away from me. This entire situation feels like contraband that has been caged and locked away from me, and I finally have a piece of the key.

"There's a story, I swear."

"And..." I urge as we begin to walk once more.

I'm getting hard just thinking about Nia sitting on her bed watching it, and I trip over some sand. My mind can barely register anything past the idea of her watching that goddamn movie.

She laughs at my stumble. "Grace told me you guys would like it as a bachelor party present. So, I was going to give it to you." Her tone is all business.

"Were you, now?" I say, quirking an eyebrow. "And did you and Grace watch it together?"

"You pig."

"I feel that's a legitimate question."

She stops mid-step and I'm so close to her that my chest bumps against her back. Then she stays there, unmoving, her head tilting to face me. We're maybe an inch or two apart, my head hovering next to hers, both of us looking straight ahead.

"You're starting this again," she whispers. Her breath is so close it makes my hair stand on end. Every bit of pressure in my body rushes directly down to my crotch.

"Starting what?" I ask.

"The suggestive, seductive whispering."

"*You* started the whispering."

"Listen, I told you things I shouldn't have last night," she says. "Let's get over it."

I chuckle, my breath moving a tendril of hair hanging next to her ear. She inhales sharply at this. Does she really regret everything? I take a step back.

"Stop that," she says.

"Stop what?" I whisper back. I'm starting to feel like a yo-yo being thrown down and wound back up, just wrapped around this woman's finger.

"That weird grumble guttural sound you make," she says. "I heard enough of that last night."

I didn't even know I made a sound.

"I liked finding out more about you," I say, and I mean it. I loved the honesty, the raw admissions about our personal lives, and everything in between. There's a moment now where she stares into my eyes. She steals a glance down to my lips. It reminds me of how she looked last night—hungry and wanting.

"We don't talk about that," she whispers.

"What?" I whisper back.

"You know what."

What is she referring to? I open my mouth to ask, but I feel a quick slap on my back that jolts me away from my focus on Nia's smooth lips.

"Corinne," Nia says through a shaky breath, a large grin spreading on her face. It's fake and I could sense that from a mile away. I wonder if Corinne can too, but even if it's possible, her own face doesn't give a hint of being any the wiser.

"What's going on?" she asks. "Are we sharing secrets?" I have never wanted to hear Corinne's peppy voice less in my entire life. In fact, I'll even go so far as to say I've never wanted to see a tall perky blonde in a small pink bikini as little as I do now.

Corinne is much smarter than she lets on. I swear I can see mischief lurking behind those absurdly large, winged black sunglasses.

I try to speak again, but a loud ringing from Nia's tote bag interrupts.

"Do you always keep that at max volume?" Corinne asks. Nia tries to flash another fake smile, but I roll my eyes at the ridiculous effort of it all.

"It restarted and I guess the volume triggered back to a default," Nia says, digging through her bag, pushing past items as the ringtone wails on. How do women find anything in bags that big?

"The bottomless bag," I comment to Nia, smirking.

"I keep forgetting to check it this morning," she says before yelling, "Finally!" once she locates the phone. Then, with a quick glance at the screen, her face shifts from triumph to shock.

"Woah, uh, I should probably take this."

"Everything okay?" I ask.

"I have about ten missed calls from my brother."

I try to see what's on her screen because I'm a nosy fucker, but the light of the sun and my lack of sunglasses causes me to squint and only be able to make out vague details. All I know is when she goes to her messages, I see paragraph upon paragraph of texts sent from the other person.

Finally, with a small twist of her wrist, the sun stops reflecting off the screen just long enough for me to see one simple and clear text at the bottom: Call me now.

18

NIA

FIVE YEARS AGO

Some childhood games never die, and making blanket forts with your siblings is one of them, though building them in a hospital waiting room when one sibling could become a parent at any moment might be when the term "grow up" is applicable, which is exactly what my sister Sarah is whining to all of us as we pass pillows around.

It's late at night—or maybe early in the morning—on Christmas Day, and all the Smith children are throwing hospital sheets and pillows across aisles of chairs to create a blanket palace fit for the arrival of Harry's daughter, Cara.

"Lawrence, pillow me!" Harry yells, causing a *pop* to his head when the fluffy brick hits him square in the jaw.

The nurse at the window tsks, but that's the extent of her reprimand. It's Christmas, after all, and other waiting room occupants in the maternity ward are helping with our pillow neighborhood.

I pile the final blanket on a stack meant to form the ceiling of a very sad parapet.

"You tried," Harry says with a smile.

"Don't insult my pillow genius," I say. "And what are you working on anyway?"

He points to the area nestled between two couch cushions as walls, a tiny throw tucked around the edges.

"A nursery," he says. I grin back but instead of a sweet moment, we have Jamie and Lawrence crawling their way over, bypassing other makeshift "rooms" in the palace.

"You're such a sap," Lawrence says, clapping a hand on his shoulder. "Who guessed baby brother Harry would be the first of us to have a kid?"

I smile to Harry. It's a happy moment, one none of us expected but exciting all the same. Who isn't excited to be an aunt or uncle? A grandparent? My heart swells and a buzz runs through me, but then it centers on my butt and I realize it's just the phone in my back pocket, begging to be answered.

I tug it out and see an email in my work inbox. My stomach drops at the name. It's been doing that a lot lately. Maybe I'm just desperate. Maybe my dry spell is finally catching up with me. All I know is that I have an email from Ian Chambers on a Sunday morning, and it just made me feel a bit tipsy.

From: ichambers@treasuriesinc.com
To: nsmith@treasuriesinc.com
Subject: Congrats!
Nia,
Good luck being an aunt. I'm sure you'll be great. Or you'll be bad. Who really knows since it's your first niece? But I bet you'll be great. Congratulations!
See ya tomorrow,
Ian

It's a simple message. Unexpected, but weirdly welcome. Maybe it's the atmosphere of this waiting room or my raging hormones, or maybe it's that he's the only person from work who congratulated the family—the only one who remembered. Whatever it is, my face lights up.

"Is that your work husband?" Harry asks, peering over my shoulder.

"God no," I say, forcing out a laugh and pocketing my phone.

"Nia has a work husband?" Lawrence gasps. "Scandalous. Nia, who even are you now?"

"Stop," I demand. "It's just a co-worker congratulating Harry."

"He congratulated *you*," Harry says.

"Stop reading my emails."

"Did I hear work husband?" a voice says. Sarah pokes her head in and crawls into the fort. She pushes a stack of pillows out of her way and plops down beside us.

"Hey, that was the kitchen!" Jamie says, one hand palm up as if to point out the stove that is now in shambles.

"Whoops," she says. Her eyes go wide but with zero apology. "But what's this about Nia being a harlot at work?"

I groan loudly, grabbing a pillow and shoving my face into it.

"And that's the microwave too." Jamie exhales. "No respect."

"Nia is a harlot?" Another voice greets us from the entrance, but it's a much deeper one this time. When the face turns the corner, we all gasp as if in some B-rated horror film.

This killer was Mr. Grant Smith all along!

My chest is rising and falling, and I'm beginning to think I have the *Twilight Zone* ride imbedded in me for the night.

"Grant, wow...uh, you made it!" Harry's tone gives off vibes of being both happy and apprehensive. I'd say I only have the latter emotion coursing through me.

Grant has been overseas for two years. What's going on in his life? Good question. If you find out, let me know. How he knows about this even happening is beyond me. He hasn't spoken a word to any of us since his move, at least not as far as I'm aware.

"Yeah, I figured I would," he says. "Girlfriend is out of town and all." His grins, and something about it rubs me the wrong way.

"Been a couple years," Lawrence says. "I thought we were only stuck with the better half of the twins."

Sarah chokes out a laugh, covering her mouth immediately. She's reveling in the compliment.

"Can't miss the first nephew, can I?" Grant says, flashing a grin to all of us.

"Niece," I correct. My eyes narrow of their own accord.

"Oh-kay, I'll go check on Mom and Dad," Jamie says. He's never been one to engage in awkward conversation. Give him a cabin and a fishing rod and he would hide from the world for years. It's a wonder he emerged from Alaska for this, but not as surprising as the other brother in front of us flying in from who knows where.

"I'll join you. One per parent," Lawrence says. They crawl their way out, leaving only me, Harry, and the twins: one smiling, the other with a look of casual ignorance. He even has the corner of his mouth twitched in a smile. I want to slap it off.

"Sure, right, so who's the mother?"

"Rude," I mutter.

"Her name is Riley," Harry says.

"Yeah, but who is she?" Grant asks, laughing under his breath. "How have I never heard of her?"

Harry and I are quiet, but he clears his throat and straightens his posture. I wonder if he consciously meant to.

"I met her nine months ago," Harry says. "We don't date now, but it's still my daughter, dude." His good nature is faltering, slowly shifting its way back to the frown.

"We're all chipping in on a present for her," I say.

"What is this? Some charity case?"

I want to fight my way over every single pillow and strangle him with scratchiest hospital blanket I can find.

"God, Grant, you just got here and you're already being the worst," I say.

Then, with the shift of the blankets overhead, a sliver of hospital light shines in and I see his eyes: bloodshot, glazed over.

"Wait—are you drunk?" My tone is harsh, demanding, and unabashedly judgmental. I am totally judging the hell out of him.

He smiles wider and shrugs. "No, but why are we changing the subject from Harry's baby mama to me?"

"Riley," Harry corrects. His eyebrows are pulled together, a deep frown on his face. There's no shame. It's all defiance.

"Why are you here?" I ask.

"Seeing my family."

"Since when is that something you do?"

"Girlfriend on a business trip—does that mean nothing? Well, I guess it does to you, Harry." He nudges Harry, only to be shoved off.

"Dude, come on."

Grant throws his hands up. "Where is your sense of humor, people? I'm joking!"

"Sorry for not getting the joke." No, I'm not. I don't want to understand. I want this interaction to end. And, as if like clockwork, the blanket fort is torn apart, and hovering over us are the heads of our siblings, grinning down at Harry.

"You're a dad," Lawrence says.

Harry smiles ear to ear, cheeky and almost tear-filled. I've never seen such a look of pride, not even when he opened his mechanic shop.

"Go get your baby mama, brother." The moment disappears like the snap of a finger.

Harry's eyebrows pull together and he stands, staring at the oblivious brother in front of him. "Why are you even here?" he demands.

Grant shrugs with a chuckle. He's not really here, unaware of the family he's quickly abandoning once again even though he's done it several times before.

Grant doesn't even register Harry's bold middle finger as the new father leaves to go see his newborn daughter.

19

NIA

PRESENT DAY

I should have known better than to think the majority of my problems started and ended with Ian.

"Holy shit, Nia, where the hell have you been?" Harry says immediately upon answering.

"My phone died," I say. I want to glance to Ian as if to blame him for the other events that took place, but I hold back.

"Well, I'm about two hours away from you, and Grant is probably about thirty minutes ahead of me."

The sentence causes me to pause, and then a thousand questions come barreling in all at once. It's like the bottom third of a news channel. *Breaking news! Here's an alarming article, here's another, and here's why you will die young!*

And here's the news that will usher in my own personal hell.

"E-Excuse me?" I stammer out.

"Maybe he's already there," Harry says. "Hell if I know. I haven't been able to catch up with him."

"Why the... I don't..." I pinch the bridge of my nose and squint my eyes closed. Zero part of my body is processing this news well because my heart is pounding, my feet are planted like cement, and, quite frankly, I think I might vomit.

"What's going on?" a voice asks. I look up to see Ian and Corinne. I forgot they were in front of me. Corinne's arms are crossed, and Ian's eyebrows are pulled together, head tilted to the side. It's genuine concern, and my heart melts.

No, now isn't the time for admiration, Nia.

I hold my hand up to them as if to signal to give me a moment.

"What?" I ask.

"He saw the invite on your fridge and stole my car." *My fridge? Harry's car?*

"I have so many questions," I say.

"Your conversation with him yesterday put him on edge. I figured he needed to get out of the house. So, I took him to your house. I was trying to fix your car."

"You took him to the house of the one person he didn't like at the time?" I scoff.

"I was trying to be a good brother, so sue me!" he bellows back. We don't fight like this. We never raise our voices, let alone have legitimate arguments. It's making my heart both race and break all at once. "I wanted to try fixing your car again because you're too stubborn to pay for a new one, and I also wanted to help our idiot brother who I'm fairly sure is on fucking drugs while driving on the interstate."

"What?!" I yell. It's like with every sentence Harry says, it gets more and more difficult for me to process anything. *Please tell me this is the nightmare part of a hangover fever dream.*

"He stole my car. I'm driving yours—which, yes, is fixed. You're welcome."

My dear brother Harry, the one with a heart of gold, wanted to fix my car because he's just that kind of person, and he succeeded because he's just that good of a mechanic. Then there's my other brother, Grant Smith, who, in all his privileged glory, thought it would be a good idea to steal this kind soul's pet project.

No wonder Grant is so far ahead. Harry knows how to max out the speed of any car and maneuver it with skill, but my trash vehicle is nothing compared to Harry's souped-up monster, his pride and joy. No wonder he's pissed.

I pity the fool who steals Harry's car.

"He's going through a lot," Harry grumbles. In true Harry fashion, he's still trying to see the good in people. I, on the other hand, may murder Grant the second he shows up.

"It kinda seems like it's his own damn fault," I shoot back. "I mean, what do I do? I'm here with a bunch of people. How am I supposed to handle a psycho at the same time? And what does he even want?"

The words visibly startle Ian and Corinne, who exchange a look.

"You wouldn't answer your phone." Harry says. "He just wanted to talk to you. Apparently, he thinks driving all the way to Florida is the way to do it. Look, I'm coming to get him and bring him back."

"He's driving down here just to talk to me?"

"Has Grant ever done anything that made sense?"

I exhale. "I'll see if I can get him in my room before he wreaks too much havoc." This is not how I wanted to start my hungover afternoon. In fact, seeing Grant at all is not how I wanted to start any day moving forward.

"I'll keep you updated," he says. "Like I said, just two hours out."

There's a moment of silence between us, and I know we're both taking in the situation. It's absurd, but it doesn't matter how long of a pause we take. It's still happening.

"Thank you for warning me," I say.

He grunts back something along the lines of, "Yeah."

"See you soon. I'll call you when he gets here."

I hang up, holding the phone tightly in my hand. My knuckles are white, my heart is pounding, and I'm slightly light-headed, but now is not the time to succumb to weakness. I need to be the strong one, because in less than an hour, I will most likely be face to face with a brother I haven't seen in years. What do we even say? How do I address him? What is he like now?

The last time I saw him, his eyes were bloodshot and his t-shirt was littered with stains, but he was still flashing the grin of someone who is confident in how ridiculously awesome their life is. It was at the birth of my niece. He didn't say goodbye. He didn't announce that he would never come to another family event. He just left.

I shake my head and try to focus. I need to go to the front of the resort and wait for him. I need to cut him off before he can do anything too stupid.

"Nia?" Corinne asks.

My head shoots up to her and I inhale. "I need to handle some things," I say. "Just go meet up with Grace and them, but don't tell anyone."

"We're here to help," Ian says without missing a beat, and Corinne gives a strong nod.

"You don't want to get involved in this."

"Yes, we do," Ian says firmly. I rarely hear this tone from him unless he's in court. It's powerful, strong, and sends shivers down my spine.

Can I not go two seconds without admiring him?

"Fine," I accept. "I need to go to the front."

"I'll take your things back up," Corinne says, reaching out for my bag. I slide it off and hand it to her along with my room key. She runs off, and Ian and I look to each other.

"So, tell me what's going on," he says, and I don't know what else to do but oblige.

We walk back through the lobby and I tell him everything

—at least, everything I can tell. I say how I don't know a lot of the details, how I don't even know what he'll be like when he gets here. Ian listens intently, his brows furrowed as he nods with each piece of information he gets. He asks no questions, just listens. I wonder what's going through his mind. I wonder if every good thought about me is being washed away, and it hurts me a little to think so.

Corinne joins us shortly after, handing me back my key. "Drama!"

"Yep, just like Disneyworld, Corinne," Ian says.

The silence between the three of us isn't uncomfortable. It's solemn, as if we're holding a funeral for this day, which has effectively gone to shit, but the moment doesn't last long.

We hear a loud rumbling, the sound of an overworked engine, and the revving of a vehicle with too much power for one car. It is definitely Harry's sports car driven by a person who doesn't understand how to control the car's infinite limits. It whips around the corner, streaks of black and red zooming through, halting in front of us with a screech.

Ian touches the small of my back and a swoop of nerves drives through me faster than Harry's beast of a car. I'd watch that nasty movie and imagine Ian a thousand times over if it meant I didn't have to be here.

The car's door rises up. It's a feature I distinctly remember Harry being psyched about, but instead of Harry's grinning face peering out of the car, it's a much more haggard, unshaven man.

Grant's face is slack, and his eyelids are drooping. I guess an eight-hour drive on drugs will take a toll on your energy levels. But, even apart from that, he's showing visible signs of age. His hairline has receded, and his once luscious dyed auburn hair is now back to pale blond, overshadowed by wisps of gray and white.

He walks around the side of the car, not even bothering to

close the door behind him. He's wearing gray sweatpants and a navy shirt. I see some familiar stains on the sleeve. Could he be more of a cliché?

"My own welcoming committee," he croaks out with arms spread wide. "That's a long fucking drive, and so many fucking idiots on the road." He's irritated, and I wouldn't doubt that he had road rage the entire way here; he looks like he's close to raging now as it is. "Well, aren't you a sight for sore eyes." Grant tosses a half-hearted wink over to Corinne. She grimaces in response.

Even coming down from a high, he's still trying to be a ladies' man, but it's becoming clear to me now that he was less of a gift to women and more of an egotistical womanizer. I look up to Ian. His hand is still resting on the small of my back, but there's a bit of a grip to it now, and his jaw is set. I can't help but notice his eyes piercing my brother. Ian's hair is curled and suave—not at all ragged like Grant's—and his strong jaw ticks with every second.

They couldn't be more different.

"God..." Grant grips his head, grinding the palm of his hand into a closed eye. When he opens them again, they're bloodshot. The bags don't help his appearance either. "Please tell me there's a bed here."

"Well, we're at a resort, so I would hope so," Ian shoots back, and my brother blinks before taking a stride toward Ian with his finger out. I can feel the explosion coming on.

I dart forward and press both hands to his chest. "Hello, Grant," I say loudly, trying to turn his attention to me.

"Little Apollonia," he says, calming a bit, though his face remains red. The nickname makes my spine stiffen slightly, and I find myself rising to a fuller height without even thinking about it.

"That's me. Guessed correctly. Good job," I say, patting his chest.

He stares at me, trying to take me in. Then his eyes narrow. "I have a bone to pick with you," he grumbles.

I hear Ian's sandals clap forward behind me, but I hold my hand out and stop him in his tracks.

"Who's your giant watchdog?" Grant asks, peering to Ian. I look over my shoulder. His hands are curled into fists by his sides, accentuating his forearms and large chest. His blue eyes are narrowed, but a slight smile still tugs on the corner of his mouth. I don't know whether he's mad or delighted at how irritated Grant is.

"You're the pit bull trying to attack me." Ian laughs.

This comment makes Grant's face grow so red it's almost purple. He tries to walk forward again, but I push my hands into him.

"Down, boy," Ian says with a smirk. *Damn it, Ian.*

"He's a friend." I exhale. *Yes, he's a very hot friend who is, for some reason, very protective.* "Let's go upstairs. We can talk there. I have a bed and everything."

He shakes my hands off, runs his fingers through his hair, and straightens his posture, shaking out his shirt as if that could possibly improve his appearance.

We walk forward and he spots Corinne again. "Are you coming with us, darling?"

She scowls at him. "Unfortunately."

When Ian follows behind me, Grant lifts an eyebrow. "He's joining us too?"

"I'm the best part of the welcoming committee," Ian says, throwing him a wink. I mouth a "Stop" to him and he shrugs nonchalantly.

What am I going to do with this man?

In His Eyes | 163

IN LESS THAN THIRTY MINUTES, after an unnecessary number of snarky comments from Ian, Grant finally passes out on my hotel bed, snoring like a bear in hibernation. An hour after that, I go down to the lobby for Harry. He is flustered and forcing out a grin. I wrap him in a hug but immediately pull back.

"Oh god, you're sweaty."

"I didn't exactly have time to fix your air conditioning."

"Fair."

We walk back up to the room where he takes a moment to stare at Grant before exhaling and joining Ian and Corinne on the patio. The four of us look out at the beach with the sliding glass door shut and the curtains closed to both block out the sun for Grant and ensure we can't see my mess of a brother.

Harry and Ian share niceties, but not much past that. I'm hoping it's been too long for Ian to remember the last time they met, but Harry is not nearly as oblivious. That's what I get for having a schoolgirl crush on this man and not concealing it from my brother like any other rational person might.

"You guys can stay for the night," I say. "That drive is long, and he probably needs time to get normalized again or whatever."

"Do you know if he has any more?" Ian asks Harry, who shrugs.

"He didn't have anything in his pockets when he came in, not even a wallet," Corinne says. The three of us look to her, and she leans against the railing with a smirk. "What? I patted his pants down. He didn't seem to mind."

"We won't be a burden," Harry reassures me. "We can probably put something on TV and that'll occupy him. You guys go out and do whatever you were going to do. Don't worry about us."

Ian's face immediately lights up and a grin spreads across it like a kid finding secret candy in a couch cushion. I don't like this face.

"We actually have the bachelor party tonight," Ian says. *Oh no.* "You should come!"

"Absolutely not," I say, hands slicing the air as if calling a foul. "No. No way. The last thing Grant needs is a strip club."

"Nah, we won't do the strip club. Nobody wants to anyway," Ian says with an unconcerned shrug.

"We're not busting in on your party." Harry laughs, and Ian's smile still beams with enjoyment over the whole thing.

"Just let me talk with Cam," Ian says. "We only have three people here. Two more will make it a party. Plus, I can keep an eye on your brother the whole time. I don't drink."

Harry twists his mouth to the side, apparently considering the offer. *Oh, good lord, is he going to accept?*

"No, this is ridiculous," I say, stepping between the two of them. "The man in there just drove down here on drugs with no wallet and we're going to reward him with a night out on the town?"

"You only focus on the fact that he's lacking ID?" Ian teases. My face flushes and I turn away.

"Maybe Grant needs a guys' night," Harry says.

"Are you serious?" I twist toward him. "For real? You're going to agree with Ian?"

"Ian!" Harry snaps. "That's right. I remember you!" *Good man. At least he plays it off well.*

"Is nobody listening to me?" I cross my arms and tap my foot. I'm having horrible flashbacks to my childhood with a very unbalanced boys-to-girls ratio.

Corinne is in the corner of the patio, smiling at me as if this is a simple thing for the boys to figure out. *Woman, this is a serious problem. How am I the only one realizing just how crazy this is?*

I wave my hands. "No night on the town. No big party. No."

"Unfortunately," Harry says, taking in a deep breath then exhaling, "it's two against one." There we go—the ol' sibling card.

"Don't you dare play that game with me," I say, lifting my index finger close to his nose. He pushes it away. I see Corinne giggle behind him.

Et tu, Brute?

"We'll be back before you know it," Harry says. "Scar-free."

I look between Ian and Harry. They both have the same puppy dog frown on their face. Harry's is cute, but Ian's is positively heart-wrenching. What is this stupid soft spot I'm developing for Ian again? Why does his five o'clock shadow make me want to run my fingers across it? Why can I not stop imagining that jaw against my thighs?

"Arrest-free," I add. I hate not being in control. I hate this so much. But, hell, I probably couldn't stop them if I tried, and I can't deny the draw of those icy blue eyes.

"No promises," mumbles Ian. I shoot him a glare, and he throws his hands up. "Kidding."

20

IAN

I like Harry. The first thing he says to me when we leave to find Cameron and Wes is, "You're the dude who crashed our dinner a few years ago."

"Bingo."

"And how long have you liked my sister?"

"How long ago was that dinner?"

We exchange grins and continue down the elevator.

As it turns out, we catch Cameron while he's pregaming with a flask down by the beach. He and Wes are already tipsy, and although Wes mentions something about picking up strays again, which I happily ignore, they both seem pretty excited about the addition of two new people. Lucky for me, they are also too tipsy to even ask who these men are after my haphazard lie stating that I met them at a bar.

Perfect.

Grant eventually wakes up, and he seems a bit more stable. His eyes are red and he is less than thrilled to see me, but Harry knows the right things to say to calm him down. I think the news that he is about to go to a bona fide bachelor party makes him more excited than able to muster up hatred for me.

Although, the mention of us skipping the strip club causes the return of irritation once more. He's a yo-yo that will be hard to "walk the dog" with tonight, but I'm always up for a challenge. Plus, they didn't make me a yo-yo champion for nothing.

Man, summer camp was awesome.

I take one last look at Nia before leaving. Her eyebrows are pulled tight in the center. I throw her a smile, and surprisingly, she returns it.

"Here's my phone number," she says, handing me a piece of paper. "In case you need it. Just keep me updated."

"You're giving me your number?" I wiggle my eyebrows and she blushes.

"Don't abuse it, Ian."

I type the number into my phone and shoot out a quick text. She looks down at her screen and scoffs. I'd kill to see that smirk every day.

"You sent me, '*Hey girl*'?" she says, holding up her phone.

"Entrancing, I know."

"Good lord, just go."

———

THE BAR IS NEARLY empty when we arrive, but the groom insists on starting the party immediately, so it's shots all around. Grant takes both his and mine. I almost protest, but whatever. I'll just keep on eye on the old bastard.

Ian: Just arrived.
Nia: Cool.
Ian: Crowded bar.
Nia: No need for constant updates.
Ian: Ordering drinks.
Nia: Why are you like this?

It takes Grant a total of thirty minutes to finally talk to me again.

"You like little Apollonia?" Grant's slurred voice rings over the music. Already drunk—what a surprise. Did the bartender seriously not card him? I suppose he is looking a little worse for wear and even older than he actually is.

"She's not too fond of me, but I pride myself on the fact that I can eventually wear anyone down." There's a moment of quiet before Grant bursts out into laughter. It must have taken him a second to get the joke.

"There we go," Harry says, patting Grant on the back.

"Ian!" Another familiar voice rises over the crowd and *holy shit* here comes the motherfucking goat man, barreling toward us with open arms. He attempts to hug both myself and Harry, but thankfully his reach isn't long enough.

"Surprised you remember me," I say, taking out my phone.

Ian: Goat man.
Nia: Goat man?

"How could I forget you?" he says, squeezing my cheeks between his thumb and forefinger. I twist out of his grip, causing his fisherman's hat to topple over. Harry picks it up and hands it back.

"Who are your friends?" the goat man asks.

Ian: Hey, do you remember his name?
Nia: Who?
Ian: Goat man.
Nia: Is it Billy?
Ian: Are you telling a joke?
Nia: Maybe.

Harry waves, but Grant stares at him with eyes glazed over.

The man squints. "What's with your pal?" he asks.

"Uh, watch out, he's had a rough day," Harry says, but Grant seems less than concerned about the local wonder coming toward him.

"Not your fault, eh?"

"No, it was," he admits. I shake my head and am surprised to see that Grant catches the motion. "What, are you going to judge me, pretty boy? What makes you think you're any better?"

"I'm not," I say. "We all have our demons. Hey, I won't judge yours if you won't judge mine."

"I don't believe you," he says with narrowed eyes.

"I don't care." I shrug. Grant seems like he's getting angry again, but the goat man puts a hand on his shoulder and hops onto the bar stool next to him.

"Why don't we all share?"

Ian: I think this bachelor party just turned into a therapy session. Or a teenage girls' slumber party.
Nia: What color are you painting your nails?
Ian: Bright pink.
Nia: So, what are some of their secrets in this so-called therapy session?

I lift my head, tuning in to the conversation I've been too distracted to hear.

Ian: Cam went to circus school for a semester before dropping out.
Nia: Get real.
Ian: Wes says he regrets a tattoo on his butt. He tried to show us. I think it might be Ramona's name.
Nia: Is it in a heart with an arrow through it?
Ian: Absolutely.

Nia: Should you be sharing all of their secrets?
Ian: Harry steals your cookies.
Nia: Knew it.
Ian: And what's your secret?

At that, the texts stop. *Damn it.*

We all gallivant from one bar to the next, eventually ending at the pier as planned. My feet hang over the side of the dock with Grant seated next to me. Harry and Cam wade through the water, and Wes and the goat man bury themselves in sand, making sandcastles that look like more penises.

"Sorry for earlier," Grant says.

"You shouldn't have driven," is all I can get out.

"You aren't going to accept my apology?" he asks, narrowing his eyes.

"Temper, temper," I respond, lifting my eyebrow to him but ignoring his comment altogether. "You might want to quell that."

"You're an ass."

"Tell me, do you feel bad about anything?" I ask. "Anything at all?"

His eyes shift to me and he swallows before looking out at the ocean. For a moment we only hear the waves and the laughing of the men below. Looks like Cameron has buried Wes with makeshift sand boobs over his chest.

"You're bold," Grant says.

"I like to think I'm charming."

He scoffs. "I hate you."

"So, do you?" I ask again. "Regret anything, I mean?"

"I hate myself a little more every day."

I remember being that person. I remember feeling like the world is on your shoulders and you can't shove it off. Every day gets harder and the guilt pushes you so far into the ground until you're burying yourself in it, slowly letting yourself drown under the weight.

"Eventually, you won't," I say. "You'll rediscover what life is and then you'll grab it by the balls and never let it pass you by again."

Grant stares at me. He's swaying under the influence of who knows how many shots, and he's blinking slowly. I wonder for a moment if he's going to fall off the pier, readying my reflexes just in case, but he smiles and nods.

"I hope you're right."

"I'm always right," I say, and he rolls his eyes.

Ian: Your brother isn't half bad.
Nia: You guys are getting along? Cute.

> *Cute.*
> "You're a menace," he grunts.
> "I get that a lot."

Grant grins, and I think we may have just become friends. Imagine that.

Ian: I miss you, Polly.

21

NIA

I'VE BEEN LEANING ON THE RAILING OVERLOOKING THE PARKING lot for at least thirty minutes, maybe more. Maybe less than that? Who knows; time has begun to blur.

I glance down at my phone, peering over the texts Ian and I have exchanged tonight. The most recent states they're on the way back. It's the message immediately preceding that one that I keep mentally stumbling over.

I miss you, Polly.

Shit.

Corinne stayed with me after the boys left for their night on the town and we watched television. We settled on the Florida channel with repeating advertisements for boardwalk Ferris wheels and local putt-putt courses. There was even a vampire-themed putt-putt. It's the middle of July, but sure, why not?

I wonder if the boys ended up going to a strip club. I believe Harry would surely balk at that, but then again, maybe he wouldn't. I don't want to picture my baby brother getting lap dances from naked women. He's named after Harry Houdini, for God's sake. That fact alone should halt a woman in her tracks. I'm pretty sure my parents' creative juices were spent when they named the last of us. *Thanks a lot, guys.*

I lean my head on the cool railing. Do I trust Ian to watch over them? Maybe I do. He doesn't drink for some unknown reason, but whatever the case, he's dedicated to the cause. When Ian says he's going to do something, he sticks to his guns and rarely strays from the path. The motivation of that man is incomparable to anyone else, and while I've always believed Harry was the purest of heart, I'm starting to wonder if Ian is giving him a run for his money.

For years, Ian has been nothing but a nuisance to me, and I've always considered that to be pure entertainment for him. But, has he really liked me? Has he *loved* me?

No, what a ridiculous notion. I've been the one pining after him, not the other way around. Because, if it were the other way around, how would I feel then?

I don't know.

The door opening from behind me makes me jump.

"You doing okay?" Corinne asks through a yawn. I nod in response and she leans on the railing next to me. "You don't seem okay."

"I'm worried," I admit.

"About your brothers or about Ian?" She says it in a teasing tone, but I answer honestly.

"Both."

A pregnant pause lingers between us and she lets out a sharp laugh. "Huh."

"Huh?"

"Well, it's interesting," she says, twisting her mouth to the side. "I wouldn't have guessed that."

I exhale. "Me either."

Cameron's hulking Jeep pulls into the lot and my heart rises into my throat. I feel like I'm going to both vomit and pass out all at once. I just imagine my brain yelling, *Alright, shut her down, folks!* And honestly it might be for the best if I just fell over right now, ignorant of the world.

The car door on the rear driver's side opens, and Wes falls out. His groan when his hands hit the pavement is audible even from here. *There's one.* Cam follows suit, his hand placed on Wes's shoulder like some drunken conga line. *Two.* Then there's Harry, laughing one of his belly laughs reserved for good company. *Thank God. Three.* From the front passenger seat stumbles the much-too-old-for-this swaying figure of Grant. *Four.* He seems drunk, but that's to be expected. He doesn't look as weary as when he arrived this afternoon. The driver's door opens, and a long and muscled leg extends out. My heart pounds louder, and it's a wonder Corinne can't hear it trying to beat out of my chest. *Ian. Five.*

We rush to the elevator and I press the button, convinced it's broken based on how long it's taking to arrive. No matter how many times I signal it, the light is still the taunting, dull orange. It finally arrives and, with more feverish button-mashing, rumbles down to the ground floor. Grace definitely lied when she said this was a five-star resort.

The doors slide open and there they all are. Harry is still laughing, and he's helping support Cam and Wes with their arms thrown over his shoulders. Wes is an especially big man, but Harry can go toe to toe with him in stature, so the cooperation looks effortless. Ian is single-handedly dragging Grant by his side, and the smile upon my brother's face is genuine and unfazed by the fact that he can barely walk.

Ian and I lock eyes, and it feels like something I've never experienced with him—or at least not in a few years...

His eyes cut through to me like a stab directly into my chest; I feel the dagger sinking in, driving deeper, and, like I'm close to death, I'm at a loss for breath.

"Polly, I have delivered," he says.

"What are you, a pizza man?"

He wiggles his eyebrows. "Why? Is that a scenario you're interested in?"

Irresistible man.

We ride up the elevator with most of the men groaning the whole way and Ian next to me near the back. I can smell the sweat, cigar smoke, and sand. The outside of his palm bumps mine when Grant shifts beside him. The heat rising from his body warms me. I've experienced a lot of the ocean's cool night breeze and his touch is comforting, like the blanket of Georgia humidity, a feeling of home wrapping over me once more.

"I want to barf," Cameron groans. It jerks me out of my thoughts, and Wes grunts in what sounds like agreement.

"Almost there." Ian's tone is deep, and it's obvious he's been in command all night. The low voice is intoxicating, running over me, sending nerves coursing throughout.

He adjusts Grant hanging from his side by shrugging my brother's arm farther up on his shoulder. Grant leans in to grumble something inaudible to him and Ian laughs.

"Dude, thank you," Harry whispers. Even from the opposite side of the elevator, his breath reeks of alcohol and flat soda. I sniff to see if maybe I can smell anything resembling a strip club, but then I remember I have no clue what strip clubs smell like.

"Don't forget you promised me you would cut your hippie hair earlier tonight," Ian says. "I'm holding you to it."

"I don't remember that." Harry squints at him. The squint must be too much to handle, because he ends up closing his eyes the rest of the way.

"He didn't promise that, did he?" Grant asks.

"Nah," Ian says.

"You devil," Grant growls.

Ian's return smile is kind and gentle. There are no judgments, no sneers, no nose pointing at the ceiling in disgust at everyone's sloppy behavior. Instead, he's joking with my brothers, and it looks so natural. I've never seen Harry or Grant mesh so well with anyone outside our immediate family. It's jarring, but my chest feels warm.

We proceed out of the elevator with the grace of newborn giraffes exiting a clown car. Wes waves goodbye and somehow finds the correct hotel room. After he stumbles inside, I count once more. There's Corrine and me plus the four men left.

Cameron's index fingers massage his temples, making him look like a caricature of a mind reader.

"Are you trying to remember your room number?" Ian asks.

"It's here somewhere," Cameron slurs, peering to each room on the hall. "I'm going to wake Grace up, aren't I?"

"I am totally on board with irritating Grace at one in the morning." Ian laughs at his own idea and holds his hand out for Cameron to place the room key in his palm. Ian walks to the correct door and shoves him in. *Three men left—my men.*

"You two can stay in my room," Ian says. "I think Nia needs some shut-eye tonight."

"I won't sleep anyway," I say, putting my hands on my hips and eyeing the two drunk brothers with a shake of my head. "They can stay in my room."

"Polly, you worry too much." He chuckles. The sound sends flutters through my stomach, but I lift an eyebrow in protest.

"Yeah, Polly," Grant slurs. "You're a worrywart. Worry, worry, wart, wart."

"Act your age, old man," I shoot back, index finger extended as if I'm his mother instead of his younger sister. He holds his hands up.

"You can come with us," Ian says. He finally meets my eyes again and it makes my stomach lurch, freezing over my insides until they're ice cold and hardened. My nipples quickly follow suit, and I'm hoping my shirt is thick enough to hide them.

"Sure," I agree. *I agree?!* Who am I? What am I getting myself into?

And why is lightning zipping through my every limb?

"If you need any help, just knock on my door," Corinne says, making me jump. I had almost forgotten she was there.

She scans the card to her room. Then it's only me and Ian —and two drunk men who need more drinks almost as much as I need to be alone with Ian Chambers.

Which is to say, *absolutely not at all*.

22

IAN

Ever since Nia barreled into that lobby with her ivory cheeks flushed pink and heavy breaths accompanying every intake of air, there's been some unexplainable tension between us.

I've felt this type of shift in a relationship before, but I must be misinterpreting my pseudo-Spidey-sense because this feeling is one that comes at the conclusion of a night of close contact and suggestive talk. I've been on dates before. I've had one-night stands. This spark is the electricity of a woman longing to sleep with me—except Nia just isn't that kind of woman.

Yes, I must be misinterpreting.

I lead Grant and Harry into my hotel room and let them lumber to the bed. It's just barely able to fit the both of them, and I'm realizing now that my bunk may be in the bathtub tonight. Nia is quiet when I glance over to her, but when our eyes meet, that familiar sensation washes over me once more.

Her brown doe eyes are large and dilated. Her bottom lip is pouting as if she's resisting the urge to let it slip into her mouth.

Her fingers run through her hair to move it to rest behind her ear.

My breathing quickens and I try to mask my sharp inhalation as blood rushes downward. She's so damn sexy, and she probably doesn't even know it. I'm familiar with harsh, demanding, controlling Nia. I've never seen this timid version of her. I want to take it all in.

The men on the bed are already passed out on their sides. Harry exhales small breaths of air, but Grant's obnoxious snoring directly oppose him like he's in competition with his brother. Even in sleep, he needs to be the alpha.

Slowly walking over, I wiggle a pillow out from under them and stuff it under my arm. I nod toward the bathroom and Nia does as I intended, tiptoeing in.

I'd be an idiot to imagine this will lead to anything. It would almost be unfair to the rest of the world if the universe granted me this one wish. Plus, I'm not pushing it. She doesn't want me.

I shut the door behind us, immediately tossing the pillow into the tub.

"Who says this isn't a resort?" I say, grinning from ear to ear.

"Are we sharing that?" she asks, pointing to the bathtub with the lone pillow slumping against the side.

"What? Do you think I'm a monster? I always offer pillows to the ladies."

I step one leg into the tub and lower the rest of myself in, stopping midway to pick up the pillow and toss it to the other end. Nia makes her way in as well with a less graceful motion. I instinctively reach for her forearm to steady her, but she doesn't need it. The reaction earns me a smile, though, and my chest is like a tiny bonfire igniting and popping embers through my limbs.

"Nice to know you're such a gentleman with bedding," she says, keeping her voice low.

"Are you imagining me in bed?"

She rolls her eyes, but a smile still peeks through. "You're ridiculous."

"You're blushing," I point out. She wasn't, but now her face flushes a bright red.

"Sometimes you say things that offend me."

"Oh really?" My jaw drops in mock surprise. "I had no idea."

"Let's count that as one of my answers for our twenty questions game."

"But I didn't ask a question."

"You didn't have to."

I shift in place, trying to wiggle into a more comfortable position, but it's impossible given both my height and how uncomfortable this situation is. My long legs, though bent at the knee, still reach the opposite end of the tub. Nia settles between my shoes, and we stare at one another—yet another pause filled with what feels like so many unsaid things.

"Okay, twenty questions then," I say. "Your turn."

She squints, pulling her knees to her chest and wrapping her arms around them, humming softly. "Hmm," she muses. "Tell me your deepest, darkest secret."

"Oh, are we going there?"

"We're going there," she says with a devilish grin I don't think she's ever thrown my direction, nor would I have imagined her wearing it around me in my lifetime. "Spill, Ian."

I want to admire her smile more, but my gut clenches at the question.

Some people may struggle when asked their "deepest, darkest secret" because their life has been so awesome and uneventful, while others may instantly think of an exact event that crushed their naïve excitement about the world. I am one of the latter.

Thoughts of a car barreling toward me, my friend beside me with wide eyes and a mouth ready to scream, glass flying everywhere...then nothing, only the blinding lights of the hospital.

I gulp and let my finger rub against the lip of the tub. I'm desperate to have Nia know me for who I am, and I've come close to telling her before, so what am I scared of?

"Nah."

"You said the other night you would tell me." Her eyebrow lifts and my stomach drops.

How long have I waited to see her look at me like that?

I take the plunge.

"I told you about my car wreck." She nods. I'm surprised she fully remembers it after her night of drunken debauchery. I long to relive our other intimate, sexier conversations, but I'm now bound to this type of intimacy instead. "I survived. My friend didn't."

There's a pause between us, but Nia doesn't gasp or pet my arm or even ask if I'm okay. She stares at me with a hard expression as if waiting for me to continue. There's nothing she can do to change my past and she's not trying to apologize for it —and this is why I like her.

"I was drunk," I continue. "He was kind of tipsy too, but I...I should have known he wasn't fit to drive, you know? They say it happens in slow motion, but it really doesn't. It's like lightning then thunder. There was the initial crash, then all I remember is seeing those little pieces of glass flying around. You know when you see lint in sunshine? Or maybe it was dust from the airbag. I don't know. The next thing I remember is waking up and being told I'd been in a medically induced coma for a month and I no longer had a car or a friend."

She leans forward, hand brushing up my calf, to my knee, and then to my thigh. Her fingers run over my wrinkled flesh— the cinched skin peeking out from under my shorts. It feels fitting that Nia is the one I'm choosing to tell, and it's comforting that she isn't just hearing; she's understanding.

"Is that how you got this?" Her fingers stroke the healed, grotesque wound, her tone soft and barely audible. I sit up, and the porcelain squeaks and echoes beneath my shoes. My head hovers near hers and when we make eye contact, I nod in response. Her hand leaves my thigh and before I can miss her touch, her finger taps the scar over my eyebrow. "And this?"

I chuckle. "Oh, no, that's just a guy who punched me in a bar fight."

The air in the room settles instantly and we're both laughing. She puts her finger to her lips and slaps my shoulder to shush me.

"You got mouthy?" she whispers.

"Of course I did."

"I'm not even surprised."

I notice that, within the past minute, Nia has scooted in toward the center of the tub. She still sits between my legs, just a foot or so away from where I'm trying to hide the growing pressure against my zipper.

"My turn," I say, loud enough for her to hear but trying to be considerate of the sleeping drunks on the other side of the door.

"Sure, go for it."

"What's up with Grant?"

"What *isn't* up with Grant?" She exhales with a light laugh. "He's a drunk and apparently into drugs now. He's a mess." There's a pause and she lets out another sigh. "But, thanks for being nice to him. And to Harry."

"They're good guys." I shrug.

"Don't let what I'm about to say go to your head," she says, "but I don't think you're that bad of a guy."

"I find it offensive that you had to give a disclaimer before complimenting me." I pause. "What happened with us?"

"What do you mean?"

"We were kind of friends and then...nothing. For my last two years I worked at Treasuries—what happened?"

She avoids eye contact, breathing in and out. "I don't know."

It's uncomfortable, and I get the sense that tonight will not be the night I get an honest answer from her. "It's because you realized how damn cute I am, isn't it?"

A restrained smile beams on her face. "No."

"You took a bit to answer that."

She says nothing, looking at me, but tracing the outside of my leg.

My hands wander to her ankles, stroking her soft skin and letting my fingers explore her bone. I test the waters more and slide up to her calves, caressing the curves of them, tightening my grip slightly to get my fill of her. I reach her knees then, trying the boldness once more, my hands resting on the outsides of her thighs.

I wait for the moment she'll stop me. I'm anticipating a snarky remark and blatant offense. However, she doesn't move an inch. Every muscle in my body, from my jaw to my feet, tenses. Her eyes focus on some spot behind me. Maybe she's contemplating her escape through the door, but Nia will be the first person to voice her opinion, and I wonder if she's letting me in.

I try not to breathe heavy and seem like a desperate man longing for more, but it's impossible. I've spent years craving to know how her skin would feel, questioning what she tastes like, imagining what my name would sound like on her lips as she moans with pleasure.

Her eyes dart to mine. I expect she was constructing a pros and cons list in her head, adding checkmarks and crossing out qualities of mine. In the end, once she's made her decision, Nia doesn't back out. She's either in or she's not.

"Do you want me?" she asks. It lacks any hint of seduction

or desire. It's all business, and if there's anything I'm good at, it's negotiation.

"Yes," I say with a curt nod.

"How bad?"

"If you think you've been offended before, you have no idea how offensive I can truly be."

At these words, her hands grip the nape of my neck and she jerks me toward her. Our mouths smash together, and I let out an involuntary groan. Her lips are full and perfect as we move against each other. I run my hands through her hair, taking in her scent of coconut hotel shampoo and the beach air that's cemented itself onto her.

I use my other hand to grip her waist and tug her toward me. She arches her back and pushes into me, inhaling sharply before taking a fistful of my hair. I shouldn't be surprised Nia dominates the situation. She only takes action on things she can control. Unfortunately for her, so do I.

As her hands run over my jaw and drop to my collar, I'm already clutching her hemline and pulling her shirt over her shoulders. In the second we part so she can toss the clothing aside, I trace my fingers just below her bra, down to her waist, settling on her pelvic bones. It's both everything and nothing I imagined. She's lithe and surprisingly strong. Her shorts hit just below her belly button and the length rides up her thighs, bunched from how we've maneuvered closer together.

Before she can drag me to her once more, I lower down to kiss her neck, her collarbone, and the peak of her chest. I nip at the thin, lacy bra, and her shaky breath hitches. I drag the other side down then switch sides to kiss around her nipple. I tease her and wait for I don't even know what. Begging? A moan? I will take any sign she wants me just as much as I need her, and at that moment she runs her fingers through my curls and pulls me closer, demanding action. I have to suppress my groan of satisfaction as I roll my tongue over her erect nipples. I swirl around, taking her in and nipping once more. Her head falls back and a mix between an exhalation and a whimper leaves her mouth. Knowing I can elicit such a submissive reaction drives me forward, and I'm determined to hear more.

She leans forward again and pushes against my arms so I'm sitting up.

"Hey, I was doing something there," I whisper, attempting to lean back toward her chest.

"Let's go back to my room," she demands.

Well, fuck me.

I nod, rising out of the bathtub without a second thought.

We tiptoe through the door, looking back to make sure her brothers remain sound asleep. They're still in a snoring competition and probably wouldn't wake up even if a car busted through the window right now.

I close the door behind me as she pulls out her own keycard and scans it, granting us entry into her room.

Before I can even reach for the lights, we're already at each other again. I'm kissing her neck and she's running her hands down my chest. I'm trying to keep my cool while also hoping to God she isn't regretting this.

Just as the thought crosses my mind, she reaches her hands downward and slides the button on my shorts through its hole. A sharp moan exits my throat and I lift an eyebrow. "You like being in control, don't you?"

She ignores my comment, all the while tugging down my zipper and spreading her palm against my length. I shift to press it into her as she rubs the base, lightly cupping my balls then releasing them. It's so fucking hot and bold that I can barely get any words out.

"Goddamn," I say, voice straining as she pulls the band on my underwear down and holds my penis, pumping her hand up and down and using her thumb to circle the head every time she reaches the top. I wonder where she learned to please a man so well. I'm used to passive women who remain shy and take serious reassuring just to allow themselves to be seen naked. Nia is different. She takes what she wants with no apologies.

She lowers herself down to her knees, allowing her tongue to meet the head of my cock.

"I want to make you come," I say. I feel her smile against me. I love how she seems eager to please. I love the power struggle and how she's relentless in her efforts, but this is what I've been wanting for years. I want to hear her moan and see her fall apart beneath my touch. She might like to be in control now, but I will teach her what it means to beg.

23

NIA

Ian, Ian, Ian.

His name keeps bouncing around in my head, unable to completely focus on one part of him before my hands discover another. His strong arms, his large hands, the peaks and valleys of his abs, and his large—very hard—cock.

I want him. I want him *bad*. I wanted him a few years ago and I want him now. He was, and still is, arrogant, pushy, and too charismatic for his own good—yet he's also kind, incapable of prejudice, and somehow weaseling his way back into my thoughts. I need to push that aside, though, because this isn't the time for admiration. It's time for something different. At this moment, I want to take advantage of his energy, his ego, and every bit of confidence he exudes and place it all in the palm of my hand...and stroke it, and lick it.

"Nia," he says again, strained and trying to stay quiet. I like taming the beast, making him say my real name with zero undertones of sarcasm. "Nia." This time the tone isn't pleading, but demanding instead. He pulls me up, removing himself from my mouth, and I'm immediately dissatisfied.

"I want to taste you," he says, pulling me up to my feet and twisting his palm into my shorts without even bothering to unbutton them. He presses his two fingers against my wet lips with only the thin fabric of my panties as a barrier. The sensation is instantaneous. His fingers are deft as they encircle the outside, rising up until he reaches my clit. I extend my hand to find his dick, but he clutches my wrist and pushes me away. "No."

The warmth from his breath sends more of me spiraling, and I take in short breaths. "Let me touch you," I beg, trying not to sound too desperate, but I want him back in my hand. I want to feel just how hard he is in this moment…and all for me.

He removes his hand from under my waistband and takes both of my wrists, pinning them behind me. "Just relax, Nia." A kiss on my neck. "Relax for me." I can't. My heart is pounding, and my legs are itching to wrap around him. I want to cause him to be unhinged until he can't help but bury himself into me.

His hand strokes my spine, ghosting from my neck down to the small of my back. My head rolls back and I close my eyes. "Yes, just like that," he croons, moving down to pull my nipple into his mouth once more. "You're so sexy."

He guides me into the room until the backs of my knees hit the bed. I fall backward. When he gets down in front of me, I push my hands into his curls. I've always wondered what his hair feels like, whether his locks were soft or coarse, whether they were twisted enough to curl around my fingers. I was correct on all accounts.

He glides his hands from my ass around to the front where he slowly unbuttons, unzips, and shimmies my shorts down my legs. They land around my ankles then he throws them to the side. I smile down at him, pushing his hair back so he can look at me. His ice blue eyes are hungry, shooting through me as my knees give in.

He spreads my legs apart, and I feel exposed having him stare directly at my underwear. I wish I had worn the ones that match my lacy bra, but how was I supposed to know anyone would see them this week?

Ian places his face directly across from my pussy. He turns his head to my inner thigh to kiss, lick, and slide his finger closer and closer to my center. I exhale, eagerly awaiting the inevitable, almost unable to keep my patience in check as he moves his mouth over my underwear and extends his tongue against them. It's so close and I can feel his hot breath against me. I swallow back any noise I might have made.

His middle finger reaches to the edge of my panties and slides it over, exposing all of me to him. He wastes no time before sticking his tongue into me and pulling back out to lap me up.

He knows his craft well. With each flick of his tongue, another wave of shock rolls through me. He quickly locates my clit and devours it. I feel two of his fingers enter me and my head falls back before I can will it not to. My eyes close when he rolls his fingers inside me, continuing to dart his tongue across my skin. Nerves in my thighs are radiating down to my legs and my toes curl.

I don't want to come yet. I want to keep experiencing every pleasure Ian is willing to give me. I'm not sure how we got to this point or how I'm allowing him to drive me to a state of madness when only days ago he was driving me insane for completely different reasons. All I know is that with every stroke of his tongue, my stomach is falling deeper.

I clench my muscles, trying to hold off as best I can, but he groans, his tone rumbling against my body. "Don't hold back. Come for me."

The words provoke a whimper from me, and I clamp my hand over my mouth, trying to stifle any additional noises that may arise—and they definitely do. Ian continues to lick me, faster and faster, pumping his fingers against me, and my voice is muffled against my hand.

Ian. Ian. Ian.

"Say my name," he commands, driving into me aggressively.

Ian. Ian. Ian. I can't get the words out. They're screaming in my head, but I'm too distracted to say anything.

"Say my name, Nia."

Ian. Ian!

"Ian!" My exclamation pushes me over the edge. A wave of euphoria washes over me, my muscles tremble, and all the tension releases under the weight of my orgasm.

Ian grips my legs, kissing every inch of me as his mouth drifts by until he's beside me, my head nestled into the curve of his neck.

"That okay?" he whispers, kissing the top of my forehead.

"It wasn't too bad."

He chuckles. "Not even a thank you?"

"Thanks," I murmur between heavy breaths, which only makes him grin. I'm both elated and irritated that he's as happy as he seems, and yet I want to spread that smile wider. "I want to return the favor."

He hums to himself, looking down to glance at my body, which is now only covered by my lopsided bra that is failing at its job as it is still pulled down and exposing one of my boobs. "Maybe next time," he says.

"How do you know there will be a next time?" He's much too cocky for his own good.

"Because."

"Because why?"

"Because Nia Smith wouldn't call out my name unless she meant it."

This man has me wrapped around his stupid, wonderful,

orgasm-inducing finger, and I wish I could rip it off. Then again, how would we have a next time if I remove something so precious?

24

IAN

Four years ago

"This is a horrible gift, right?" Cameron asks me.

"No, it's a great gift for people who live in the 90s, or people who like dismembered animals."

"I never really thought of it like that..." Cam holds the pink rabbit's foot keychain up to his face, scrunching his nose and pulling his lips back in a grimace. "Yeah, that does kind of ruin it."

"I bet someone would find it fun," I say. My feet are propped on Gary's desk as I swivel around in his chair. I take a gummy bear from his large candy jar and pop it in my mouth. What he doesn't know won't hurt him.

"So, what *are* you going to get her?" I ask. "A teddy bear? Or—possibly!—a ring?" I let my jaw fall open, but the sudden point of his finger elicits only a tiny bit of guilt from me.

Cameron isn't going to propose to his girlfriend. I know that, Cameron knows that, and Abby must surely know that. He wouldn't settle for anyone less than perfect, or someone who's such a jerk. Abby is like cool ice against hot asphalt—

always seconds from melting and constantly surrounded by steam.

"That's not funny," Cam says, plopping himself back at his desk and scrolling on his laptop, probably trying to find another gift just as genius as the rabbit's foot. I reach into Gary's candy stash once more and toss two more gummy bears in my mouth.

The designer's den is dark with the exception of Cameron's desk lamp and every third overhead light, available in case of emergency. Cameron won't say it yet, but he doesn't want to go home. Hell, neither do I, but I have far different reasons. He's just unhappy in his relationship, whereas my demons run deeper.

A stray light shines through the doorway and I lean farther back in the chair to catch sight of its source. I hear a door close and the clopping of heels on the concrete as Nia's head pokes around the corner.

I should have known.

"What you two still doing here?" she asks.

"We're shopping on Amazon," I say, grinning. Nia smiles back, dawdling around the corner and walking down the aisle toward us, her purse swinging by her side. She's wearing her typical outfit: tight pencil skirt hitting her knees, loose cotton blouse tucked in, and heels high. She's both professional and sexy all at once. How she balances the two is a mystery to me, but it's a puzzle I enjoy all the same.

"At work?" she asks. "Go home."

I'm tired, it's late, and all I want to do is follow that comment up with *Can I go home with you?* However, I'm also not a big enough idiot to provoke the one person who could convince the right people to get me fired.

"I'm not shopping," Cameron says from behind his laptop.

"Liar," I shoot back. He glares.

I reach into Gary's jar of goodies once more and pull out a

particularly squishy bear, twiddling it between my thumb and forefinger.

"Don't play with your food," Nia says, rolling her eyes. "It's not even yours." Her hand twitches and I wonder if she wants to slap it out of my hand. Instead, I take it to my teeth and grind the gummy slowly.

It's silent for a moment with just the sound of Cameron tapping on his laptop trackpad and my intentionally obnoxious chewing of the candy. My eyes do not leave Nia. With her head turned toward Cameron, I take every moment I can to look at her long, curled locks, pinned in a half up-do. How do women do that? And why do they think it looks different enough to finagle? Seems like more trouble than it's worth to me. But, also, I'm sitting here admiring her exposed neck, so maybe that answers my question.

"Any plans tonight?" I ask her, adjusting my legs to be propped higher on Gary's desk, accidentally knocking over a cup full of pencils.

"Come on, Ian. Get your feet off the desk," she groans. I drop them.

"Polly, sometimes I like it when you tell me to do things," I say. Even in the low light of the office, I see her face flush red.

"And is this one of those times?" she asks with a slight stutter to her tone.

"It's always one of those times," I say. I love watching her glare at me—the narrowing of her eyes, the furrowing of her brow, and the small scrunch of her nose as she purses her lips.

I spot the pink rabbit's foot on the edge of the desk and swipe it up, spinning the keyring on my finger.

"Hey, want a rabbit's foot?"

Nia pauses then shrugs. "Sure," she says, holding out her hand. I drop it in, grazing my fingers over hers. She snaps her hand closed around it, causing me to jerk my hand back with a grin. "I had one of these as a kid," she says, rolling it in her palm. "They always freaked me out, but it's morbidly fascinating, you know?"

I love seeing this side of Nia, getting little details about her life. Piece by piece, bit by bit, year by year, I find out more. I want it all.

"You're an odd person, Polly," I say, popping my feet back on the desk. When she glares, I don't move. I lift an eyebrow in challenge. It's silent. Dare I say we're having a "moment"? She rolls her eyes. I wonder if she read my mind.

"Go home, you two," she groans, turning on her heel and leaving. Once I hear the front doors close, I twist in my chair toward Cameron.

"See?" I say. "I told you some woman would appreciate it."

"Whatever," he huffs. "She can have it. Now help me find something better."

I browse on my phone for more meaningless gifts, but all I can think about is if Nia will actually keep the one I gave her, and whether or not she felt the buzz between us just now.

25

IAN

PRESENT DAY

I can still taste her the following morning, and I need more.

I promised Nia this wouldn't be leaked to anyone, and I will keep that promise as long as it means last night was not a dream.

The entire group meets for brunch, and I try my best to make eye contact with Nia.

Half of the attendees are clutching their heads while all the women fork food into their mouths.

"So, Ian, who are the strays?" Ramona asks, lifting an eyebrow.

I dart my eyes to Nia's. Are they a deeper brown than usual? Is she looking at me with desire, or is she back to being pissed at me for every move I make? I don't know if she's ready to reveal that her crazy brother drove down here in a rage, or that her actually sane younger brother is hungover from the festivities. I wait a second to see if she'll respond, and as I'm opening my mouth to speak, she beats me to the punch.

"This is Harry and Grant. They're my brothers from out of town."

Utensils pause, some stopping mid-scrape on the china. I wonder if anyone will say anything at all.

"Oh, dude, I didn't know that!" Wes finally breaks the silence to raise his hand. Harry completes the high five and they go back to eating as if nothing happened.

I can tell Nia is nervous. Of course she is. This isn't her wedding week, and these aren't Grace's friends. But, Grace throws up a hand for a high five as well, and no other words are exchanged on the subject.

"So, bachelorette party tonight, huh? Going crazy?" Wes asks, nudging Ray.

"Got strippers?" Cam chuckles, shoveling eggs into his mouth.

"Probably." Grace winks. "But only because you guys did."

We all exchange quick glances—which seem to go unnoticed by most of the women—and return to our plates. Let them think we're tough, manly men. They don't need to know we hung out at the pier and actually had decent conversation. Yes sir, we surely did experience lots of boobs and ass.

Well, at least *I* did.

I can't stand the idea of Nia around strippers. What do the performers even do at female-focused strip clubs? Spin their penises around in patrons' faces? I almost lose my appetite, but the scent of bacon wafting into my nose tempts me back to it. I'm still not happy about it, though.

"Do you think they'll wear banana hammocks?" Cameron asks, waving his fork. "Bright yellow? Hairy men with gold chains?"

"Ew, gross." Ramona scrunches her nose and glances to Corinne, who shrugs with a laugh.

"Could be a good time," she comments.

"Nia, are you pumped about strippers?" I ask. Her eyes meet mine and narrow in response. It's the same old glance I'm accustomed to, except now I feel a current between us as if we're connected by an invisible wire, humming with electricity. "What do you go for? Firefighters? Mailmen? Lawyers?"

"Shut up," she shoots back. Ramona is already holding her hands up in protest, but I don't feel hate brimming from Nia. I see how she shifts in her chair. She's trying her best to hide it, but I know my words have set her off. I bite down on my fork, grinning. I wonder if she's wet beneath that skirt.

"It is two days before the wedding," Ramona says. "I am not having your silly bickering ruining these wonderful, beautiful people's party." Her index finger points back and forth between the two of us, but when our eyes meet once more and the corner of my mouth lifts in a smirk, Nia shakes her head and goes back to her food.

Grace lets out a small giggle, and Ramona exhales.

"Well at least the bride finds it funny now."

26

NIA

I tried to see Harry and Grant off in the morning, folding some snacks from the breakfast bar into napkins and saying things like "Well this was fun" and "I'll see you when I get home!" but all the men insist on inviting them to the beach for volleyball and discreet, flask-based day drinking.

"Nia, we're already down here," Harry insists. "Plus, I already had a mimosa for breakfast so I can't possibly drive."

"Grant can drive."

"We have two cars, remember?" Grant's arms are crossed with a pair of swim trunks in his fist.

"Where did you get those?" I ask, pointing at them.

"Gift shop." His thumb points to the corner of the lobby where there is indeed a small kiosk with candies, salty snacks, sandals, and swimwear.

"I can drive my own car back," I continue, ignoring the tangent. Harry is shuffling his feet on the linoleum, causing tiny squeaking sounds.

"Stop that," I say, and he rolls his eyes in response with a smile. I open my mouth to say more, but a voice calls from the sliding glass door whirring open at the end of the hall.

"Are you guys coming or what?" Ian stands in the threshold, and I'm trying not to drool. He's shirtless, because why the hell not? As he draws nearer, I see the familiar veins trailing down his forearms, curling up to meet his protruding wrists and long, deft fingers...fingers I want inside me again.

"Nia, please let us stay," Harry groans, drawing me out of my thoughts. "Cara's mom has her for the next two days, and I *love* the beach."

"Man, she's not our mom," Grant huffs, tossing the swim shorts over his shoulder. "We're staying. Room key, sister." He holds out his hand, palm up, and gestures for the keycard. I narrow my eyes, reaching into my pocket and laying it in his hand. If it were anyone else, I wouldn't. The last thing Grant needs is some type of vacation as a reward for his behavior. This feels like I'm enabling him, but at the same time I wonder if maybe it wouldn't be so bad for him to hang out with men like Ian and Cameron. They're good people, honest guys, but I also know just how stubborn Grant can be—almost as stubborn as myself. He won't be leaving any time soon, invite or not.

"Thank you," he says in a singsong voice, waving his hand for Harry to follow him to the elevators, which he does. There's something about Grant that compels people. It's his swagger, his confidence, or maybe it's the fact that he's our eldest brother.

The elevator door closes behind them and electricity sparks in my spine, all the way down to toes. I feel my gut give a slight tug and I know Ian is still looking at me—at *all* of me. His eyes wander from my neck to my chest and down my legs. Those blues could have X-ray vision, seeing through my clothes and taking in my naked curves, my hard nipples, and my steadily rising temperature, which threatens to make my face turn a bright red hue. I'm trying to keep my wits about me, but by the time Ian's eyes land back on my chin, lips, and then eyes, I'm breathing heavy.

His eyebrow lifts. "How about that 'next time'?"

My chest clenches and I inhale sharply. I laugh, looking both directions to cover whatever this conversation may appear to be to outsiders. The same older couple from the bar that insists on looking like twins are eyeing me, and I wonder if they're the siblings from *The Shining*. I can feel their judgments from a mile away. I would tell them, *It isn't what it looks like*, but this tension between Ian and me is *exactly* what it looks like.

"Seriously?"

"We could." He pulls a card from his pocket. "I still have *my* room key."

This beach trip is starting to lack a lot of the "beach" aspect, but I'm too excited to care.

"Fine," I say, walking away, toward the elevator. I can hear his steps following behind me.

Even when we load onto the elevator with an unassuming younger couple, no doubt on their honeymoon given how frequently they're touching each other, I feel no regret about this decision to go with Ian to his room. I'm positive he is not looking for anything more than a vacation fling, and neither am I. Who are we to deny each other this pleasure?

Then a quick thought has me considering that maybe this isn't a fling. He's proven himself to be caring with my brothers, one of which does not deserve praise given Ian's first impression of him, but Ian forgave him with such grace that I wonder if maybe this man is actually capable of wanting more than a quick brush of his dick against my hand, which is exactly what he does now in the back of the elevator. He leans back and I flush red. He chuckles at the sight of it.

We exit the elevator and rush to his room. He barely has the door open before I'm pinned against it. We're still exposed to the outside hallway and I'm both self-conscious and excited. He can't even wait two more seconds to have his hands on me. They trace up my sides, to my shoulders, gripping my elbows to lift my hands above my head. He nuzzles his head in the crook of my neck and groans.

"Now?" I ask.

"Now." His voice growls deep in his throat. He places a kiss on my collarbone and lifts his head to look down at me. His height is substantial and dominating, and although this sends a jolt of pressure from my stomach down to between my legs, I don't want a domineering man right now. He presents a challenge, and I want to rise to it.

I raise my eyebrow, empowered by his forward nature. He knows what he wants and so do I. I want Ian Chambers. I want his arms, his hands, his muscular thighs, and his tongue everywhere he pleases.

His hand roams down to my hips then threatens to go lower but stays at my pelvic bone.

"Spread 'em," he says with a grin. I grin back and start to shift my thigh outward.

"Oh shit," a voice says from beside us, and we simultaneously whip our heads to the hallway where a jaw-dropped Ramona clutches a plastic bag and has her hand over her heart. "Oh god, I'm so sorry. Uhh..." She stumbles over her words, looking between us then averting her eyes. "Wow. Okay. Um..."

"What is it, Ramona?" Ian demands. His voice has an edge to it, and I instinctually lift an eyebrow. God, I need this man inside me right now.

"We were just—um—going to prepare for the bachelorette party," Ramona says, her hand curved over her brow like a shield blocking her from the sight of us on the verge of ripping each other's clothes off.

But of course. The bachelorette party. Definitely a more pressing matter.

Sure. Absolutely.

Not.

"Yes." I twist my wrists and Ian releases them. Totally

normal thing to do in front of his sister. "Grace needs us. Obviously." I roll my eyes, attempting to be nonchalant. I smooth my skirt down and laugh a little, as if this is just a game. *Ha! What a silly moment, Ian's sister! You just walked into us playing policeman.*

Spread 'em.

I don't look at Ian, and I do not exchange any pleasantries. I wish I could say, *Thank you for making me wetter than any other man ever has been able to* or *I'm desperate to pleasure you*, maybe even *I'll moan for you again soon*. But, no—I turn, *shake his fucking hand*, and walk away.

I hear Ramona laugh and say, "See ya, loser," before rushing up next to me. "You're so full of surprises, Nia. I knew you had some freak in there."

"Where's Grace?" I ask, ignoring whatever she said. Honestly, I don't even fully register it until moments later. *Freak?* "Wait—what does that mean?"

27

NIA

Grace, Corinne, and I sit on the edge of the bed as Ramona lays out the next few hours of our life. She insists on starting early, which is unexpected for all of us. Grace is still yawning from her afternoon nap, and Corinne is blinking in her bathing suit, smelling like sand, undoubtedly taken from the beach. I'm trying not to huff like a child as I balance both listening and pushing down my heightened sexual frustration.

I'm still picturing how Ian looked at me, how he groaned in my ear, the rough hands wrapped around my wrists as I relinquished control. It's weird to feel so vulnerable, but the combination of Ian's reassurance in treating me with care and pleasuring me until I was numb between my thighs makes it a bit easier to succumb.

Does he actually want me now, or is he riding on the high of control—of knowing he's finally captured me despite my best efforts to resist? Do I care? I'm just not sure I can handle him.

"I think I want waffles," Grace says, squinting at Ramona, who was in the middle of stating how insanely drunk we will be by the end of the night.

"The bride wants waffles, the bride gets some frigging waffles," Corinne says, shaking Grace's shoulder.

Ramona waves her pencil at Corinne. She's only holding it like a baton in order to direct us because there is no paper in sight. "You're absolutely right, tall blonde."

"I like tall blonde," Grace declares. "I approve."

"Am I short blonde?" I ask.

"Cute blonde," Corinne corrects.

"I like cute blonde as well," Grace says again with an air of royalty in her tone. "It is so."

"There are worse ways to start a night." I fold my arms across my chest and sigh. Although, I could have started my afternoon with Ian, so there are also better ways this night could be kicked off as well.

"I have to pee," Grace says, patting her knees and then locking herself in the bathroom.

"Good time to break," Corinne agrees. "Let me at least put on shorts." They leave and I'm left alone with Ramona. *Why does it feel like the Chambers family is always cornering me into conversations?*

There's an awkward silence followed by Ramona popping her lips and grinning.

"Do you want to talk about it?" she whispers.

"No," I shoot back.

"Do you like him?"

"Are we in middle school?" I chuckle.

"Fine." She raises her hands. "None of my business then." Ramona and Ian have too many similarities, one of which being the fact that, even though they say they do not want to know something, their face says otherwise.

"Just because you try to seem uninterested doesn't mean I'm going to tell you anything."

"Damn." She snaps with a grin. "That works on everyone else."

"Doesn't work on me," I whisper.

"Apparently it did for my brother."

At that moment, the room door opens, and Corinne, now dressed in loose-fitting shorts but still in her bathing suit top, halts mid-step.

"What are we talking about?" she asks.

"Nothing," Ramona says, twisting her pencil nonchalantly. I avoid eye contact.

"Secrets," Corrine hisses, her eyes narrowed as she points between us.

The toilet flushes, water runs, and Grace comes out of the bathroom. "I heard whispering."

"They're sharing secrets." Corinne crosses her arms.

"Secrets, secrets are no fun," Ramona calls out, tossing her head from side to side.

"*You're* the one keeping secrets."

"I don't know what you're talking about."

The conversation has circled enough that most of us are confused, which satisfies Ramona enough for her to start talking about the evening yet again.

I stop listening, and for once I don't care about schedules or itineraries or the whens and wheres of the day. I'm not mentally begging for my planner. I'm only thinking one thing: *I want Ian Chambers.*

Four hours later, I wish I would have listened to Ramona's plans more intently. Our heels clip-clop loudly as we teeter toward a large, lime green building surrounded by palm trees. It's the size of a warehouse with the edges adorned by neon purple lights flashing off and on in spurts and never at the same time. It creates a ring around the place that would be inviting if I didn't know what was inside.

It's very obvious that we are a bachelorette party. We're walking in a line, arm in arm, with pink penises pinned to our outfits. Ramona forced a crown onto Grace, who has already taken it off twice, only to have it shoved back on by her maid of honor.

We walk forward on the brightly painted sidewalk made to look like a yellow brick road. The double doors ahead of us are blacked out, and I'm struck by the memory of the sex shop. I'll give this place credit—at least it gives off the vibe of *Yay fun!* instead of *We won't tell your friends you were here.*

"Do you think they have a short man in green at the door?" Corinne asks.

"With a sliding speakeasy peephole?" Grace says.

"If I would have known this was where we were going, I would have worn sparkly red heels," I say.

The other ladies are dressed in tight-fitting bodycon dresses that hug their curves as if tailored just for them, while I'm re-wearing the same red dress from the other night. Admittedly, it does look good on me, and I am sporting heels that are much higher than any I would wear on a normal basis. In fact, I was so surprised by how well the outfit came together, I almost snuck to Ian's room beforehand, but Ramona has been playing the role of helicopter mother hen so well I couldn't spare time to even use the restroom without a swift knock on the door asking if I was finished already.

She skids to a halt, causing the rest of us to stop like dominos.

"Girls, this is our mecca."

"Mecca?" Grace says. "Come on, let's just head back to the hotel. We don't have anything to prove to the guys, right?"

"Who doesn't want to go to a strip club for their pre-wedding celebration?" Ramona gawks.

"Ramona, if your mecca is a male strip club then we need to discuss your sex life," Corinne says, looking down the line at her. Corinne and I are on the opposite end with Grace being our connection to the curly-haired wonder leading this raid into sexy-man-land.

"Mine is very active, thank you. In fact, I think all of us have pretty active sex lives." Maybe I imagine it, but I swear she throws a wink my way.

"Speak for yourself," Corinne mumbles.

"Okay, then three out of four," Ramona scoffs.

Out of the corner of my eye, I catch a discreet glance from Ramona, but I ignore it. This is turning into a mess already.

With that, we all lift our feet and walk down the yellow brick sidewalk like the motley crew we are: Grace, the girl ready to be home; Ramona, the scarecrow, not in need of a brain but the sense to read her audience; Corinne, the tin woman clearly needing a heart in her sex life; and me, the cowardly lion, not ready to take on the naked men who await me.

I could probably take on one naked man—but he's still back at the hotel.

———

THE INSIDE ISN'T *that* bad. There's only one massive problem, and it isn't the giant dicks being shoved in my face—it's the lack of them.

Ramona didn't do enough research. Imagine our shock when we pay our forty-dollar entry fee and skip through the foyer only to see the green-lit stage occupied by a fully nude woman.

"Oops," Ramona says slowly, looking at the rest of us. Corinne shrugs, and Grace is already laughing.

I always imagined strip clubs as they appear in movies, with naked women in G-strings and winning smiles. I was right for the most part, but I didn't anticipate the fact that, although clubs in movies don't have pussy on display, real life absolutely might.

How charming.

We grab a table away from the stage where men are gathered, some leaning forward on their elbows. I feel like I've walked into a different world where I don't belong, a male fantasy in which I'm intruding. Any minute now, someone will surely ask if we're in the wrong place, right?

What would Ian think?

I pull out my phone, giving in to my temptation.

Nia: I don't think I'm in Kansas anymore.
Ian: Where are you?
Nia: In a state of immediate regret.

I throw my phone back into my clutch and clear my throat.

We order waters that are much too expensive, and Ramona circles her finger to signal for shots. She mouths something to the server that I interpret to be "lemon."

"Oh, I don't think I need a drink," Grace says. Her laughter is stilted, and I think that's what gives her away.

"Holy shit," Ramona says breathlessly.

It's weird how women just *know*. If a woman looks naturally happy, if she cups the ridge of her stomach, and if she refuses a drink at an event like this, there's only one explanation. Poor Grace checks all three boxes.

"Grace, are you...?" Corinne starts.

"Cameron doesn't know yet," Grace quickly responds, gulping down a large swallow of her water and slamming it back down on the table. "I mean, I think he'll react just fine, but...the wedding, you know. I don't think he needs to worry."

Ramona screams, and I cover my ears. I think even the current performer halts on her pole before squeaking down.

"HOLY SHIT!" Corinne yells. They're both smothering

Grace with their long arms wrapped around her, and I'm grinning back at her.

"You're gonna be a killer pregnant woman," Ramona says, her speech slightly muffled as she speaks into Grace's shoulder.

"Are you saying I already have hormones resembling those of an angry pregnant lady?" Grace says, her eyebrow quirked up. A smirk spreads on her face and there's no denying that she's far from offended.

"You craved pickles and peanut butter just last month," I say, sipping my water through a smile as Grace smiles back.

"Wait—why aren't you surprised?" Ramona asks with a suspicious side-eye.

"I can be the DD," I offer in an attempt to change the subject.

"Secrets!" Corinne hisses with a wink.

I am saved when the shots arrive, tiny tumblers filled to the brim with neon yellow liquid. I pick mine up and sip just to try it. The sugared edge is off-putting, but the drink itself is dangerously delicious. I only taste the hint of alcohol after the lemon-flavored treat has settled on my tongue.

"Hang on, hang on, we have to toast!" Ramona says, releasing Grace and clutching her drink, raising it in the air. Corinne, Grace, and I follow suit.

"To Grace, the best mom."

"The best mom," we all chant together, clinking our glasses. Grace blushes and sets her glass down while Ramona and Corinne tip theirs back, inhaling the contents in one go.

"Nia, are you seriously not going to drink?" Ramona asks. It's less of a question and more of a demand.

"We need a driver," I say.

"Nah, that's why we have the boys," she says, "but if you *really* want to pretend you're responsible, we can sit you in the driver's seat later to make you feel like you've contributed to the night. Now drink up."

I hesitate, looking down at the drink. I've never been one for shots, but this one does taste particularly good.

Why not?

I tilt my head back, bring the glass to my lips, and flip the bottom up. It slides down smoother than I expected, but the aftertaste of alcohol is much more prevalent than it was a moment ago. I guess that's what happens when you take in the entire glass in one fell swoop.

I shake my head and join in the laughter once I see everyone else looking at me.

"What about Grace's?" I ask, pointing at the solo shot waiting to be devoured by some brave soul.

"It's yours," Grace says, sliding it across the table toward me.

"No thanks," I say, waving my hand in protest. My head is already swimming from the last one. I can't tell if it was how quickly I shook my head or if I'm just a complete lightweight. Either way, drinking for two seems like an awful idea.

Corinne shrugs, grabs the glass, and tips it back.

"I'm tall—it takes a lot for me to get drunk. I'll drink for two." That is all Grace needs to seem satisfied, and it's the perfect cue Ramona needs to order four more.

My phone buzzes and I pull it out with too much excitement.

Ian: Are you going to be a bad girl tonight?
Nia: Do you want me to be?

28

IAN

I SHOULD HAVE KNOWN THE BACHELORETTE PARTY WOULD BE more of a mess than our bachelor party. Every one of those girls has the ability to strike a match and light a torch for the others to follow. My sister, the wild child; the bride, the feisty redhead; Corinne, the bandwagon partier; and, Nia, the irresistible, stubborn, beautiful woman.

God save the man who tries to mess with their party tonight.

"Go fish," Cameron grunts. We're sitting in the hotel restaurant at a large round table in the corner. There are couples sitting at the bar ordering drinks and even a gaggle of girls flirting with the bartender and his long hair. I'm dipping chips into our spinach artichoke bowl and trying not to think about the girls and their possible mishaps.

Nia sent her last text an hour ago. My muscles have been tense ever since then.

"How do we even play this game?" Grant's knuckles smash against his cheek. He looks tired, and I wonder if he's suffering from withdrawal. He's gotten grumpier in the past day, and I can't help but notice the copious amount of sweat rolling down his forehead, though maybe that's just how he normally looks.

"You've played Go Fish before," Harry says, throwing in a card and taking one out.

"I don't think you're playing it right," Wes says, scratching his head before running both hands through his floppy hair.

"*You're* not getting it." Grant's voice is muffled through his fist.

"You put in a card then take one back out," Harry says with a laugh. "What is there to get?"

"Let's just play Uno," I say. "In that game, you don't even have to mess with the whole picking one back up deal."

"Fuck you," Grant snaps, slamming his hands on the table and throwing his chair back. He's charging toward the exit, and Harry is already huffing.

"Sorry guys," he apologizes, scooting his chair back. "We'll probably head up for the night. Let me know how things go and if you need any help."

He's referring to the girls, because it's been an unspoken understanding all night as to why we're sitting in a bar playing a game meant for children, and it's not because we're passionate about Go Fish. Even the grandma on the back of the cards is grinning up at me with her dentures. *Lady, I don't need your looks.*

"You bet," I say.

We're all silent, throwing cards in, picking them out—honestly, I'm not sure any of us *do* know the rules—then a phone buzzes. The three of us flip our phones over on the table to check whose it is. I desperately want it to be Nia. Maybe she was bold enough to send a nude. Not sure how she would manage, but a man can dream.

"Hey, Ray," Wes says. I jerk my head to him. He blinks, nodding, then chuckles after a couple seconds, looking around the table at each of us as if saying, *Are you hearing this shit?*

Except, no, no we cannot, and my anxiety is growing by the second. "A strip club? Really?" His eyes widen but a grin is plastered on his face, stretching from cheek to cheek. "A *female* strip club? How did you end up there?"

Ramona took them to a female strip club. I can't help but bark out laughter at the thought of how uncomfortable Nia probably is at a place like that. That explains her text from earlier.

"I can't understand you, dear. It's a bit loud," Wes continues, pressing his finger into the opposite ear.

Then we hear a slurring voice yell through the phone, "I SAID, COME PICK US UP."

And with that, we're all up and out the door.

I claim the driver's seat, much to Cameron's chagrin, stating, "You wanna get there fast? I'm taking the wheel," before double-checking we're all buckled, putting that sucker into drive, and skidding out of the parking lot. I'm accustomed to my sports vehicle beast, and this hulking Jeep doesn't do much for someone in a hurry. Even as I'm barreling down the road following the GPS suspended from the windshield, Wes is in the back seat laughing into the phone. I'm unsure how serious the situation may be, but with Wes still having a good time, I guess I shouldn't be too concerned.

"Is that so?" A laugh. A shake of his head is seen in the rearview mirror. I'm swinging the car around every twist and turn.

What am I doing? I shouldn't be worrying. Nia is a woman with a good head on her shoulders. I'm sure she's the sober one and Ramona's call is just a false alarm because she wants to see her husband. Those two can't be away from each other more than twelve hours.

But Wes will still rush to her side. There's a reason all of us sat in the hotel playing a boring card game. At the end of the day, we just want our women safe.

Sure, Nia may not be *my* woman, but I did have my mouth to her pussy less than twenty-four hours ago, so yeah, I'd say even if you disregard the nine years of wanting her, on some level, she might be my woman.

The GPS says I've arrived at the location and it's on my left. I crank the wheel over and jump the curb into the parking lot.

"Jesus!" Wes yells from the back seat.

"If you're going to drive a Jeep, you're practically obligated to jump curbs," I say.

"Honey, are you meeting us outside?" Wes asks into the phone, clutching the 'oh shit' handlebar up top.

I'm unbuckling, putting the car in park, and stepping out. My eyes scan the parking lot and I see none of the women we're looking for.

Until I do.

There she is with white-blonde hair tied into a top knot, dress riding up her thighs, and one leg out of the driver's seat in Ramona's car. She's laughing, both hands on the wheel at ten and two like the good, responsible girl she is. I'm wondering why we were called if Nia is sober enough to drive, but when I get closer, my stomach sinks.

With the smell of alcohol drifting off of her, it would be far-fetched to think she's anywhere near sober.

She doesn't notice us yet. She's play-revving the engine like the wheel is motorcycle handles and her mouth is open, a smile upon her face showing pure elation. Heat rises up from my chest. One of my fists is clenched by my side, and the headlights from the car are less blinding than the headache growing in my temples.

And then, I don't see her anymore. I'm blinking my eyes open. I'm in a bed. My legs are covered with a quilt. I see an empty chair in the corner, a purse leaning against its legs, a blanket draped over the back. A door is open. The linoleum is almost as stark white as the lights shining above me. It's difficult to make out the rest of the room, but there's ringing in my ears followed by the feeling that something must be very wrong.

I'm being told my best friend passed. Wreck. Not my fault. Of course not my fault, they say, but I know better, and I don't want to be told otherwise.

"Nia! Nia, drive! You said you'd be our DD!" a voice yells from the passenger seat, breaking me from my memories. I walk closer to the car and bend down to see Corinne sitting beside her. Nia is laughing, cranking the wheel in a mocking revving motion again.

The words bust out of me before I can consider anything else.

"What the fuck is going on?" I ask. I reach my arm in and turn the headlights off. My headache should lessen, but I'm only getting more heated by the second. "Where are the keys?"

Nia's head twists toward the open door, eyes glazed over. Is she even sober enough to recognize it's me? Then her eyes widen, her eyebrows rise to her hairline, and a wide grin replaces the light-hearted smile from earlier. Her cheeks are full, flushed, and beautiful, but she's still in the driver's seat, reeking of alcohol, and my heart is still pounding. I can't stop it.

"Ian!" she yells, pulling one hand off the wheel.

"Ian!" Corinne echoes, opening the passenger door and clomping her heels across the pavement and around the car.

"What are you thinking?" I ask Nia, and her brows furrow inward.

"What?" she mumbles. I see the keys resting in her lap, and I take them.

"Ian!" Corinne's voice rings again as she draws me into a hug. Her height is comparable to mine, and I'm not used to women hugging around my shoulders rather than my waist. I instinctually pat her back, but my eye contact with Nia does not break, her confusion clear.

"Ian, Ian, this is a *female* strip club!" Corinne says, bouncing on the heels of her stilettos.

"Congratulations," I deadpan, eliciting a small giggle from her.

"Ian!" Wes's voice calls across the parking lot.

Oh my god, if I hear my name called one more time...

I jerk around to see Ramona's arm slung over his shoulders as she stumbles forward, laughing like a hyena. The strap of her dress is hanging off her shoulder and she walks barefoot with both heels in her hands.

Fantastic.

"Give me a second!" I yell back.

The doors to the club are thrown open and Grace walks out, striding forward in a straight line, unmistakably sober as can be. Cameron follows behind her, one hand on the small of her back.

"What the hell, Grace?" he says.

"Give me a second to gather my bridesmaids, Cameron," she shoots to him. Her mouth is in a straight line as she points to Wes and Ramona. "Will you help him, please?"

"I need to pee," Nia whines from below me. Her eyebrows pull tighter in the middle.

"I'll go with you!" Corinne says, holding out her hand for Nia to take.

With a jerk of her other leg, Nia stumbles out of the car. I bend to grab her other arm. As she's lifted out with both our efforts, she groans a little. Her skin is soft, but with every breath, it seems like the alcohol smells stronger. My head swims.

Nia was going to drive. She knows better than that. She knows how *I* feel about that.

"Oh, are you guys going?" Ramona yells, seeing Nia and Corinne trot back toward the black doors of the club. "I need to go too!"

"We're ten minutes from the hotel." Wes laughs. "Can you guys not wait?"

"Bye!" Ramona yells back over her shoulder. Wes tosses her a wave she cannot see then all three women disappear through the doors.

Wes, Cameron, and I look to Grace, who stands with her hands on her hips.

"What?" she snaps, and all three of us jump. There's nothing like an angry bride.

"Nothing," Cameron says, hands in the air.

"Why aren't you drinking?" Wes asks. "Figured you would be the worst."

"Over your wife?" she shoots back.

"Well, she's a given."

Not even a moment later, Ramona is stumbling back out through the doors. Wes and Grace run—at least, Grace runs as well as someone can with heels—and catch her before she falls.

"Where are Nia and Corinne?" I call out. She shakes her head with a laugh, knees bending as if she can't contain the hilarity of it all.

"Corinne is just doing Corinne things." She giggles. I don't have time to register what that could possibly mean before Ramona is yelling over to Grace.

"Why didn't you drive?" she asks, squinting at her as if she can barely see her best friend.

"You called Wes, remember?" Grace says, her tone clipped. "I told you not to. I said I could drive."

"That's right!" Ramona yells, attempting to snap her fingers in realization, but she's forgotten how to, which I wasn't sure was possible. "Protecting that baby bun!"

Fuck.

"What?!" Cameron bellows from behind me.

Double fuck.

I don't have time for this.

I storm toward the entrance, swinging the doors open like I'm barreling into a saloon, and I see Corinne locking lips with some woman, hands roaming up the stranger's thighs.

"Where is Nia?" I ask.

Her head jerks away from the woman, who seemed to be having a fairly decent time. I recognize her instantly—the black-haired beauty with the big tits from the hotel bar.

Go you, Corinne.

"Bathroom," Corinne says breathlessly, and I throw a salute her way.

"At ease, women."

My feet carry me to the women's bathroom. There's a call from behind me, maybe the bouncer or the ticket guy asking why I haven't shelled out the obscene amount of money required to gain entrance. Either way, I slam the women's bathroom door open and, thankfully—or, thankfully for the other women in the club—the only sight I see is Nia against the wall, knees curled to her chest, giving me a shy wave.

I inhale sharply. I'm too exhausted to fight. I can't bring myself to argue with the fragile woman in front of me. I just want to wrap her up in my arms and carry her home.

"Let's go, Polly."

Nia is the woman with a solid head on her shoulders. She's the woman with control and responsibility. She's the woman I need, not just the woman I want, but with the memory of her cackling in that front seat, I now wonder if maybe I had the wrong impression.

Maybe she's isn't the one for me, and that realization hurts like a bitch.

29

NIA

IF I HAVE TO WAKE UP ONE MORE TIME WITH A HEADACHE pounding like fireworks on the Fourth of July, I'm going to lose it. My only form of solace is that I awake with a cup of black coffee on my bedside table and a light breeze blowing the curtains inward from the open sliding glass door.

"Hello?" I ask.

The patio creaks and Harry's head pops in, baseball cap backward on his head and strands of blonde hair sweeping in front of his face. A toothbrush pokes out from between his teeth.

"Goob mornin'," he says, padding across the room.

"What time is it?"

He holds up an index finger, leans over the sink, and spits.

"Time for us to leave, I think." A plastic grocery bag with clothes rests on the desk next to a wallet, two sets of keys, and a cell phone.

"Why?" I ask, propping myself up on my elbows. I point to the coffee. "Is this mine?"

Harry nods, brushes some more, and spits again.

"Well, for one, we weren't invited to this wedding." He

pockets the wallet, phone, and one set of keys. I notice my pink rabbit's foot on the other ring.

"Are you leaving my car?" I ask.

"That leads me to my next point," he says. "Grant can't exactly drive since he doesn't have a wallet, so I'm taking him back."

"You're not staying?"

He laughs. "Nah. This was fun and all, but I have a daughter to tend to."

"And Grant?"

"He's getting breakfast with the other guys." Harry walks over, the mattress dipping under his weight as he sits on the side of the bed. "I'm going to talk to Mom and Dad about rehab."

Rehab. It feels like both a dream and harsh reality that we're even discussing the word.

"Good call," I say. "Wow, this is a lot deeper than I figured this week would go."

"Yeah, some deep shit," Harry says, patting me on the leg and rising again. "Well, you've got your car here. It's fixed for the time being, but you should probably still buy a new one. I don't trust it."

"Neither do I," I mumble. "And, you know, I've been really liking Cameron's Jeep. I'll look into one of those or something."

"Wow. Did you just admit you need a new car?"

"Oh hush." I swing my legs over the side of the bed and stretch. I'm still wearing my dress. It's pretty wrinkled, and I'm sure my makeup and hair are worse for wear as well.

"One small step for mankind, one big step for Apollonia Smith."

"It's just a car, Harry."

"First, a man. Now, a car. Who are you?"

I halt mid-step, a t-shirt inches from my reach, but I'm somehow unable to grasp it. "What was that?" I ask.

"Ian. Aren't you guys…I don't know, a thing?"

Are we? I think back to last night. He didn't exactly seem *happy* to see me. I was drunk—my pounding head will attest to that—and it was much worse than the night before.

"I'm not sure," I admit.

Harry grins. "I am."

It's weird how Harry seems to know me better than I know myself, or at least what I want.

"I feel like a teenager again," I say to him. My ankles twist around each other and I find I'm biting my lip at just the thought of Ian.

Harry's arms are crossed, and his mouth is pointed to the corner of his face in some knowing smirk.

Butterflies, jitters, nervous energy flowing through me…I don't know what this is, but I want to explore it. I finally want to explore Ian.

30

NIA

THREE YEARS AGO

"So, we just left."

"You left?"

If I had to pick one thing I dislike the most about Ian—which includes various things—I would say his stupid *I was a total badass in my twenties* stories take the cake.

"At least you're a better person now," Cameron says with a chuckle, scribbling on his tablet as he leans back in his chair.

"Maybe. But, yeah, no tip," he says, as if dining and dashing isn't one of cruelest things you can do to someone in the service industry. "Nothing."

"Okay, I'm done with your ridiculous showboating today." I exhale and go back to typing. Ian sits across from me, his laptop resting on his thigh with his ankle crossed over his other knee. Cameron is in the chair next to him, engrossed in his design work. The chairs are the white standard ones awarded to the staff members with an office. I tried to decorate my space by hanging some canvas paintings of oceans. They're supposedly meant to calm people, though with the number of irate employees who storm into my office, I'm realizing their effect is more for me than the people complaining about the food on snack Fridays.

"Why do you hate me so?" Ian asks, adjusting his posture and grinning. It's that same charming grin that puts his gorgeously straight teeth on display. I'd be lying if I said my chest didn't flutter at the sight of it. After years of enduring his smiles, you would think the emotions would fly away just as quickly as they appeared, but nope, not a chance.

"Because you're infuriating," I say.

"Was," Cameron says without looking up. "He *was* a horrible person." He blindly reaches to pinch Ian's cheeks, and the grin widens. Cameron twirls his pen between his fingers and clicks the lock button on his tablet. "So, are we in detention? Because it sure feels like it."

The two men have been in my office for approximately an hour and have accomplished nothing. I hadn't even noticed until Ian's stories became more and more ridiculous as time rolled on.

"I wanted your opinion on the new company handbook considering you're fairly tenured employees. Plus"—I point my finger at Ian—"the lawyer is nice to have."

"Oh, so now I'm nice to have?" Ian settles into his chair and closes his laptop. I swear, this man is testing my patience.

"Is that why we've gotten nothing done?" Cameron says. He's smiling at me. In the course of only a couple years, I'm already suspicious of Cameron Kaufman. He's starting to learn how to push my buttons almost as well as Ian. But, despite his cocky nature, he's supposedly a talented junior designer, so at least he's adding value. His potential promotion to become creative director has come down the pipeline more than once.

"You and I can sit down alone," Ian suggests, and even though he appears indifferent, I can tell he's trying to conceal a smile tugging at the edge of his mouth.

I can't count on one hand, two hands, or even all ten of my

toes how many times he's tried to conceal his challenge of authority. He knows he's defying every employee handbook published since his arrival, as this would surely qualify as workplace harassment if I wanted to twist it as such. *I wrote that damn handbook.*

Even so, it's hard for me to give him a write-up because, if I'm being honest with myself, those twisted smirks improve my afternoons more than I'd like to admit. Ian makes me feel wanted—something I never feel in my life outside of work—and it's harmless enough for me to pretend no lines are being crossed.

Sometimes, I'm a bit ashamed I let this kind of thing slide, but then I see his grin and my guilt very discreetly melts away. Nothing will ever happen. I can banter with him if I like, right?

"I like employee input," I say, narrowing my eyes. "That's why it's necessary for Cameron to be here."

In fact, employee input has zero effect on the creation of this document. There is absolutely nothing Cameron could say that would change my dress code policies or the laws impacting employee termination and due process, but I'm logical enough to know there needs to be a buffer between Ian and me.

Cameron lifts his wrist to check the time and pats his knee. "Well, would you look at that, it's quittin' time. This was a fun waste of an afternoon. See you tomorrow, bud." He claps Ian on the shoulder and throws me a wave over his arm.

Ian blows out a low whistle, and I shrug because I can't think of anything else to do.

"Then there were two," he says. The statement should be casual, but it sucks the air right out of the room.

I look down to my screen and type out words for an email I will undoubtedly trash later.

After a moment or two of silence, he clears his throat. "We paid, you know."

"What?" I say, glancing up at him with a raised eyebrow.

"That story—we went back to the restaurant. My friends wanted to experience the whole dine and dash thing, but we definitely went back and paid. I wouldn't do that."

The confession drops my stomach and I gulp. He could have touched me and I'm not sure it would have had the same effect. Call me weird, but honesty is more attractive than any other factor. I find myself inhaling slowly and continuing to type.

Harry always says I should be more open, and I know it would make me a much more effective human resources professional. I like to think I roam around the office striking up conversation with enough employees to be relatable, but with Ian, it's never been as easy for me. I almost *want* to hate him at this point. It's comfortable, familiar, and knowing he's a good guy doesn't help me accomplish that.

"Why tell lies then?" I ask.

His ice blue eyes stare back at me. They're shifting down to my lips then up again. I lean back in my chair to put extra distance between us.

He shrugs. "It's not as much fun when people know I'm actually a decent person."

"You are the most difficult person I've ever had the misfortune of knowing," I say.

"I accept the compliment."

He grins, and I smile back without my consent.

31

NIA

PRESENT DAY

Harry and I walk down to breakfast, and the grin across my face doesn't falter for even a moment. He's trying to discuss which route home will be more scenic, but I'm too caught up in the nerves radiating down to my fingertips to contribute anything—not even a *There are some good peach stands on the way!* because round peaches only make me think of the nasty things Ian and I could, and should, be doing together.

The moment we walk into the hotel bar, I can feel Ian's presence. The scent of his cedar body wash finds me like an arrow searching for its target, and when his blue eyes lock with mine, I know it's hit a bullseye.

But just as quick as my heart was to embrace the sharp head of the arrow, it crumbles under it when I realize that gaze holds no sense of play. Ian doesn't lift a challenging eyebrow or have that tilt in the corner of his mouth that holds some unspoken secret.

Ian sees me, and then he goes back to his omelet.

What the hell?

I remember nothing but happy things from last night. He

and the boys came to pick us up, we all laughed, and then...*what else?*

I don't know.

"Don't ome*let* that food go to waste," I say with a smile then immediately cringe. What the heck did I just say? Even Harry looks at me with his teeth gritted and eyebrows pulled inward as if telling me how bad of a try-hard I am right now.

What can I say? Ian isn't looking at me with puppy dog eyes or spitting sarcastic comments my way. This is unnatural.

"We hittin' the road?" Grant grumbles, his fork nestled between his lips, grinding at his bottom teeth as if irritated that it's there to begin with. He looks like he could be sitting on a porch overlooking a lawn littered with broken cars with the way it's toothpicking in and out of his mouth.

"You bet," Harry says, tugging off his hat and running his fingers through his locks before snapping it back on, bill backward. "Let's get kicking."

Ian stands, towering over both of my brothers, and wraps them in a tight three-way hug. It might be more endearing if I weren't so startled by how uncharacteristically silent Ian is—and how the hug is not for me!

What. The. Heck?

He doesn't meet my gaze when he says, "I'll walk you guys out."

"That's my job," I say with a strained laugh. It only gets a reaction from Harry, who swings an arm over my shoulders and pulls me in tight.

"You're embarrassing yourself," he whispers. I shove my elbow into his chest.

It's odd—if I didn't know any better, this walk to the parking lot might look like a tight-knit family parting ways at the end of a long adventure: the brothers, their sister, and the welcomed-with-open-arms brother-in-law. But, it's not. Just three siblings and the estranged tall man hovering behind them like a shadow of either protection or doom. I honestly don't know which.

"Be safe," I say, leaning down through the window as Harry revs the engine. His eyes flutter shut as if he's finally found solace in the sound of his sports car. He's been through too much these past few years. He's got the zen of a monk, and I envy it.

In the reflection of Harry's pitch-black, buffed-out car, I see Ian behind me, hands in his pockets and a small smirk on his face.

Grant shifts in the passenger seat, unbuckling and buckling his seatbelt until he seems satisfied enough to lean forward and toss a wave at Ian. "Hey asshole, you should drop by sometime."

With my elbows still poised on the window, I whip my head around to see Ian giving a half-hearted salute back to Grant. I expect him to flash me a grin or a wink or any single thing that would make this seem like it's actually Ian standing behind me, but it's like a body snatcher has come and ripped the sarcastic, devious Ian from the world and replaced him with someone I don't know—or, more accurately, someone not interested in me for the first time in years.

I have to be imagining this.

Harry clears his throat and I back away from the car, almost bumping into Ian. I would have if he hadn't moved out of the way so quickly—a movement which seemed deliberate. I feel like he would have stayed there were it any other day.

No, I'm just overanalyzing. It's nothing. He's just tired. We were both up late.

But also...why isn't he gripping my top, pulling me close, or even having snide conversation with an undertone of sly naughtiness?

We wave as Harry whips out of the parking lot and onto the main road. Then there's just the sounds of passing traffic, carts rolling into the hotel, and the distant ocean waves. Still no quips from Ian. He finally looks at me, gives a half-smirk, then shrugs and walks back toward the hotel.

Well now I'm irritated.

"I don't think I've ever seen Ian Chambers so quiet," I say, walking behind him, trying my best to keep up with his long strides.

"I'm quiet?" he asks.

"Don't play dumb."

"I'm just tired." The automatic doors to the entrance slide open and we walk through. The lights hum and buzz above us, and it's just one extra layer of sound that isn't him being an asshole. I didn't realize how much I would miss his stupid comments until they were gone.

"Yeah, sorry we kept you out late." I try to steer us back to the issue at hand. Something happened last night that I don't remember, and I'll be damned if it stays up in the air.

"Don't worry about it," he says.

"What happened last night?" I ask. Ian walks toward the elevator, and I follow.

"Don't you have to go to the beach or something?" he asks.

Is he trying to get rid of me?

"Really—what happened?" I ask again. He pushes the button to the elevator, and when the doors ding open, I follow him in. This ride doesn't carry the same weight that it did yesterday. It's just the two of us, but we're not pressed against the walls of the elevator or sneaking secretive touches. I'm staring at him and he's finally looking back at me, eyes narrowed, slowly letting out an exhalation.

He's smoldering because it's impossible for him not to. It's the stubble, the eyes, the strong arms peeking out from under his sleeves...all of it—though I get the sense that he's not intentionally trying to turn me on.

"The rest of the wedding crowd will be coming in today," he

says, running his hands through his curly locks. "I should really get some sleep. I was up late."

When he keys into his room, I'm stuck standing there—dumbfounded, confused, and heartbroken.

Again.

32

NIA

Two years ago

I'm turning thirty-three, and I'm processing the paperwork for a twenty-seven-year-old woman who had a riotous affair with her thirty-five-year-old boss.

I'm getting too old for this.

It's Friday and our company is having its usual get-together in the renovated warehouse. Ian and I are the only people still working in the main office, and my door is shut as we discuss the issue at hand. Our creative director, Cameron, and his junior designer, Grace, are sleeping together—or, *were* sleeping together? The details are fuzzy.

Ian stands beside me, hands on his hips, exhaling at the write-up on my laptop. He's normally on board with investigation, but his best friend seems like the exception.

"We don't need to look further into this. We'll file it and call it a day," he says, crossing his arms and pacing to the other side of the desk.

"Not doing your job now?" I ask. I don't like it when Ian and I butt heads professionally. Sure, on a more personal level, we're like oil and water, but in a work environment, we don't usually have issues. For an HR and lawyer duo, I could have worse.

Except, in this mood, I definitely feel less confident in our partnership.

"She's not pressing charges, so why are we bothering?" he asks.

"This sets a precedent for future co-worker relations."

"Good," he says. "Then let's develop a policy that actually makes sense."

I'm quiet, leaning back in my chair and rocking. "And what do you propose?" I ask.

"Work relationships allowed as long as it's not between an employee and their manager."

"Except that's exactly what just happened, so how do we follow through? If we're going with precedent and all."

It feels odd to speak with Ian about work relationships. I've spent years staring at his jawline, his chest, his ass... It's inappropriate, but I've kept it to myself for the most part—except for telling Harry, who is relentless with his jokes. I think even Cara has picked up on it. If I hear her say, "Who is Ian?" one more time, I might commit myself.

"I'm just saying that, for example, if you and I were to get together, there would be no ramifications in this imaginary policy."

My stomach curls in on itself. My posture tightens. I can feel nothing else but anxiety coursing through my veins mixed with something akin to butterflies. How do I react to that? This isn't a conversation I want to have.

Just as I'm contemplating saying something—anything— his eyebrows lift as if he just realized what came out of his mouth. It was inappropriate, yet the confidence of it all is what turns my nerves into a Slinky, slowly bouncing its way down my body.

"It's hypothetical," he says quickly. His hands drop to his

sides and he lets out a forced, stuttered laugh, looking at some corner in the office. He can't meet my eyes. "I...wow, I'm sorry. That... you know I don't date co-workers."

"Yes," I say. It's the only thing I can get out. I shake my head. I try not to let out an equally awkward laugh, but instead I think it's best to keep the conversation rolling.

"Nia, I didn't mean to—"

"Don't worry about it," I say. I force a smile, rolling my chair forward to absentmindedly check email. There's nothing new, unless you count my steadily increasing jumbled thoughts.

We do need a new policy, but even if this were a different proposal and *any* office relationship were banned, how off limits would it be, exactly? Cameron and Grace got away with it —but, *no*. What the heck am I thinking? I look up to see Ian walking back around. His scent is intoxicating. In my peripheral, I see his toned forearms, his large veined hands, and the bit of bulge just barely visible below his brown leather belt.

He's attractive. That's never been issue, but in this moment, with all these possibilities right in front us—the fact that Grace and Cameron skirted the ramifications of their work affair— I'm second-guessing every thought I've had about him. I feel weak. My nipples harden, and I cross my arms to hide them.

"We should get going," I say. "We'll finish this Monday. I'm sure Beer Friday can't possibly go on without you."

I stand and we're close—more so than I intended. His eyes look down and bore into me. I can see his chest rising and falling as mine mimics the motion.

I wonder—not for the first time—what it would be like to press my lips against his. Would I feel his stubble brush over my chin? Would I feel a forbidden sensation, overwhelmed by butterflies and the heavy hands on my waist? His breath is close...almost close enough to capture.

My hand twitches against the crook of my arm. They're crossed but begging to be released—into his hair, onto his jaw, down his chest... If I were a more reckless woman, he could take me on this desk. My back might hit the keyboard and I would wonder if my ass might send a couple nonsensical emails with things like "sdnghuighdi" or "fbdsfdsg." But, hey, we all make sacrifices for a hot fantasy.

I'm ready to get on my toes and move closer. I even feel myself rising a centimeter, but then he lets out a laugh, and the moment feels split by some invisible axe. The room's temperature shifts, and I'm brought back to the present moment.

Fuck.

Fuck.

Shit.

What the hell was I thinking? What the absolute *shit* did I almost do?

It's weird, though—he lets out a chuckle and looks into another corner. Yeah, he's definitely avoiding eye contact now.

"You're...this is..." He laughs again, and I feel so mortified. I have humiliated myself. Me, the responsible employee, the one with a solid head on her shoulders, almost just let go. I could have lost everything.

"What?" If I can just pretend that moment, whatever it was, didn't happen then maybe it will go away.

"I didn't mean to make you feel uncomfortable," he says.

"I don't know what you're talking about."

"I don't date co-workers," he repeats. "I swear I wouldn't do anything like that."

I jerk my head up to him. He's cringing at himself, and I want to tell him I was the one to make that moment awkward, but I can't bring myself to do it. He can't know I almost caved. After years and years of whatever he's been hinting at, I don't want him to have the satisfaction of knowing I could have tossed away every moral I have for him.

How absolutely stupid am I?

"What are you getting at?" I ask, lifting an eyebrow as high as it can go as if to shove my head in the sand, pure ostrich-style. Maybe he knows I know. Maybe he doesn't, but I'm not taking chances.

"Nothing," he says on an exhalation. He shoves his hands in his pockets and walks to the door, looking back before opening it. "We'll work on the policy Monday."

"Sure," I shoot back. I don't look up from my computer when he leaves, though I do notice he does me the courtesy of closing the door. As such, I cup my face in my hands and let myself break into nervous shakes.

I'm angry. I'm sad. I'm disappointed in the woman I've become. I almost lost control. That isn't me. That can't be me. But…a small voice in my head wonders what could have happened. I know there's something there. At the core of it all, I'm a smart woman, and I've learned how to read Ian. He flirts, but it must have deeper meaning. He teases other employees, but it's me who takes the brunt of it. I'm the one he visits the most. My office is practically his office—much to both my disdain and my comfort.

I can't sit here and brood over this. I need to get out. I need to experience some type of social interaction that doesn't involve a handsome man or employee relations that somehow feel too close to home now.

I pack my bag, shoving my laptop in with its charger and placing it in the corner. Maybe for once Beer Friday will do me some good. Ian is there, but I can easily blend into the crowd. We just finished a project. The warehouse will be packed.

And so it is. I try to make small talk with the accounting department, the sales guys, and even our receptionist, Saria. She seems less than interested, but she always seems disinterested in conversation with me. HR can't win them all.

I'm abandoned, and the feeling of loneliness overtakes me. I don't care about how others view me or about having close friends. I depend on my family for that. Even so, after tonight, it feels almost insulting.

Maybe I'll go home and cuddle with the cat. Maybe I'll even throw on *The Office*. Then again, maybe not. At the thought of Jim and Pam, I think maybe I'll settle with something else like *Rambo*. My brother says it always makes him feel empowered. I think Amazon has camo headbands...

I head to my car, contemplating calling my brother for more suggestions involving men who mean business, and distantly I see Ian near his car. And then—Saria, with her pleather skirt and tucked-in shirt, standing just beside the passenger door, balancing sexy and professional all at once. He has a nervous smile on his face as she crawls in, or is it anticipation?

He's taking her home.

Tears well in my eyes. My neck feels hot, even though my hands are cold and clammy.

He doesn't date co-workers.

Why would he tell me that if it was untrue? And of course he's secretly with the youngest woman here. She must be, what, more than ten years his junior? And he's the lawyer, the hot one with all the power, loading her into his car.

This is disgusting, and it hurts. It hurts to know I was right all along. All these years, all this back and forth, and all I am is the HR professional he can get a rise out of.

How hilarious that must have been, to tease the stiff, to break her down just enough so she almost caves—and then he goes back to his secret, younger girlfriend.

He's a tease. He plays with people, and I'm the idiot who actually thought he liked me.

I'm at work. I'm a professional.

And I'm turning thirty-three.

Grow up, Nia.

33

NIA

PRESENT DAY

The remainder of the day is a whirlwind of wedding stuff. That's as elegantly as I can put it: *stuff*.

It's not that I'm opposed to weddings or that I don't intend to get married one day, but I was also just dismissed by a man I've tried to convince myself not to like as he made advances toward me over the past few years.

Talk about irony.

I wish I could take it all back—the night of passion between Ian and me, feeling comfortable with him, promising a round two. He told me this is what he wanted yet somehow I'm the one left upset and, quite frankly, angry.

It seems almost unreal to be as sad as I was, but hours later when I'm lying on Grace's bed, I'm less sad and instead angry. I'm still mulling over the thought that maybe, just maybe, Ian Chambers has broken my heart. Again.

I clench my fists tighter.

That fucker.

"Have you spoken to your future baby daddy yet?" Ramona

asks Grace, bouncing on the end of the bed with her legs crossed and fingers typing away on her phone.

"No," Grace replies. She's at the desk, compact mirror open in front of her while she tilts her head side to side as if considering what type of makeup she's going to wear.

"You probably should," Corinne singsongs from the sliding glass door, peering out at the ocean with a small flute of champagne relaxed in her hand.

"I'm gonna try this thing where I pretend to make him my husband first," Grace says, inhaling sharply and shutting the mirror with zero makeup achieved. The rehearsal is in a couple hours; I didn't think it was possible to be nervous about a fake wedding, but I'm also not marrying someone tomorrow.

Grace twists in her chair, gripping the back with both hands. "Who wants to go eat tons of donuts? I'm pregnant and eating my feelings."

We all stare, and Ramona is the first to respond with, "Yes, where can we get donuts right now?"

"Practical question," Grace says, pointing a finger at me. "Exactly what I expected from the maid of honor, and I love it."

"Oh god, yes, I could totally go for donuts," Corinne responds, plunking her flute down on the TV stand.

I'm sprawled out starfish-style, and while it's difficult to justify moving from this bed that feels like a sea of clouds, I also don't feel it's appropriate to say, *Sorry bride, I'm too irritated to speak, but thank you for the offer of donuts.*

Instead, I say, "Absolutely!" and force a smile that's almost as stiff as dry concrete. Thankfully, my lips move as directed, and there I am standing with my purse slung over my shoulder and what I can only imagine is a twitchy smile a la the Joker from *Batman*.

"Wait," Ramona says, running to a tote bag slung over the desk chair and rummaging through it. She pulls out a pair of sunglasses. When she places them on, they overtake her face, giving her the look of a giant fly.

"Protection," she says. "Everyone will be looking for the bride, so we need to be sneaky."

She turns around and pulls out three more pairs of sunglasses, and I'm starting to think this bag is some type of magical wizarding purse belonging to Hermione or Mary Poppins.

"Protection, protection, protection," she repeats each time she places a pair in our hands.

"That advice would have helped Gracie here a while ago," Corinne says.

Grace shoves the glasses up the bridge of her nose and lifts a fiery eyebrow. "Watch yourself, girls. Mama's coming through."

I put my sunglasses on and wonder why we're going the Clark Kent route. These glasses aren't some invisibility cloak. Grace's hair color alone can be noticed from a mile away.

But I also wonder if this would conceal my identity from Ian if he were to pass by. *Since when am I spineless?*

I answer my own question when, to my absolute misfortune, the second I walk through the door, Wes and Ian are at the opposite end of the hallway, leaving his room.

Since now. I am spineless right now.

I look at the parking lot over the balcony railing, trying to seem aloof. The men's hands are full of decorations, and before I can wonder why, Ramona is already pumping her arms and powerwalking over to them.

"Okay, you remember where this goes, right?" she starts. I hear Wes groan, then nothing. My brain processes zero sounds moving past their lips. It's like a ringing goes through my ears when I shift my gaze to the one man I promised myself I would not look at. The world freezes, and I am instantly, unabashedly staring at Ian like some creep behind binoculars.

Normally, his eyes would be locked on me as well, icy blues tearing through me with an accompanying sly grin, equally unashamed—but not this time. Not right now.

Ian laughs at something Ramona says, shrugs as if to dismiss her, then starts walking toward me. I need to say something. He can't just walk past me without saying anything, right?

"Hey." *Wow, that's the absolute best I can do?* I am an adult and I only know how to say things like *Hey*.

"Hey," he responds. Good—at least I'm not the only awkward one here.

"Can we talk?" I ask. He looks to Wes then back at me as if requesting permission. What does he think? I'm some seductress evil witch dragging him to my cave to make boyfriend soup?

"Yeah, sure." He shrugs. "Hang on a sec, Wes."

"Oooh, someone is in trouble," Wes says, poking his bottom lip out. This earns him a small shove from Ramona.

"Do *you* want to be in trouble later?"

"No ma'am."

Ian follows me to the end of the hall. The lightbulb above us is flickering, which seems a bit out of place for such a nice resort—though I'm starting to question this fact at all—but then again maybe it's reflecting how faint my relationship with Ian seems to be. I am a Shakespearian tragedy waiting to happen.

We reach the end—far enough that the others probably cannot hear us—and I turn on my heel to face him. His expression is stoic as he stares back at me. I catch a whiff of him, and his scent runs through me like a devil's pitchfork poking every inch of my senses, stabbing my anxiety.

"About last night—"

"Nia, I don't really want to talk about it." He averts his eyes, finding some part of the railing to focus on.

I cross my arms. "Well, I'd quite like to."

"What do you want to know?" he asks.

"Something has changed. Yesterday—or more like the past decade—you've been the biggest bother of my life. Now look at you." I throw my hand out, palm up, waving it up and down from his head to his knees. "You're a shell of the ridiculous Ian I know. What happened last night?"

"You were drunk, and you tried to drive," he says. "That's what happened last night."

"What?" I ask, baffled. What is he talking about? I didn't drive.

"Nia, come on."

"Come on, what?" I say incredulous. "I didn't drive."

"I'd just told you something the night before, the one memory I don't tell anyone," he says, leaning in to whisper, though it comes out as more of a hiss. I lean back instinctually. "I told you I lost my best friend, and then, not even a day later, I find you behind the wheel, drunk off your ass, laughing with your foot on the pedal of a car." It's like with every word, I can feel the tension getting thicker and thicker between us. His eyebrows furrow in the middle. I feel sick. "Now, I'm not self-important enough to think you would have my feelings about drunk driving in the back of your mind at all times, or that you would do it maliciously, but...don't play stupid. You're not stupid, or at least I really thought you weren't."

"Ian, it's not what it looked like, I swear." I'm trying not to sound like I'm pleading, but the hurt in my voice isn't nearly as bad as the pain I see in his eyes.

He did tell me something meaningful, and he thinks I immediately disregarded it. Of course he doesn't want to talk to me.

"I just don't think this is going to work out," he says, and it's like someone punched me in the stomach.

"I'm sorry," I say. My voice catches, but I try to clear it

discreetly. "I wasn't going to drive. We were joking. I know what that means to you. You have to believe me."

"I don't think I can." He turns to leave, decorations shoved under his arm, but I reach out to grasp his elbow.

"Well, wait, hang on. Can we just talk about this?"

He rounds on me, figure towering over my small frame. If I weren't so infuriated, I might be scared. "What is there to say? I don't have time for irresponsible drunks."

I freeze and my breath hitches. Is this how he feels? Does he truly think I would endanger the lives of everyone around me—especially after hearing his story one day earlier? Not only does this assume I'm ignorant, it also implies that his story didn't resonate with me. How heartless must he think I am to believe that didn't affect me?

"That's extreme," I say quietly.

"Sorry. I just... It's a lot to think about."

"Clearly."

"Sorry I annoyed you for nine years," he mumbles. "Don't worry, I won't bother you anymore."

He turns to leave again, and this time I don't reach for him or ask for more clarification. I have all the clarification I need.

The world around me seems dulled. I only distantly see the outline of Ian walking away, meeting Wes, and approaching the elevator doors.

The other women down the hall start moving, and I take that as my cue to join them. I'm still lost in my hazy dream state, but the hum of speech finally hits me when I feel a hand on my shoulder and hear Corinne say, "You okay, Nia?"

"I won't bother you anymore."

I'm nothing to him.

"Yeah, I'm just exhausted from last night." My vision is glazed over and I know I'm speaking in a monotone voice, but I can't muster any inflection. "Just nursing a headache." Admittedly, my hangover headache disappeared a few hours ago when I popped ibuprofen, but it is starting to come back rapidly.

Corinne glances from Ian waiting at the elevator and then back to me.

"Guys, I'm so silly. I forgot my purse!" she suddenly says, slapping herself in the forehead with a goofy smile. "Geez! Hey, Nia, come with me? We'll circle back with you guys in a few minutes!" She couldn't be more obvious, and I'm sure Ian and Wes hear the awkward exchange from the elevator, but they don't turn around. Before Grace or Ramona can protest or ask any questions, Corinne's hand is entwined with mine and she's tugging me back to her room, scanning the keycard, and shutting the door behind me.

"What?" I ask. It comes out harsher than I meant it to, but I can't bottle my frustration any more.

"You look dead," she says, tilting her head to the side, and I let out an offended exhalation. "Hey, just being honest."

"I'm just tired," I say.

"Lies. You went on and on about Ian last night, and now he's acting like he doesn't even know you."

"I did not." I do faintly remember gabbing about him. It's hazy, but at one point I might have said, "He's a god." Judging by Corinne's expression, that's probably an accurate memory.

"That's not what it—"

There's a knock at the door. Corinne opens it, and both Grace and Ramona slide in through the crack.

"Secrets, secrets..." Ramona whispers, shutting the door behind her.

"You didn't forget your purse," Grace says, her arms crossed. Then somehow, as if through telepathy, all of their gazes shoot to me.

"Is my brother being an idiot?" Ramona says, bored, as if this is the last thing that could be news for her.

My heart skips a beat. I already miss Ian's snarky

comments. They're infuriating, but they're also clever and flirty. He has the type of grin that lights up a room—until he opens his mouth, of course...a mouth that was on mine just one day ago.

Grace's eyes grow wide and she runs to the bed, hops on, and slides a pillow underneath her chest, feet waving in the air behind her. She looks like a little girl at a sleepover, ready for a good time.

"Spill!" she says, fingers spread in a *Go!* gesture.

I consider saying nothing, but for once I also wonder if maybe I should. I've never had this many female friends, never had a group all looking at me like I'm the next hot gossip tea to fill their cups. Is sharing everything standard procedure with female friends?

"He thinks I was drunk driving."

Ramona's face drops. "Oh no."

34

IAN

"I'm gonna be a dad."

"Yep. Daddy Cameron."

"Daddy Cameron," he echoes.

"I think your aunt brought her dog," I say. Cameron is lying on my hotel bed, staring at the ceiling with enough intensity to rival a hawk. Wes and I finished setting up the ceremony stage, and after showering, we're just waiting for the rehearsal to commence and for the groom to stop brooding. I look at my watch. *Thirty minutes of wallowing remaining.*

"Makes sense she would do that," he says, not breaking eye contact with the uninteresting tiles above. "She loves that dog."

"I did see it's wearing a bow tie, so at least he's dressed for the occasion."

"How thoughtful."

"No, it's weird," I say. "Don't encourage her."

"You're right. Also, hey, I'm going to be a dad."

"I think I heard that somewhere." I chuckle.

"Oh, right."

Even though he's in some zoned-out state of shock, a small

smile still tugs at the corner of his mouth. I wouldn't say he's overjoyed, but the man is happy. Anything to do with Grace and their now growing family makes him happy.

Their family members have been arriving since this morning. Thankfully, Cam and Grace didn't invite many people, so him hiding out in a hotel room isn't the rudest thing he could be doing right now. Plus, this is helping me to avoid Nia as well.

I can't deny it—I'm still crazy about her. I want her to tell me to shut up, I want to see her rolling eyes fueled by disdain for every word that comes out of my mouth, and I want to take her shorts off again. But, that's beside the point.

There are few triggers in my life anymore. The accident ten years ago taught me not to take life so seriously, and I've been good at sticking with that outlook. People can take me for who I am, bullshit sense of humor and all, but I learned valuable lessons from my experience. For example, even if someone looks okay to drive, they may not be. I should have known better. I was smarter than that.

Nia is smarter than that. *Isn't she?*

"Do you think I'll be a decent father?" Cameron asks, breaking me from my thoughts.

"Well, you sure haven't offered to swaddle me in a while, so I'm a bit biased."

"Shut up."

"So, what is the plan for the next half-hour?" I ask. "Are we continuing to hide out like a bunch of cowards?"

"Seems so." He sits up, pulling one arm across his chest then the other, twisting to look at me. "I should go, shouldn't I?"

"I'm not saying you're being a pussy, but you're being a pussy."

He gives me the finger. I probably deserve it.

ONLY THE WEDDING PARTY, the parents, and some immediate family attend the rehearsal ceremony—though, from what I understand, this is most of the attendees anyway.

Cameron's aunt, who has her chihuahua tucked under her arm, much to the dismay of the hotel staff, coordinates the faux ceremony. She says the groomsmen will not be walking the bridesmaids down the aisle, as there is an uneven number. We're to wait up front and watch the bridesmaids.

Great. There's no escaping Nia now.

I take my place next to Cam, nudging him in the side. "Ready to see your baby mama?"

"Fuck off."

Cam is testy today. *Noted.*

Down the wooden stairs leading to the beach come the three bridesmaids. There's Ramona, her curly hair pulled back in a bun, and then Corinne, tall and elegant. My gut jerks and I'm taking in Nia before I even register that I was looking for her to begin with.

Even in casual rehearsal clothes, she's stunning. She's wearing a long skirt that rolls behind her in waves with the wind. I can tell by how feverishly she's trying to pat it down that she's regretting the decision to wear it on such a blustery evening, but with the slit revealing her upper thigh, I'm quite satisfied.

I want to speak with her, but my brain fights with my heart. She's not who I thought she was. I've always admired her responsible, no-nonsense personality. I've always thought she was perfect. After spending all this time pining after her, could I shift my attention to someone else?

Every person has their flaws, but there are some I just can't overlook—no matter how long I've adored her. The only thing I can do is look at the ground and pretend she isn't there.

It's then I notice the precious chihuahua peeing on the

stark white runner right in the middle of the aisle. Grace's frustrated screams follow shortly behind.

THE REHEARSAL CEREMONY leads directly into the rehearsal dinner, and we're gathered in the same resort bar we've frequented for days now. I'm sipping on my water, zoned out as Grace's mom and her stepdad, Nick, discuss plants and farming *to* me more than *with* me.

I'm trying not to stare at Nia, but it's difficult. At least after this week I won't have to see her again. Thank God we don't work at the same office anymore. I don't think I could stand it.

"You see, avocados are a fruit," Nick says. "Most people don't know that."

"It has a seed," I say.

"Bingo!" He laughs. It's how I would imagine Santa Claus would sound: jolly, warm-hearted, kind. "Brownie points for the best man."

He's nice enough, but I can't handle fruit talk right now. I bid him farewell then push past the crowd back to the elevator. I'll order room service and a small travel-sized bottle of rum, or maybe even a full bottle. We'll see what they have.

At the bar stand Cam and Grace, arms looped around each other as he places kiss after kiss on her forehead, running his hand over her belly. She's grinning from ear to ear. I wonder if I'll ever find something like that. I shut my eyes. *Don't think of Nia.*

Full bottle of rum it is.

"Hey, where are you going?" Cam calls, elbowing through the small group of old men chortling over who knows what. They look like turtles poking out from their shells. "We were about to do some karaoke. They're setting up the stage and everything."

"It's been a long week," I say, forcing a smile. "Plus, your family is here. I'm sure they'll want the spotlight I've been hogging." I toss in a wink for good measure, and this seems to satisfy him enough.

"Okay..." He hesitates a moment. "Well, get some sleep. I'm depending on you tomorrow."

"Sure thing, bud." I feel horrible. I don't feel like a great best man, but also...I don't exactly feel like a great person at all right now.

I make it to my room without anyone else stopping me and immediately call room service.

"Alcohol," I say immediately after I'm asked for my order.

"Sir, what type of alcohol?" He seems bored, or irritated. I'm unsure. My life is essentially filled with people giving me a combination of the two.

"Your pick," I say. "Also, do you guys have cheeseburgers?"

"Yes, sir."

"One of those too."

"And how would you like that?" he asks.

"You pick."

"And the side? Is that my decision too?"

"Funny."

"I try, sir."

I hang up, and there's instantly a knock on my door.

That was inhumanly quick.

I yell for whoever it is to come in before realizing they probably need a key. I rise out of my chair and am greeted by my sister, brows furrowed in the middle and a frown reaching from her nose down to her chin. I didn't even know real-life frowns could be so sad-looking and cartoony.

"I heard what happened," Ramona says, inviting herself in.

"Oh." I sigh. "Okay."

She sits on the floor beside me, legs crossed over each other like some child preparing for story time at daycare. It's reminiscent of when we were kids and I'd pretend I was presenting a case for her, the jury. I remember I would steal her Barbies and put them on my train track set, tied tight with a rubber band so she couldn't get them loose, then present it like a reenactment. *"So, as the jury can see..."*

I wanted to be a lawyer even before I knew what it really entailed.

"Nia wasn't going to drive, you know," she says.

"Not the first time I've heard that, Ray."

"I know things are still hard for you," she starts, and I let out a stilted laugh. This conversation is oddly foreign to us. Even in the months following the car crash, while Ramona stayed in the hospital with me as often as she could, we only talked about school, or her new boyfriend, Wes, or whatever celebrity gossip she found interesting. Neither of us had the energy or strength to discuss why I was in that hospital bed in the first place.

"Are you putting on your psychologist pants?" I ask.

"No, I'm just trying to be a good sister." She exhales, and I stare at her. She must take this as a sign to keep talking, and I allow it. "Travis's death wasn't your fault. Please tell me you know that. Even after ten years, I feel like you don't."

"I don't," I say.

"You were just in the passenger seat. Both of you were drunk. There's no way you could have known."

"He told me he was good to drive," I mumble.

"And I'm sure he truly thought he was."

I nod, but I don't know if I hear her comment fully.

"You can't keep holding on to this, Ian. Nia didn't drive, and she really likes you, you know. And she's smart. She's good for you. She would never do that—especially after you told her."

"She was behind the wheel—"

"Yeah, but so were you when Dad drove you around in his lap as a baby. Were your little, chunky baby legs going to reach the pedals?" She laughs, causing me to choke out a laugh as well. "We said she could be DD earlier in the night. Then we joked about it later because she clearly couldn't. Trust her. And, if you can't, then trust *me*. That car wasn't going anywhere."

Is it possible to feel elation, confusion, and resentment at one's self all at once?

"She likes you. Do you know that?" Ramona says, attempting to rise up on her feet again. I reach out my hand to help her up, and she walks over to the desk, no doubt eyeing the sacred DVD.

Nia likes me. I keep repeating the same words over and over like a skipping record. *Nia likes me. Nia likes me.*

The way I treated her this morning, the way I pushed her to the side like garbage…it was wrong. It drives me crazy to know I was so wrong.

"She likes me?" I echo.

I turn and find Ramona lifting the pornographic contraband. "Ew, why?"

"Gift from Nia."

"Gross."

"She likes me, you said?" I ask again, bringing the subject back.

"Why are you surprised?" she says. "Your names are anagrams of each other's. You're practically soul mates."

"Ian doesn't use the same letters as Polly," I say with a grin.

She rolls her eyes. "I also see why she hates you."

"I thought you said she likes me?"

"Yeah, it's all very confusing." Her hands wave in the air. "You were right—she's complicated."

"I like complicated."

"I know you do." She narrows her eyes. "I think it's because of how simple our family was. You know—"

"No more psychologist stuff, Ray." I point a finger at her face threateningly, and she laughs.

"Come on." She swings her arm around my waist. "Let's go watch some bad karaoke."

35

IAN

Eight months ago

What have I completed on my last day of work at Treasures Inc.? Let me think: I played air hockey in the warehouse, I stole freezer food from an anonymous employee because the fish sticks were too tempting (and who cares if I take a two-hour lunch?), I annoyed Grace in her office until she kicked me out, and I scoured the building looking for Nia until I realized she wasn't here.

It felt odd that she conducted my exit interview yesterday. Generally, she's very active on an employee's last day, but not today. Not with me.

I sit in the break room later, surrounded by co-workers; I can't recall half of their names. I've been here almost nine years, and the staff has drastically changed with our spike in growth the past year. Veterans left for bigger and better things, and the only people I really know anymore are Grace and Nia.

Grace carries a small cake to the round table, nine candles lit to signify my years here. They all sing a rendition of "Happy Birthday," except they've replaced it with "Happy Last Day." I laugh as they all expect from me, but it's all wrong. None of it feels like a proper exit. Not without Nia.

We pass out the cake, with Grace cutting the pieces. A scowl rests on her face. I'm sure she has work to do, but she's trying her best to be a good sport, just like me.

"Hey, so where is Nia?" I ask. I force a chuckle, like it doesn't really matter and isn't driving me insane, but with her raised eyebrow and smirk lifting the corner of her mouth, I can tell she knows me better than that.

"She took the day off," she says, shoveling another piece onto a paper plate. "Gary, this is your last piece." She hands it to the plump man in the corner who looks like a child being denied his lollipop.

"Weird," I say, just low enough so people can't eavesdrop. "She normally makes a big deal out of last days."

"For real." Grace's eyes grow wide, letting out an exhalation. "If she were here, I wouldn't be doing this stupid cake-cutting job."

"Hey, it's my party."

"Yeah, and you're fully capable of using a knife too."

"Did she say why she isn't here?" I ask, trying to maintain a nonchalant manner, but it's not working. I feel betrayed. Even with our ups and downs, she's been my constant at this company. If only she knew she was the reason I'm leaving in the first place.

"Nah, just needed a day, I guess."

I can see through Grace, or maybe I'm just projecting my own insecurities that Nia is definitely absent because it's my last day and she's finally done with my shit.

"Don't feel too bad," Grace says, walking to the sink to wash the knife as people slowly leave.

"No, I feel absolutely stellar," I comment flatly. My tone is laced with sarcasm, but I can't help it. Today was going to be the day I filled her in on my not-so-secret secret. Nia needs to know I'm leaving for her. We argue, sure, but I want to finally try for something more. I'd argue with her forever if I could. She's the only woman I want, and now we're no longer coworkers. The barriers are gone. We're free, able to do whatever we like.

Whatever we like... If only she knew. If only she would have me.

"Well, she'll be a bridesmaid in my wedding, you know."

"That's eight months away," I say.

"Okay, grumpy Gus, I'm just saying. You'll at least see her again."

"Well, there's that."

She waves the dripping knife at me. "Hey, my wedding gift to you is a second chance."

"Shouldn't I be gifting you something?"

"Nah, I'm good." She winks and wipes the knife down before putting it back in drawer.

Grace and Cameron's wedding.

I'll see Nia then, and I will let her know.

Because she has to know.

I won't stop until it's crystal clear.

36

IAN

PRESENT DAY

I've heard every song under the sun tonight.

"Don't Stop Believing." *Classic.* "Sweet Caroline." *Sure, I can join in with that.* "Livin' la Vida Loca." *Totally on board.*

I would generally jump in with karaoke, but I'm a bit drained from the week.

Wes is singing "Ring of Fire" and pointing to various people in the crowd as if signaling that the song is dedicated solely to them. I'm wondering if he really understands the meaning of the song when I smell the familiar scent of lavender.

Nia appears in front of me, and heat rises to my face as my body tenses. I don't know what to think anymore.

"Hi, Nia," Ramona says from beside me, but when I give her the side-eye, she turns around to order a drink—and probably to pretend she isn't listening. At that, Corinne mimics the movement. It's just me and Nia, facing each other like some cowboy showdown with two women hunched over the bar like two stone gargoyles.

"We need to talk," she states, and it isn't a question. It's funny how she thinks she can just show up and demand to speak with me, as if I'm malleable enough to bend to her will. Normally, I would be, but I still don't know what to think about any of this. Maybe I just need time. Maybe I still don't believe her. Maybe I don't want to take the risk either way.

"I don't think so," I say.

"Please," she says. Her eyebrows tilt downward, concern plastered on her face. Sure, I want her—bad. I can't just turn that switch off, but everything still feels so raw.

"No," is all I get out, hoping to go back to bad karaoke but probably damning myself to more psychologist talk from Ramona. I don't care. "I don't want to listen. Sorry."

Nia grits her teeth behind closed lips, and her jaw grinds from side to side before she finally nods. "Fine. Fine." With one last look, she walks off, taking her cool, comforting scent with her.

"Well, that wasn't awkward," Ramona mumbles, turning back around with eyes wide, rolling her tongue to drag the tiny straw in her drink to her mouth.

Corinne turns back around and says nothing, which is probably smart on her part.

Wes's rendition of Johnny Cash ends. He gives a low bow, pulling his arm into his chest and waving to the crowd as if he's just waiting for a bouquet to be thrown to him. With the way Ramona suddenly bursts into clapping and whooping, I'm willing to bet she would do it if she had one on hand.

"Thinks he's a rock star, huh?" Corinne chuckles.

Out of the corner of my eye, I see Cameron and Grace slide beside us.

"How's your night going?" Grace asks, looking around a hollering Ramona to give me a smile.

"Couldn't be better. Really happy for you guys." The words are genuine, but they hurt. When I look at Grace and Cam or

Wes and Ramona, I know they're soul mates. It's the way both couples look at each other, the smiles and gentle kisses they exchange—or, in Ramona and Wes's case, the way they're immediately eating each other's faces the second they're reunited. It's the truest love, and for some reason, I feel cheated of that.

"Where's Nia?" Grace asks, looking around then lifting an eyebrow at me.

"Why do I feel like you're accusing me of something?" I ask, taking a small step away from her.

"Should I be?"

"Alright, alright, alright," the DJ bellows from behind the tech booth, cutting off our conversation. "We *all* went down with that ring of fire!"

"Wait, is he insulting me?" Wes shouts.

"Ian, what did you say to her?" Grace asks, but we're interrupted once more by the DJ's voice crooning into the microphone.

"Next up, we have Nia Smith!"

What?!

Most people walk up skipping and filled with drunk abandon, but not Nia. Up she walks with her hands by her side and chin held high, forcing confidence from every pore.

Cameron laughs. "What?! This is great!" He bursts out in hoots and hollers, as do Wes and Ramona. I don't join in. I'm too shocked to move.

What is she doing up there?

If I walk away now, maybe I can catch some late-night sitcom reruns or devour the cold cheeseburger still waiting for me in my room. Then again, why would I do that if I have a real-life sitcom right in front of me?

The karaoke accompaniment starts. It's a light guitar, and the beat is bouncy and fun, almost like a mambo. It's accompanied by staccato claps. Then, up on the screen flashes the name of the song: "Tequila" by The Champs.

"Is she seriously singing 'Tequila'?" Grace laughs.

"Hell yes," Cameron says with a grin.

For the unacquainted, "Tequila" is a two-and-a-half-minute song filled with massive instrumental breaks and only one word, repeated three times: *tequila*.

Nia holds the microphone in her hand, bending her knees up and down to the beat, trying to seem like she's enjoying it, but I can see her eyes darting around. She's scared shitless. A few people laugh.

Then she speaks.

"This song is dedicated to Ian Chambers." She scans the crowd, spots me, and shakily extends a finger. "That's right, lawyer man."

"I'll be outside," I say to Ramona, pushing myself away from the bar.

"Oh, come on, Ian—" She reaches out to grab my elbow, but we both halt at the voice speaking through the sound system.

"No." Nia's demand reverberates. The whole bar quiets, and the only sound is the inappropriately exciting karaoke music. "You're going to sit your handsome ass down, Ian. I have a microphone. I have the stage. Now you *have* to listen."

The guitar in the background is now accompanied by the song's signature saxophone. The karaoke screen counts down the bars until the first singing section—just a very slow bar filling up with color.

I back up and sit down on the edge of a stool.

With all the glances pointed in my direction, I'm surprised there isn't a spotlight shining on me.

"Now listen up." Nia's voice booms through the sound system. "I'm sorry, Ian. I am so, so sorry. I know how much that...that *thing* hurt you." She's looking around, trying to stay vague while also getting her point across, but it's just looking like maybe foul play was involved.

The tech guy steps out from behind the booth and reaches out for the microphone. "Ma'am, this highly is inappropriate."

Nia jerks her head to him with a glare that could scare the pants off of any man. Her grip on the mic tightens, whitening her knuckles instantly.

"I selected this song," she growls. My heart jerks back at the sound. *Jesus.* "And I will be performing it just like every other patron in this bar performed theirs." Although Nia is small, the additional foot granted by the stage gives her a fairly imposing figure. The tech guy steps back with his hands lifted in surrender. Hell, if I were him, I would too. She looks like a madwoman with a gun, except she's got a microphone and she isn't afraid to use it.

"Now, as I was saying." Nia's head swivels back to me. "Ian, yesterday was a misunderstanding. Don't misconstrue it as anything more. I was an idiot, but I would never want to hurt you. Never you. You're smart. Hell, you're the smartest man I know. You're the only man who can put up with my shit and send it right back in—hang on—" The music pauses for a beat and she choruses, "Tequila" in the most monotone voice ever before continuing.

"Well at least she got the lyric," Grace mumbles.

"So, anyway—"

"What in the hell?" I'm loudly interrupting her before I even register the words coming out of my mouth.

Nia blinks then gives me a smile. "Oh, so you're talking to me now? Good."

"No." I shake my head, resting my fingers on my temples and taking a step toward the stage. "What the absolute hell? Get down from the stage, Nia."

"Absolutely not," she says. "I have a microphone, and you do not."

The song is definitely mocking me. The sax rips louder, the guitar is upbeat, and the claps are enough to drive me insane.

"The rooms on this floor can probably hear everything you're saying." I sigh. "Get down."

"Yeah, but we can hear each other, so what's the problem?"

"Good lord."

"Did you not hear me earlier? I'm sorry." With her apologetic glance, it's hard to find the words to reply.

I storm to the stage—audience be damned—and whisper to her under my breath, "This is not the time or place." Unfortunately for me, whispering to her still echoes through the sound system. *Right. She's still holding a microphone.*

"When will it be the right time?" she asks. "When else would you listen to me and have a—wait a second..." The song stops for a beat. "Tequila."

"Who the hell is running this bar?!" I shout, twisting around and throwing my hands in the air. "How are you still singing?" The saxophone in the song is rolling like mad, hitting every high note. "Take away her mic. This is ridiculous."

I shoot a glare to the tech guy, but he backs up again, muttering, "I'm not messing with this psycho." Nia must look like some rabid dog, and this man is just trying to do his job.

"Very professional," I sneer, hands on my hips. "And the woman is a little over five feet tall, man. She is *not* a psycho."

"So you do believe me," Nia says.

"No. Yes. I don't know," I say. My hands drop to my sides. I'm close to stepping off the stage before I hear a small, pleading tone come through the speakers.

"Please. Ian," she says, slowly, calmly, desperately. "Please hear me out."

Her brows pull inward and her shoulders slump. The microphone is dropped to her side, limp in her hand as she tilts her head. I can tell she's at the end of her rope. So am I.

The saxophone stops. The guitar solos. Then a chorus of

"TEQUILA!" sounds from the entire crowd followed by immediate cheers. Nia does not join in on the final lyric.

Amongst the excited hums coming from satisfied, entertained bar folk, I can still hear Grace at the back of the bar yelling, "Best. Rehearsal dinner. Ever."

37

NIA

"Nia," Ian calls after me. His steps echo across the wooden patio.

I lean against the fence separating the resort pool from the ocean sand. I needed to feel the cool air and listen to the rush of the tide. I needed to get away from the stifling bar, but Ian followed me.

His steps slow as he gets closer. I turn away from the ocean. Ian is walking apprehensively, most likely testing how close he can get before I break down in tears.

"Say what you need to say, I guess," he says.

I cross my arms over my chest, and a smile stretches from one side of his mouth then spreads across his entire face, a slow shift from concern to genuine satisfaction. "What?" I ask.

"This feels wrong." He chuckles. "You should be mad at me."

"But I'm not." This only makes him laugh more.

"But, that's us, right?" he says, moving closer, feet away from me. "I'm irritating and you get angry because you know you're too good for me."

"I'm not *too good* for you," I say through gritted teeth.

"But you are. You definitely are, and it's an absolute privilege to be near you." Following his words, he places a hand on the fence, caging me in on one side.

"You're just putting me on a pedestal," I say. "I'm sorry. I'll say it a million times. I'm sorry. I know things are rough. I know that was a hard thing for you to go through—to still go through—but you've got to believe me."

He tilts his head to the side. "You're hard-working, beautiful, *so* smart..." He trails off. "I'm sorry, Nia. You do deserve better than me. I was so quick to judge—"

"You have your reasons," I interrupt. I tighten my grip on my own elbows as I pull my arms into my chest. If I don't, I might be letting him pull me into an embrace.

"You like me."

"Maybe," I say, rolling my eyes. "It's ridiculous, really."

And it is ridiculous. Because it's true.

I like Ian. I have for years.

"Sometimes life is ridiculous." He chuckles. I look up, not having realized just how close he's gotten. His lips hover near my nose. I try to keep my head down, but he takes my chin between his thumb and forefinger, lifting my face to meet his.

Our lips touch, and all the tension running through my shoulders and spine releases. His mouth is soft, warm, and *right*. He tilts my chin higher, allowing himself to take more of me, and I let him. I lift onto my toes and deepen it. I can't uncross my arms. They're stuck, petrified into place, but I'm not mad. I'm not even irritated.

Still, with every passing second, my nerves struggle to stay contained. They're bouncing from point to point—my fingers, my shoulders, my chest, and into my throat, where I let out a small hum.

One kiss. That's all I can take.

I pull away, lowering back down on my heels. His eyes

open, and there they are: the beautiful blues. I wonder if they could be mine forever.

"Let's just get through the wedding tomorrow," he says. I smile and slump against the fence. It's hard to maintain any form of resolve when he looks at me like *that*. He removes his hand from the fence and pockets it.

"Sure," I say.

"I believe you, Polly."

Out of habit, I respond, "Don't call me that." But the nickname doesn't spark the usual hatred or catapult my blood pressure through the roof. It's almost a comfort, and the word spears through my chest, warming my body.

His hand reaches up to caresses my cheek, my jaw, then my neck.

"How about Apollo, then?"

"Maybe," I whisper. "Just maybe."

38

NIA

"Are you nervous? You're totally nervous."

Ramona clutches Grace's cheeks in her palms, staring into her eyes.

"I've been in love with Cameron since the day I met him, Ray. Okay, stop it." She swats Ramona away. "You're ruining my makeup."

I sit on the chaise nearby in my peach bridesmaid dress, legs crossed. While it may not fit me as well as Corinne's does her—she could have just walked off the runway in Paris—I suppose it doesn't look *too* bad. It's loose on the top as I expected, but my fully formed hips and ass make up for my lack of bongos.

A head pokes through the door, peering in *The Shining*-style. Except instead of a hole, it's just a crack in the door. Much less menacing, especially since the face belongs not to a crazed Jack Nicholson, but to Grace's mom, Lynette, who is on the verge of a breakdown.

"Oh god, I'm going to cry," she says, though it looks like the threat of tears is far from gone. They fell hours ago.

"Mommm," Grace groans.

Another head pokes in, chin resting on top of Lynette's. It's the lady whose been walking around with the chihuahua under her arm. She's running the show, but honestly, I don't think anyone granted her the role of coordinator. I think she just stole it, which makes me wonder if she stole that dog too.

"We're ready for you!" she chimes. "Everyone is at the beach!"

Grace stands from her chair, smoothing out the bunches in her dress. It's a beautiful mermaid gown, tight along her waist and hips then cascading out behind her in an elegant tulle train. Her illusion neckline gives the appearance of a strapless dress with lace trailing up her chest and disappearing just beneath her shoulders. Her fierce red hair is pulled into a tight ballerina bun with strands loosened to frame her face, and she'd fit right in on the pages of any high fashion bridal feature.

"Good, let's get this party rolling," Grace says.

Ramona swings open the cracked door, and both women and dog tumble in.

At the sight of her daughter, Lynette lets out a sound that's a mix between a moaning whale and a yowling cat, throwing her palm over her eyes and swatting at us to disregard her. Grace raises an eyebrow to us. "Okay, well, um, yeah...let's just get going. I've got a prince to marry." This only makes her mom howl louder.

"Hell yeah. Let's do this!" Ramona says, clapping with each word. The other lady mirrors the clapping, shaking the small dog under her arm. It lets out a low growl in irritation. Ramona sticks out her tongue.

"Don't taunt the dog," Grace whispers.

"It taunted me first."

We all crowd out of the room, crossing the resort foyer and

trailing down the short wooden pier with Grace's mom wailing through tears the entire way.

Ahead we see the rows of white resin folding chairs and, just past them, an arch with the officiant, the groom, and the groomsmen. Ian towers half a foot over Cameron. His black hair is thick and curled with one dangling strand resembling a sexy Clark Kent, which I'm sure would annoy him if it were pointed out. Or maybe he would even crack a joke at how he's just as wonderful as the Man of Steel himself. I bet it would be just funny enough to make me roll my eyes. I relish the thought.

I'm the first to walk down the aisle, and a small iris bouquet is shoved in my hands by the dog lady seconds before my feet step off the wooden pier onto the shifting sand.

I don't know whose idea it was to have this ceremony far from the shore, but they clearly did not understand how beaches work. We're in the soft sand and the legs of each chair are slowly sinking. Guests are gripping the sides, trying to right them, but every movement only makes the seats more lopsided. I can't help but smile, and when I look up, Ian is smiling back at me.

My left foot sinks a bit but I continue on as if I didn't just semi-trip down the aisle. Ian winks, and for a moment I consider that this could be my future. One day, I might be walking toward Ian not in a peach dress, but in a white one. A guitar might be playing in the background just as the ukulele is now. Maybe there will be violins, and perhaps I'll be staring into his blue eyes, getting that boyish grin flashed back at me.

The decision to like Ian was made for me years ago; I just needed to let it happen. Just like the sand around me, my desire for him has been getting deeper and deeper minute by minute and year by year. The only thing time will change is just how deep my affection goes.

I take a left at the front, settling at my designated spot near the end as Corinne then Ramona line up beside me. They balance their way through the sand like I did, but when the ukulele changes its tune and Grace starts down the aisle, I notice she had enough sense to take off her heels.

She walks down the aisle arm in arm with her mother, though while Grace looks elegant and demure, her mom is tripping through the sand on wedged sandals with leaking mascara and a trembling bottom lip.

The ceremony commences and I angle myself inward as directed by the self-appointed coordinator and her yapping dog, who is probably the real brains behind the operation. When Cam's eyes fall on Grace, his wide, dimpled grin could light up the entire beach.

When it's time for vows, there's no sign of apprehension or fear. Grace simply provides a quick, decisive, "I do."

It's difficult for me to believe our lives are dictated by fate or a series of uncontrollable circumstances. In fact, this very moment—right here standing in what feels like quicksand—is the result of thirty-five years' worth of carefully thought-out decisions obsessively mulled over in excruciating detail. But what if destiny is the true puppeteer? What if Grace and Cam were destined to meet, no matter what obstacles blocked them, employee-manager relationship be damned? If destiny is the true world power, I can tell it knew exactly what it was doing with those two.

When the officiant announces their full married name for the first time, Cameron and Grace embrace each other and we all clap.

The wedding party files out, trying our best to maintain balance. As I'm the last one, I have no groomsman to escort me, but I don't mind. I look ahead at the woman in white and her grinning man.

I wonder if destiny brought me here to open my eyes to

what life can be like when you let go. Maybe now is finally the time for me to relax, enjoy the world, and for once, not be in control, but instead roll with the waves of the ocean.

You can't control every aspect of your life. And maybe you don't need to.

39

IAN

Cameron waits less than five minutes before rushing the food bar and shoveling shrimp onto his plate with the serving spatula.

"God, I thought those photos would take a thousand years," he moans.

"We took literally ten pictures," Ramona says. "Which, honestly, is not nearly enough."

Grace cuts forward, snatching a plate as well. "As long as we have at least two pictures for our fireplace, what do I care?"

Guests are sitting at their assigned round tables under the white tent erected for the reception. Their plates are empty, and I'm honestly unsure if the wedding party was supposed to serve themselves first or wait for everyone else. Looks like we're going with the former.

"You're embarrassing yourselves," Wes says.

"No, we're not. Nia embarrassed herself enough last night to cover for the rest of us," Cameron says, grinning.

I look over at Nia, whose eyes are already locked onto mine, a shy smile twisting her mouth.

A line of guests finally file behind us by the time we've

made it through the buffet. There is a long table reserved for the wedding party near the end of the tent, and Nia and I sit on opposite ends. I wonder if she's thinking what I am—that only one word will strike a match between us, and the flame will be impossible to snuff out.

Grace and Cameron barely have time to stuff their faces before the DJ calls them out for their first dance. He must not have gotten the memo that food is serious business for these two newlyweds.

"Let's fire him," Grace says, patting her mouth with a napkin.

"Well, honey, we'll have to cut him some slack for now," Cameron says, grabbing her hand. "We can't exactly find another DJ this last minute."

"Only request cliché wedding music," I suggest. "*Really* ruin his night."

Cameron claps a hand on my shoulder. "This is why you're the best man."

THE PARTY COMMENCES faster than expected. Every person walking past our tent is graciously invited in by the bride and groom until our group grows to about two hundred drunken beach bums, resort guests, and families jumping up and down, hands flying in the air to the words of "Shout" over and over. I can sense the shift in the DJ's demeanor as he plays song after song of wedding classics like "Cha Cha Slide" and "Macarena". He has a permanent sneer of disgust. Conversely, I don't think Grace and Cameron have ever had so much fun.

I decide to sit this song out, finding an empty round table to relax at. I throw off my tie, undo the top two buttons of my shirt, and cross my ankle over my knee, stretching my arms out over the back of the chairs next to me. I sweep my eyes across the crowd, looking until I spot the white-blonde hair paired with a tiny peach dress.

Nia is over near the pop-up bar, leaning against the counter and chatting with the bartender mixing drinks. I've patiently waited all night for her to speak to me. It's been maddening to watch her walk around in that bridesmaid dress. The straps rest loose on her delicate shoulders, and the neckline slopes just low enough to give a chaste peek at the start of her chest. Once it hits her waist, it doesn't leave much to the imagination, and I've had to avert my eyes many times to quell a growing hardness in my pants. Now, though, I'm alone and too greedy to look away. My zipper may be strained, but I'm not depriving myself of this sight.

As I soak Nia in, memorizing every bit of her body, her head shoots up and looks around. I know exactly what she's feeling because I feel it too. It's that pull—the tug of an invisible wire connecting us, like some impulse to know where the other is. If we lose track of each other, we search, and we always find one another.

Her eyes land on me, and she smiles. I raise my hand in greeting. She wiggles her fingers back in a wave.

She leans in to mouth a few words to the bartender before making her way over to my lonely round table. This will be the closest we've been in proximity all night, and I can feel my blood pumping heavy at the thought of it.

I pat the chair next to me and she falls into it.

"Come here often?" I ask.

She scoffs, rolling her eyes with a laugh. "That's the best you got?" she asks. Her brown eyes are warm, inviting, and scouring over my face and bared chest. I let them wander as they like.

"What do you want me to say?" I ask.

"Something more original."

"Fine. Then...are you lost? Because heaven is a long way from here."

She rolls her eyes again—so hard that this time I think they get stuck for a moment.

"Oh, has that been said before?" I say, feigning innocence.

"You're incorrigible."

She shakes her head slowly, a smile spread from ear to ear and that beautiful, plump lip pulled taut between her teeth. I want to say something, but I'm finding it hard to form the words needed to express how unreal it is to have Nia next to me, biting her lip, one eyebrow raised and leaning against my arm. Not only is she relaxed, she's allowing my finger to stroke along her shoulder.

"Do you want a drink?" I ask, jerking my head to the bar.

"I think I'm pretty much done with drinking for a while." She leans back with her arms crossed. "Two hangovers in one week is about my limit."

"Two in a week?" I gasp. "Wild child."

"Shut up," she says, pushing my side.

"Ooh, that tickles," I croon. "Do it again."

"Stoppp," she says through laughter, elbowing my stomach.

We grow quiet and sit there in silence. My eyes roam over every part of her while she looks out at the dancing crowd.

"So, are you going to forgive me for being such an asshole?" I ask.

She shrugs. "Maybe."

"I can take maybe."

"Are you going to forgive *me* for being such an asshole?" she asks.

"Maybe." I smile.

Her head swivels toward me and she inhales sharply as if carefully considering her next words.

"I almost kissed you a few years ago," she says. "Did you know that?"

My breath catches. I laugh awkwardly, trying to conceal my surprise with as much casual ease as I can. "Wait—what?"

"Yeah." She places a hand on my knee, stroking around it absentmindedly. I stiffen. "After that write-up for Grace and Cam."

"I'm not recalling..." It's irritating to think there was a moment I lost. Jesus Christ, I need to know when Nia fucking Smith tried to kiss me.

"Of course you don't remember," she scoffs. "You were too distracted by the receptionist."

And then it hits me—*I do remember that night.*

"That was Beer Friday, wasn't it?" I ask.

I remember that fucking night.

"You told me you didn't date co-workers," she says.

It all comes rushing back to me: our chat in her office, the termination paperwork for Cameron's indiscretions looming between us, the way she looked at me. I felt weird at the time, but I assumed it was just my inappropriate lusting after Nia finally crossing some line. I remember her odd expression at the awkward situation, and I never considered that maybe her face was revealing something else. I remember saying whatever I could to make her think I wasn't coming on to her. The last thing I needed was a harassment lawsuit from my own HR manager, but I had a feeling there was something between us.

I fucking knew it.

But then Saria—the young receptionist many years my junior—stepped in.

"Saria... She tried to... Nothing happened." I remember Saria gripping my leg, sliding it up my thigh. It was uncomfortable, to say the least, and a disaster waiting to happen. Imagine the uproar of the in-house lawyer sleeping with the young receptionist. Not a chance. Then she was too drunk to drive, and I did what I always did: I drove her home, and that was it. She tried to hit on me when I dropped her off, but that was only right before she lost all her alcohol in the bushes. "I wasn't lying. I don't date co-workers."

"I believe you," she says. Her tone is to the point and indicates that the topic is closed. No discussion needed. It's simple and decisive, just like everything Nia does.

I smile. "Plus, come on, I was too in love with you to think about anyone else."

Nia lets out an uncomfortable laugh then narrows her eyes. "You say that like you really mean it."

"I am a lovesick, head over groomsman oxfords, mess of a man around you. You're why I left the company," I say.

"You left because of me?" Her mouth is slightly open, scanning me for lies.

There are none to be found, Polly.

"I left *for* you." I remember when I decided to job hunt. I knew I wouldn't be happy unless I tried to be with Nia, and she wouldn't give me the time of day as long as we were co-workers.

A smile creeps up her face, widening ever slightly. I can tell by her twitching cheeks that she's trying to resist, but she's losing the battle.

"There's a smile," I say. "I like your smile."

Her hand shifts from my knee up to my thigh. Patience be damned, I want Nia. I *need* Nia.

"Want to get out of here?" I ask.

"Yes."

40

NIA

I now wonder why I wasted any time not allowing myself to be being completely enraptured by Ian Chambers. Was it my stubborn nature? My pride? Or was it that misunderstandings truly ruin everything?

It's irrelevant now as the two of us walk away from the reception tent and farther down the beach, Ian's hand around my waist and me clutching the hem of my dress. I don't know where we're going, and we walk for who knows how long. The music from the party dulls, the light from the tiki torches vanishes, and then we're alone walking down the shore in pitch-black darkness, just as we did a few nights ago.

At some point, Ian's hand glides lower from my waist to my hip, where he stops and pulls me into him.

I can't see where we are yet. My eyes are still adjusting, and the loss of one of my senses makes the touch of his wandering hands seem that much more thrilling and electrifying. They run up my sides, trailing the stitching of my dress, following it to my shoulders, where his fingers curl under my dress straps. When he lowers one, I feel the warmth of his lips brush my shoulder. He repeats the motion, making a path from my shoulder up to my neckline. A shiver runs through me.

"Are you cold?" he whispers. The tone is low, rumbling, and though it has a hint of concern, I sense more than that—I sense longing.

"No," I say breathlessly.

I can feel the mist from the ocean hit the backs of my calves. The rolling tide rushes beneath my heels, and I'm thankful for the relief of the water. With every small kiss, I'm beginning to lose touch with reality. Am I dreaming? Is this just one of my fantasies? Maybe I fell asleep while reading. But no —the surge of water tickling my feet reminds me that the world is still moving. I am most definitely not dreaming.

I place my hands against his button-down, sliding them up to touch his neck. Every kiss planted on me triggers another tick in his jaw, another sharp inhalation of air, and a hum of happiness reverberating from his throat, vibrating my palm.

He's barely touched me, and I'm already begging for seconds.

"Is this the fabled 'next time'?" I whisper, running my fingers through his curly hair, letting each lock bounce its way between them. Full, thick, and *mine*.

"This is whatever you want it to be," he says between kisses. My legs clench as shocks travel from my stomach down between my thighs.

He lowers my other dress strap and shimmies the top down just enough for me to feel the cool air harden my nipples. He rubs his thumb over one, and nerves radiate out from my chest.

"Dirty talk," he says.

"What?" I choke out. My nipple, exposed to the breeze, isn't cold for long before he's captured it in his mouth, rolling a tongue over it. Desire takes me in waves, and I moan involuntarily, fisting his hair. He chuckles against me and I gasp at his breath.

"How do you feel about it?" he asks.

I am on a beach with a hot-as-hell man—a man who, in every other aspect of his life, just acts upon what he wants. He doesn't ask questions; he just *does*. That's why I like him, and I would expect nothing less now.

"Don't ask me questions," I demand. "Just do."

He snarls deep, immediately turning his attention from my chest and smashing his mouth against mine. I can't breathe as every one of my nerves is lit aflame. He bites my lower lip, tugging and claiming it for his own.

"Gladly," he growls.

Both of his hands grip my thighs, forcing me to jump up and wrap my legs around him. My arms clutch the back of his neck for support as he lowers us down to the hardened, damp sand.

His hands rest on either side of my shoulders as his mouth devours mine. His tongue demands entry and I grant it. Our bodies wrestle for power, but we're both much too stubborn to let the other win.

My hands rise to wander over his chest. I undo each button and trace over his abs as they are slowly revealed. They're hills, valleys, and peaks rolling across his stomach, shifting with every slight movement. After the last button, his shirt falls open. He leans up to toss it off and I reach for his belt, pulling it out of the loops and letting it dangle against the crotch of his crisp black suit pants. His hardness beneath is begging to be released.

"God, I want you so bad," he says. My hands start for the zipper, pulling it down. I lower his waistband, revealing him fully, and take him into my hands. He's large just as I remember —unsurprising given his height—and exciting to hold. I stroke, pumping my hand up and down. My movements cause him to groan and his hips buck toward me.

In one swift movement, he lowers down, rolling over in the

sand and centering me on top of him. My dress is up to my hips and he grinds himself against the fabric of my underwear.

"You're wet," he says. My eyes have adjusted to the darkness just enough to see the sly nicked eyebrow rising. "Give me your pussy."

Hell, he can have all of me at this point.

"I believe I promised you something first," I say. He exhales heavily, running a hand through my hair as I kiss down his stomach to his waist. "Do you want it?"

"Don't ask me questions." He flashes a grin. "Just do."

Even in a moment like this, he can't help but be sarcastic.

"Shut up," I snap.

"Make me," he growls.

With that, I sink lower, wrapping my hand around his cock and licking him before taking all of it in my mouth. He groans, tilting his head back as I whip my tongue across him and suck at his head. His hips jerk again, and I hear the sound of sand shifting under his fingers.

I bob my head, forcing his long length in and out of my mouth. I distantly hear him groan my name, and it only empowers me more. He's hard as a rock, hard for *me*—and then it's taken away, pulled out of my mouth as he pushes my shoulders back.

He sits up, bending at the waist and twisting us once more so my back hits the ground. He hovers over me.

This feels so familiar: his hands on either side of my body, his knees bent to capture me beneath him. Reflected in the moonlight are his bright blue eyes, the same ones that mystify my fantasies.

His fingers ghost down my stomach, lifting the skirt of my dress to my waist. He's bending down to kiss my chest again, rolling one then two fingers to bypass the fabric of my underwear and curl deep inside me. His entrance is effortless, as I'm already soaked, just waiting for him. I moan, sensations running through all of my body, from my chest to my stomach to my hips.

He's moving his fingers in and out, pushing against my soft spot, driving me more mad by the second.

He pulls out and I whine while he shifts my own underwear down, lifting my feet through them and throwing them to the side. My ass is bare against the textured sand and he lowers himself to me, teasing the outside of my lips with the head. He lowers to my ear, breathing into me, heaving out the words "I want you" through gritted teeth. He rubs my clit with his thumb, causing me to moan and arch my back into him.

"Hang on," I whisper. My hands fumble in my dress pockets —*thank you Grace for choosing a bridesmaid dress with functionality*—and I tug out a condom.

He laughs loud and hearty, taking the silver wrapper from me and rolling it through his hands. "When did you get this, you nasty girl?"

My stomach twists. "After the wedding pictures." I begged the resort minimart to sell me just the one even though they insisted on the whole box. I instead ran off with the single wrapped one yelling, "Charge my account!" before rejoining the group once more.

"You wanted me to fuck you, didn't you?" he says, rubbing circles around my clit, causing a moan to escape me. He brings this out in me—this desperation to be touched, the need to be wild, different, to allow myself to lose control.

"Yes," I whimper.

He removes his hand and I immediately feel lost without it. He digs in the pants that remain limp on the ground beside him and pulls out a silver wrapper identical to mine.

"So was I, and I want all of you."

He places one of them down next to my forgotten underwear and takes the other in his teeth, tearing the top off. The condom is rolled down his length slowly before he runs a hand between my legs. He wraps it around the outside of my calf to spread my legs farther apart and scoot me closer to him, sand shifting all around me.

"Fuck." He exhales, angling in front of me, rubbing the head against the outside of my pussy. He's requesting entry, teasing me into submission. Little does he know, I'm already a goner. I shift closer, taking him into me the smallest bit. "Fuck," he repeats, sharper and more desperate.

He pushes in only slightly before pulling back out. I clutch his hips in an effort to drag him deeper, but he resists, forcing me to endure only a taste of him with every thrust, gradually granting me more each time.

Then, all at once, he pushes in, his entire length driving into me as I let out an unrestrained moan. He doesn't stop me or tell me to quiet. He encourages me, demanding I moan louder as he fills me whole. His hand grips my knee, bending it into his chest, using it to find purchase for his repeated motions.

The nerves in my stomach clench. Every movement against me feels better and better, euphoria striking through me until the sensation spreads from my hips out to my stomach and tingles to my fingertips.

I come before I can even tell him it's happening. All I say is, "Keep going."

"Of course," he says, bending over to place both hands on either side of my head, grounding his palms in the sand as he pounds in and out of me, driving in over and over. My head, barely recovered from the first wave of my orgasm, is already at the edge of losing touch when I clench again, veins lighting up with every roll of the second orgasm coursing through me.

"Ian." I moan his name and it sends him over. I feel him throbbing inside me, pounding more until he slows to a stop. His breathing is heavy, gasping for air until his eyes open and he stares down at me. He grins, and my heart sinks down, falling against my back, cracking into a million little pieces with the remains melting and pooling around me.

I'm lost to him. This is more than fucking. This is what it feels like to melt into another person, to fall into them, to fall *with* them.

He kisses my forehead, and it's gentle yet possessive.

"I like you, Ian," I whisper.

We pull apart, and looking back at me are those ice blues, sharp yet kind and lusting for one more go—just as I always imagined.

EPILOGUE
IAN

Until recently, I never believed the old saying that time passes by quickly when you're having fun. Turns out, it's true.

What was once a simple wedding week suddenly jumped forward five months to a weekend of moving boxes and too much duct tape. I sold my empty, cold townhome to move into Nia's house, which she said was much too big for her and required a very tall, handsome roommate.

"If you need an application, I'm happy to complete one," I offered, "but I must warn you—my resume is very extensive. Too much for the standard one-pager."

"I'll need references," she demanded. She was sitting on top of me, straddling my legs as she was prone to do, her hand already halfway down my pants.

"Excuse me, ma'am, but this is inappropriate behavior to engage in with a tenant."

"Management will take your suggestions into consideration."

The days of surreal happiness were made even happier when one month later there was a chocolate cake in front of Grant celebrating him being six months sober. He flicked his chip in the air, letting it fall into his palm like a coin indicating head or tails. Lucky for him, the outcome is always favorable with the six-month engraving staring back up at him.

Three more months flew by and we were then in a hospital, celebrating the birth of Oliver Thomas Kaufman, who was delivered at eight pounds, three ounces with a stunning head full of flaming red hair. Grace and Cameron were already coordinating diaper duty, and it was no surprise they're a powerhouse with parenting as well.

After another three months, Nia and I went to the same steakhouse where I crashed her celebration dinner only a few years prior. That haphazard dinner six years earlier was the moment I knew for a fact that I was in love with her, and this night—one year after the week that changed our lives—would be the night I'd tell her I want to love her forever.

I hired a mariachi band to come play their own rendition of "Tequila" while I got down on one knee. The staff of the restaurant wasn't too happy I messed with their ambiance by drawing in a vastly different style of music, and the band was kicked out shortly following their performance.

It was funny how quickly she said yes, getting on the floor to hug my neck and peck my face with kisses, practically falling on top of me.

It was a moment I'd never imagined would happen to me, and it happened with her.

Sometimes you just have to be patient.

For a whole decade.

Actually, that's horrible advice.

Be patient for a reasonable amount of time.

Or simply be a fool in love.

NICE TO SEE YOU!

Hi there! Thanks for reading! I hope you enjoyed Ian and Nia's story just as much as I enjoyed writing it!

Sign-up for the Julie Olivia email newsletter to receive updates on upcoming releases!

www.julieoliviaauthor.com/newsletter

ACKNOWLEDGMENTS

Thank you, thank you, thank YOU, reader! This book would just be gathering dust were it not for you awesome people wanting to read it!

Thank you to my dad because I honestly don't think I should ever write an acknowledgements page without having you in it. The discipline to keep writing even on the hard days is a direct result of your parenting. Thanks for being the best role model.

To my "evil stepmother" who I firmly believe is a real life angel. I am constantly humbled by how much you love promoting my little ol' books. Thanks for being my final reader before I send the book out into the wild.

Thank you to my editor, C. Marie! This would all just sound like a jumble of words without you!

Massive thank you to my beta readers Kolin, Erica, Jenny, Aaron, Brett, and Viorelia. When enough people say "he's not really for me, but maybe some person will like him!" you know you need to make some changes the main protagonist. Hopefully Ian is a darling again.

Finally, to my real life Ian Chambers. Thank you for being

so funny that I can't help but snag one-liners from you. Thank you for telling me whenever characters sweat too much or when they get an expression wrong because I don't even know how the saying goes. But, most of all, thank you for encouraging me when I doubt myself. You're my biggest cheerleader —without the skirt.

ABOUT THE AUTHOR

Julie Olivia loves spicy stories with even spicier banter, so she decided to write them. Julie lives in Atlanta with her fiancé and their very vocal cat. She appreciates a good pair of boots and fresh lemon-filled donuts. She is easily bribed with either.

Sign up for release updates: julieoliviaauthor.com/newsletter

- facebook.com/julieoliviaauthor
- instagram.com/julieoliviaauthor
- amazon.com/author/julieoliviaauthor
- bookbub.com/authors/julie-olivia

Printed in Poland
by Amazon Fulfillment
Poland Sp. z o.o., Wrocław